"O, What a Tangled Web"

Tolkien and Medieval Literature
A View from Poland

edited by
Barbara Kowalik

2013

Cormarë Series No. 29

Series Editors: Peter Buchs • Thomas Honegger • Andrew Moglestue • Johanna Schön

Series Editor responsible for this volume: Thomas Honegger

Library of Congress Cataloging-in-Publication Data

"O, What a Tangled Web": Tolkien and Medieval Literature – A View from Poland
edited by Barbara Kowalik
ISBN 978-3-905703-29-0

Subject headings:
Tolkien, J.R.R. (John Ronald Reuel), 1892-1973
medieval literature
The Silmarillion
The Lord of the Rings
The Hobbit

Cormarë Series No. 29

First published 2013

© Walking Tree Publishers, Zurich and Jena, 2013

All rights reserved. No portion of this book may be reproduced, by any process or technique, without the express written consent of the publisher

Cover illustration *Dragon* by Anke Eißmann.
Reproduced by permission of the artist. Copyright Anke Eißmann 2011.

Set in Adobe Garamond Pro and Shannon by Walking Tree Publishers
Printed by Lightning Source in the United Kingdom and United States

Board of Advisors

Academic Advisors

Douglas A. Anderson (independent scholar)

Dieter Bachmann (Universität Zürich)

Patrick Curry (independent scholar)

Michael D.C. Drout (Wheaton College)

Vincent Ferré (Université de Paris-Est Créteil UPEC)

Verlyn Flieger (University of Maryland)

Thomas Fornet-Ponse (Rheinische Friedrich-Wilhelms-Universität Bonn)

Christopher Garbowski (University of Lublin, Poland)

Mark T. Hooker (Indiana University)

Andrew James Johnston (Freie Universität Berlin)

Rainer Nagel (Johannes Gutenberg-Universität Mainz)

Helmut W. Pesch (independent scholar)

Tom A. Shippey (University of Winchester)

Allan G. Turner (Friedrich-Schiller-Universität Jena)

Frank Weinreich (independent scholar)

General Readers

Johan Boots

Jean Chausse

Friedhelm Schneidewind

Isaac Juan Tomas

Patrick Van den hole

Johan Vanhecke (Letterenhuis, Antwerp)

Acknowledgments

This book, which began with my guest lecture on the Virgin Mary underlying the figure of Elbereth given at a student conference on Tolkien's medievalism in the Institute of English Studies at the University of Warsaw, has been a long while in the making. I am particularly grateful to my colleague Marysia Błaszkiewicz, who encouraged me to start this project and bring it to fruition. I am grateful to my fine doctoral student Joanna Szwed-Śliwowska, who read and commented on some of the papers at their early stages. Furthermore, I am extremely grateful to Thomas Honegger, an eminent specialist in medieval and Tolkien studies, and his superb team at the Walking Tree Publishers, for providing unfailing, essential support and for generous overseeing of the project's conclusion. Last but not least, my thanks go to the excellent authors of this volume – without you this book would not have been possible.

Contents

Barbara Kowalik
Introduction
Tolkien in Poland: A Medievalist Liaison ... 1

Joanna Kokot
"O, what a tangled web we weave".
The Lord of the Rings and the Interlacement Technique ... 9

Bartłomiej Błaszkiewicz
Orality and Literacy in Middle-earth ... 29

Justyna Brzezińska
Rohan and the Social Codes of Heroic Epic and
Chivalric Romance ... 47

Maria Błaszkiewicz
Tolkien's Queen Women in *The Lord of the Rings* ... 69

Barbara Kowalik
Elbereth the Star-Queen Seen in the Light of Medieval
Marian Devotion ... 93

Katarzyna Blacharska
The Fallen: Milton's Satan and Tolkien's Melkor ... 115

Renata Leśniakiewicz-Drzymała
Berserkir, Bödvar Bjarki and the Dragon Fáfnir.
The Influence of Selected Medieval Icelandic Sagas
on Tolkien's Works for Children ... 145

Łukasz Neubauer
'He has gone to God glory seeking': Tolkien's Critique
of the Northern Courage and Rejection of the Traditional
Heroic Ethos in "The Homecoming of Beorhtnoth Beorhthelm's Son" ... 163

Andrzej Wicher
What Exactly Does Tolkien Argue for in "*Beowulf*:
The Monsters and the Critics?" An Attempt at a Metacriticism ... 179

Barbara Kowalik

Introduction
Tolkien in Poland: A Medievalist Liaison

The nine articles collected in this volume adopt a variety of medieval perspectives to view J.R.R. Tolkien's work. An exception might be the paper on Melkor and Milton's Satan, which, however, makes reference to the portrayal of Lucifer in the Old English *Genesis B* so its medievalist profile is quite easily defensible, especially if we stretch the closing boundary of the medieval period in English literature to the seventeenth century, as it is sometimes done not without good justification. Another possible exception could be the discussion of Tolkien's work via his literary criticism but, again, since the argument is based upon Tolkien's famous essay on *Beowulf*, it has unquestionably medieval ramifications.

Thus, the book's unifying approach tends to be medievalist. Thomas Honegger has helpfully defined this method, calling it the 'interpretatio mediaevalia', as "the explanation and exploration of Tolkien's work with the help of mediaeval studies" (2005: 45).[1] In the critic's opinion, obviously shared by the authors of this collection, the medievalist approach to Tolkien, one among many, has considerable advantages over other approaches. The high percentage of medieval topics in the *J.R.R. Tolkien Encyclopedia* edited by Michael D.C. Drout (Routledge 2006) testifies to the continuing relevance of this direction in Tolkien scholarship. Honegger discusses such specific ways of investigating Tolkien *via mediaevalia* as the study of proper names through the knowledge of Old English and Old Norse languages or tracing parallel motifs in Tolkien's works and medieval literature. The second of these ways is amply represented in the present volume. Thomas Honegger quite rightly points out, though, that the erudition and excellence of some of the medievalist studies of Tolkien, such as especially Professor Tom Shippey's masterful *The Road to Middle-earth*, "have left little of importance to discover in this field" (2005: 54).

---

1 For the full argument see Thomas Honegger, "Tolkien Through the Eyes of a Mediaevalist", *Reconsidering Tolkien*, ed. T. Honegger, Zurich and Berne: Walking Tree Publishers, 2005, 45-66.

Still, *the Road goes ever on and on*, also with medievalist studies of Tolkien. This book contains, therefore, some further attempts of elucidating Tolkien's creative achievement by situating it in diverse medieval literary and cultural contexts. The book's specific quality seems to lie in a readiness to employ complex structural patterns and sophisticated critical constructs as well as to adopt the cultural and literary parameters of the Middle Ages in order to shed new light on Tolkien's medieval inspirations. For example, a stimulating analysis of the cultures of Middle-earth has been undertaken by Bartłomiej Błaszkiewicz with recourse to oral studies and its understanding of medieval orality and literacy. In the opening article, Joanna Kokot focuses upon Tolkien's narrative technique and explains the artistic design of *The Lord of the Rings* in terms of the device of *entrelacement* employed in medieval prose romances. Andrzej Wicher's closing paper constitutes an essay in metacriticism, approaching Tolkien's work through his own essays of literary criticism, especially the most famous ones concerning *Beowulf* and fairy-stories. Maria Błaszkiewicz explores the significance of the queen in *The Lord of the Rings* with reference to medieval notions of kingship, and Barbara Kowalik juxtaposes the role of Elbereth in the novel against the patterns of medieval Marian devotion.

Since all the contributions to this book come from Polish scholars, it may be worth noting that Tolkien has enjoyed in Poland not only an enthusiastic popular reception but also a most serious academic interest. Philologists and specialists in other disciplines, such as anthropology, history, and studies of religion, have written books and articles on Tolkien and translated his works and seminal studies of his works. Andrzej Zgorzelski, a professor of English literature, was one of those who pioneered professional literary criticism of Tolkien. He compared *The Lord of the Rings* and to the works of William Golding, T.H. White, and John Ballard in terms of the originality of their structural devices, and in successive papers analyzed the time setting of Tolkien's novel and its ingenious blending of diverse literary modes and genres.[2] Another colleague in English studies, representing a younger generation,

---

2 A. Zgorzelski, *Kreacje świata sensów. Szkice o współczesnej powieści angielskiej*, Łódź 1967, p. 81; "Time Setting in J.R.R. Tolkien's *The Lord of the Rings*", *Zagadnienia Rodzajów Literackich* 2, no. 25 (1971), 91-100; "The Syncretic Nature of J.R.R. Tolkien's *The Lord of the Rings*", *Born of the Fantastic*, Gdańsk: Wydawnictwo Uniwersytetu Gdańskiego, 2004, 150-182.

Christopher Garbowski, has become an internationally-recognized Tolkien expert. Also among the authors of this volume are scholars who have made significant contributions to Tolkien scholarship (see the biographical notes). A large volume of papers edited by Jakub Lichański, a professor of Polish philology specializing in rhetoric and Old Polish literature, represents both the wide range and the high academic status of Tolkien scholarship in Poland.[3] English-speaking readers will find basic information about the reception of Tolkien in Poland in Marcin Morawski's article in the *J.R.R. Tolkien Encyclopedia* (535-536).

I would like to dwell for a while upon what I have figuratively called a medievalist liaison which facilitated Tolkien's entry into Poland. Namely, his work may have been recommended to Polish publishers and it was then introduced to Polish readers by one of the founding fathers of English philology in the post-war period, a medievalist, Prof. Przemysław Mroczkowski, head of the English departments at the Catholic University of Lublin and subsequently at the Jagiellonian University in Cracow. Mroczkowski knew Tolkien personally and became his friend and correspondent. Both were Catholics, a significant factor that brought them together for, as Mroczkowski's daughter recalls, Tolkien much cared to be in solidarity with members of the Church further east. While Mroczkowski was fascinated by the reforms of the Second Vatican Council, Tolkien was a staunch traditionalist. Mroczkowski first met Tolkien at the British Council in Oxford in 1957. At 42 then, he presented himself to the Oxford professor as follows: "I come from Mordor, I come from Mordor." Later, in a letter to Mroczkowski's wife Janina, Tolkien wrote: "Poland for its own sake, but especially since it is your country, is ever in my mind." The personal correspondence between J.R.R. Tolkien and Przemysław and Janina Mroczkowski reveals that they were close friends. Towards the end of his stay in Oxford, Mroczkowski visited Tolkien and talked to him about translating his books into Polish. The Oxford professor wrote detailed comments on the Polish colleague's article "on the new Robinson Chaucer",

---

[3] J. Z. Lichański, ed. *J.R.R. Tolkien: Recepcja polska* (J.R.R. Tolkien: Polish Reception), Warszawa: Wydawnictwa Uniwersytetu Warszawskiego, 1996. See also a recent M. A. thesis on Tolkien's reception in Poland: Justyna Smęder, "Recepcja literatury fantasy w Polsce na przykładzie dzieł J. R. R. Tolkiena", Kraków: Jagiellonian University, 2011 (full text available at: jbc.bj.uj.edu.pl/Content/180603).

which was a review of F.N. Robinson's second edition of Chaucer. He also annotated Mroczkowski's review of *A Preface to Chaucer* by D.W. Robertson, Jr., a seminal study of medieval literature. Interestingly, on the latter occasion Tolkien expressed serious doubts about the value of scholarly books of this kind, berating himself as an unlearned man and impostor scholar, but in fact revealing a quite distinct frame of mind, one which made him turn away from academic writing and embrace imaginative literature.[4] Mroczkowski wrote reviews of the successive Polish volumes of *The Lord of the Rings*.[5] He informed Tolkien about the good quality of the first Polish translation of *The Hobbit* made by Maria Skibniewska: "the treatment of the text is not akin to the cover" (Tolkien had been concerned about the quality of the Polish edition because of the, in his opinion, awful cover design).

The scholar from Cracow had, in fact, come to know all the Inklings and portrayed this circle to the Polish reader in a personal and well-informed way.[6] His essay contains a general appreciation of Tolkien's work. Mroczkowski emphasizes Tolkien's special attitude to language: his polyglot competence (he claims that Tolkien could understand even Polish) and his boyish enchantment with the wonder of the linguistic sign. He describes Tolkien's style as one that allows us to hear the speech of past generations, so distinct in its dignity from the present barbarian jargon, and yet animated and devoid of archaisms. When asked by Mroczkowski about his principal aim as a novelist, Tolkien is said to have replied simply: "I wanted to tell a long story." Mroczkowski interprets this as running firmly against the experiments of modernist literature. Accordingly, he does not take Tolkien's dismissal of allegory at face value but recognizes in *The Lord of the Rings* the principal allegorical *topoi* of medieval literature, the motifs of quest and of combat. The Polish scholar draws attention, in particular, to Tolkien's sophisticated creation of evil, suggestive of a threat or catastrophe of cosmic dimensions (he mentions that Tolkien personally was a historiosophic

---

4 Joanna Petry-Mroczkowska, "Przybysz z Mordoru" (A Visitor from Mordor), *Tygodnik Powszechny* 2009, no. 24 (3127). Petry-Mroczkowska draws her information from the letters J.R.R. Tolkien wrote to her father. A series of nine such letters were sold in London at Christie's in 2009.
5 P. Mroczkowski, "Wielka baśń o prawdach" (A Great Fairy-story about Truths), *Przegląd Kulturalny*, 1961, no. 49, p. 4; "Dalsza baśń o prawdach" (A Further Fairy-story about Truths), *Przegląd Kulturalny*, 1962, no. 51-52, p. 9; "Powrót Króla" (The Return of the King), *Więź*, 1964, no 2, p. 97.
6 P. Mroczkowski, "Uczoność a wyobraźnia w Oxfordzie" (Learning and Imagination at Oxford), *Dżentelmeni i poeci. Eseje z literatury angielskiej* (Poets and Gentlemen: Essays in English Literature), Kraków: Wydawnictwo Literackie, 1975, 278-307.

pessimist, believing that history moves towards a final zero point), and observes that in comparison with the empire of darkness the forces of good seem to be less centrally organized in Tolkien's world.

Furthermore, defending Tolkien against his critics, Mroczkowski connects his work not only with Germanic and Celtic folklore but also with medieval epics and romances, stressing especially its epic quality. He explains the phenomenon of *The Lord of the Rings* in terms of resurrecting, by means of poetic imagination, a world buried and lying dormant in folk beliefs, literary conventions, and verbal records of the past. We know, he writes, that ancient Celts and Germans worshipped trees – this is a dry piece of information from the field of religious studies, but Tolkien perceives in these huge plants their beauty and strength, the marvel of growth and immobilized energy, and his fantasy makes him paint the picture of Walking and Thinking Trees, the Ents. Finally, Mroczkowski underlines the Englishness of the world created in what he terms Tolkien's fairy epic, manifest in combining the English love of comfort with a thirst for adventure, and of common sense with mystery.

Tadeusz A. Olszański (home.agh.edu.pl/~evermind/jrrtolkien.htm) draws attention to Tolkien's relatively rapid reception in Poland. Writing about the first Polish translations of Tolkien's works, he points out that the translation of *The Lord of the Rings* (1961-63) was, after Dutch (1956) and Swedish (1959), the third translation of the book in the world, antedating the Danish (1968), German (1969), Italian (1970), and French (1972) renderings. Remarkably, it was also the first translation into a non-Germanic language and first in the Communist Bloc. Although the earliest Polish translation of *The Hobbit* (1960) appeared more than twenty years after the first English edition, it was again, after Swedish and German, the third translation of the book worldwide. *The Silmarillion* was published in Polish in 1985, within seven years of its English edition, and was also one of the earliest translations of the book in the world. Even Tolkien's minor works, such as *Farmer Giles of Ham* and *Smith of Wootton Major*, were published in Poland as early as 1962. These first translations were made by Maria Skibniewska, at that time a leading translator from English. Including an astonishingly great number of extremely well informed and researched publications, growing over the years, and academic papers and courses, conventions, live action role-playing games, and societies, like the

Tolkien Section of the Silesian Fantasy Club, currently publishing the periodical *Aiglos*, the wide range of interest in Tolkien's work in Poland, encompassing both academics and popular fans, seems to be an intriguing phenomenon that demands an explanation.

In various Internet discussions the Poles themselves analyze this phenomenon and give various reasons for Tolkien's immense popularity in their country. They consider the difficult access to Tolkien's books, due to the sparse and small-sized editions and the resulting exorbitant prices on the black market, as well as the interference of censorship to have been powerful factors whetting the readers' appetite. They suggest, moreover, that Tolkien's fantasy world provided a welcome contrast to the drab reality of everyday life in a communist state. In addition, to Roman Catholics, whose Church has the doctrine of co-redemption and who believe that an individual can participate in Christ's salvific work through personal suffering, Frodo's self-sacrifice is allegedly more understandable and appealing than to Protestants. Also, the romantic character of the Polish nation, seeing itself, especially in the past, as suffering on behalf of the world, is held to be partly responsible for Tolkien's appeal. The Poles point out that innocent suffering and self-offering has long been part of their cultural tradition, which renders them particularly sensitive to the Romantic underpinnings of Frodo's incurable wound and his simultaneous attraction to and struggle with Sauron. Yet another factor might be an irresistible, if unconscious, nostalgia for the return of the king: after all, Poland was a monarchy in the golden ages of its history. On the other hand, there are many readers who attribute Tolkien's popularity to the sheer beauty of his works.

The present considerations suggest a very simple answer to the puzzle of Tolkien's Polish success. It all started with the personal medievalist connection, which was also, perhaps more importantly, a Catholic one: Tolkien's works appeared in Poland because he met and befriended a visiting scholar from Cracow, who subsequently asked him if he would like to see his books published behind the Iron Curtain. Tolkien writes about this in a letter to his publisher Rayner Unwin on June 2, 1958. Later in the same month, on June 19, Unwin informed Tolkien about two publishing houses, Czytelnik and Iskry, being interested in publishing, respectively, *The Lord of the Rings* and *The Hobbit*.

Two symbolic details are worth noting while thinking of Tolkien in the Polish context. One is the famous writer's place of burial: he and his wife take their eternal rest in a Roman Catholic section at the Wolvercote cemetery in Oxford, surrounded by the tombstones many of which are Polish. The other thing is Tolkien's mention of the Saxon and Polish blood running in his veins. This passing remark has recently acquired new significance through the research done by Ryszard Derdziński and Tadeusz A. Olszański on the origin of Tolkien's family name: while the two investigators do not deny Tolkien's Saxon roots, their search has firmly established the Prussian origin of the surname *Tolkien* and led to the village of Tołkiny in Eastern Prussia, now in Poland.

The articles gathered in this book are envisaged as a modest contribution to the medievalist studies of Tolkien, firmly established and much advanced in the English-language scholarship by Tom Shippey, Michael Drout, Thomas Honegger, and by the contributors to collections of essays such as *Tolkien the Medievalist*[7] or by authors of works such as *The Keys to Middle Earth*,[8] as well as a continuation of a similar kind of studies conducted in Poland by Przemysław Mroczkowski and his followers. The contributors are mostly academics specializing in English literature and one historian specializing in the Old Norse period, and are affiliated with various institutions of higher education all over the country, their academic ranks ranging from PhD candidates to full professors.

To conclude this introduction, let me give the reader a few more highlights of what is to follow. Thus, Joanna Kokot explains some of the intricacies of timing in *The Lord of the Rings* by tracing the narrative composition of the book in terms of the technique of interlacement used in medieval Arthurian romances. Bartłomiej Błaszkiewicz employs his competence in medieval orality and literacy to reflect upon what kind of culture would have been created by an immortal species like the Elves and how the cultures of other species of Middle-earth are related to the Elven culture. Justyna Brzezińska provides a reading of the character and actions of Éowyn against the social codes of heroic epic and chivalric romance. Maria Błaszkiewicz explores the notion of the queen to reveal why

---

7 See Chance, Jane (ed.), *Tolkien the Medievalist* (Routledge, 2003).
8 See Stuart D. Lee and Elizabeth Solopova, *The Keys to Middle Earth: Discovering Medieval Literature Through the Fiction of J. R. R. Tolkien* (Palgrave Macmillan, 2006).

women are not necessarily to be thought unimportant in *The Lord of the Rings*. Barbara Kowalik interprets the invisible presence of Elbereth accompanying Sam and Frodo in their epic adventure as being analogous to the place of the Virgin Mary in the world of actual medieval believers and literary characters like King Arthur, Sir Gawain, and Robin Hood. Katarzyna Blacharska analyzes the nature of evil in Tolkien's world by comparing Melkor with Satan of John Milton's *Paradise Lost*. Renata Leśniakiewicz-Drzymała takes us to the world of medieval Icelandic sagas to throw further light on Tolkien's works for children. Łukasz Neubauer reads *The Homecoming of Beorhtnoth Beorhthelm's Son* through his thorough knowledge of *The Battle of Maldon*, the poem as well as the historical event. And, finally, Andrzej Wicher compares Tolkien's style of criticism with the school of New Criticism and illuminates Tolkien's art by way of *Beowulf* and Tolkien's view of the Anglo-Saxon epic.

"O, what a tangled web we weave", one wishes to cry out with Joanna Kokot, extending her metaphorical quotation of Walter Scott from the interlacements of *The Lord of the Rings* to the innumerable acts of sub-creation and interpretation in which all lovers of the word untiringly engage.[9]

---

9 The quotation comes from Walter Scott's *Marmion*, canto vi, stanza 17.

Joanna Kokot

"O, what a tangled web we weave". *The Lord of the Rings* and the Interlacement Technique

Abstract

The references in J.R.R. Tolkien's *The Lord of the Rings* to Old English and Old Norse epic are numerous and conspicuous. There is yet another tradition underlying the text, though, namely that of the medieval chivalric romance, recognizable already in the motif of quest undertaken by Frodo and his companions in order to destroy the Ring. It is not only the type of action that suggests the affinities with the medieval genre, but also the compositional technique of interlacement, noticeable especially in the second volume of *The Lord of the Rings*. The paper examines the way in which particular subplots are interwoven after the breaking of the Fellowship of the Ring. As it appears, the compositional arrangement results not only in the creation of a complete world (as opposed to the open reality of the Arthurian romances), but also suggests an order underlying the seemingly chaotic world, at the same time suggesting an analogy between the created universe and the text in which it is retold.

In his essay "On Fairy-Stories", while discussing his earliest literary fascinations, Tolkien writes:

> I had very little desire to look for buried treasure or fight pirates, and *Treasure Island* left me cool. Red Indians were better: there were bows and arrows (I had and have a wholly unsatisfied desire to shoot well with a bow), and strange languages, and glimpses of an archaic mode of life, and, above all, forests in such stories. But the land of Merlin and Arthur was better than these, and best of all the nameless North of Sigurd of the Völsungs, and [Fáfnir] the prince of all dragons". (*L* 63)

Afterwards he adds: "But the world that contained even the imagination of Fáfnir was richer and more beautiful, at whatever cost of peril" (*L* 64). It must be immediately apparent to anyone familiar with Tolkien's work that these childhood fascinations found their continuation not only in his scholarly interests, but also in his literary texts, among others in *The Lord of the Rings*.

Apart from the numerous references to Old English and Old Norse texts, there is still another tradition underlying *The Lord of the Rings*, which links it, more or less loosely, with medieval literature. It is the tradition of the medieval chivalric romance, readily identifiable in the motif of the quest. Like the knights from the later Arthurian romances, the protagonists of Tolkien's text have a task to fulfil (even if the task does not consist in finding the Holy Grail, but in destroying the unholy Ring), whereas the journey itself is as important for the story as the final trial. The journey thus becomes a pretext to introduce new places, which in the traditional romance are presented as rather isolated *loci*, while in *The Lord of the Rings* they become spots on a more complete map of Middle-earth; new people whose role may be merely episodic in relation to the whole plot, and new subplots which constitute ramifications of the main sequence of events, often provoked by some incidental meetings or additional tasks to be fulfilled (as happens when the Fellowship breaks with Frodo and Sam following the original task, and the others getting involved first in the battle in Helm's Deep and then in the defence of Gondor).

And this brings us to the principal compositional device that was characteristic of the later medieval Arthurian romances (with the exception of Thomas Malory's version), that is, the interlacement technique.[1]

Interlacement as a compositional technique

It is a commonplace that the successive romance writers rarely invented new plots. They rather based their stories on the extant ones, enriching them with new elements, re-working and re-ordering them. Thus one of the principles underlying the development of the Arthurian romance is that of coalescence. The subsequent romancers not only used older tales and motifs, but they also linked the originally separate and independent narratives into more and more extensive wholes – the process ending with the appearance of the romance cycles with the ambition to gather together all the sub-plots of the Arthurian world.

---

1 Even if, as Richard C. West suggests (78), it is doubtful whether Tolkien was directly influenced by chivalric romances, and it might have been more contemporary texts that inspired him, the fact remains that the roots of the interlacement technique reach back as far as the medieval genre.

Thus what in Chrétien de Troyes' romances was just a series of unrelated adventures – even if there was a common frame of reference for them, that is King Arthur's court – turns with Robert de Boron and other romancers into more complex narratives, while the so called "Vulgate cycle" (written in the 13th century) brings all the plots and themes together in one vast narrative (a similar endeavour was undertaken by Thomas Malory two centuries later). The world of the Arthurian romances thus gradually turns into one coherent whole, with significant links established between the originally independent episodes, suggesting connections between the hitherto unrelated plots.[2]

> Thirteenth-century prose writers, and especially those who took it upon themselves to exploit and expand the rich legacy of Arthurian romance, had the same ultimate purpose in mind: they [...] wanted to make the narrative more meaningful by giving it a "causal" perspective, but the method they adopted was a typically thirteenth-century one, paralleled in several other aspects of late medieval thought and imagination. It consisted less in explaining the action in so many words than in forging significant episodes, it aimed at establishing, or at least suggesting, relationships between hitherto narrated themes, it illustrated, better perhaps than any other contemporary form of art could have done, the scholastic principle of *manifestatio*. (Vinaver 68)

It is only in the fifteenth-century work by Thomas Malory that the adventures of King Arthur's knights are told as a series of complete and autonomous episodes, constituting both a temporal and a compositional sequence. In the thirteenth-century romance cycles particular subplots are interwoven, so that "no single section [...] is self-contained" (Vinaver 71). Individual adventures or plots are presented as concurrent, and to preserve this characteristic of theirs the technique of interlacement is utilized and becomes the dominant principle underlying the composition of the high medieval Arthurian cycles, so that the concurrence of the plots finds its equivalent in the way of telling them.

Thus a given plot is interrupted to give room to another, which in turn may be suspended in favour of still another one – the narrator returning to the seemingly abandoned adventures and again interrupting his tale to introduce or to

---

2 The process of coalescence is discussed thoroughly by Vinaver (56-62), where the scholar follows the development of the Waste Land plot. The initially independent motifs are linked together by the subsequent romancers, resulting in a more and more elaborate pattern of motifs, endowed with additional meanings due to their being brought together. The argument is mainly against the thesis of Jessie Weston and her followers who assume the existence of a hypothetical "prototype, containing the main features of the Grail story – the Waste Land, the Fisher King, the Hidden Castle with its solemn Feast, and mysterious Feeding Vessel, the Bleeding Lance and Cup" (Weston 3).

continue a next plot. The plots do not have to be interrelated – there is often no motivation for bringing them together in one text (even if on a higher level they may comment upon one another). The shifts from one adventure (and protagonist) to another are clearly marked in the text by the phrases announcing the suspension of one plot and turning to another:

> Come morning, Sir Gawain took his leave and continued his wanderings until he fell in by chance with Agloval and Girflet, son of Do. Four days they journeyed uneventfully, and on the fifth they parted each to his solitary course. And here the tale leaves them and tells of Galahad. (*Quest* 80)
>
> So Lancelot found help for his wound [...]. But now the story stops speaking of him, and returns to Sir Gawain and Gaheriet. (*Death* 37)

The same complication can be seen in the adventures of one particular protagonist. The knight-errant rarely participates in one single causally linked sequence of events at a time. He is apt to abandon one quest for another, one adventure for another, only to resume it after some time, so that a romance protagonist usually takes part in a number of plots simultaneously. The adventures do not follow each other, they interweave, forming a complicated design, with ramifications in many directions, and apparently devoid of a single unifying motivation.

They sometimes meet – two different adventures merge into one, the fates of two knights cross, a couple of plots find a common ending. But there is no rule, and obviously no regular plan underlies the whole. The text becomes similar to the favourite setting of the romance adventures – the forest, with its labyrinth of paths and new adventures for the travellers to meet on their way, where one can easily get lost and unexpectedly find oneself following one's own or somebody else's track. Both the ramification and the merging of particular plots, together with the interlacing of the narratives of the plots as well as the protagonists' rambles from one adventure to another (having accomplished none) – all this results in a "maze of adventures, quests, and battles" (Vinaver 69), a maze "that cannot be taken in at a glance, something that at first looks planless, though all is planned" (Lewis 194). As Eugene Vinaver notices, the thirteenth-century Arthurian cycles can be compared to ornaments, seemingly disorderly, with no consistent organizing principle, but yet perceived as ordered – even if abstract – patterns (78-81). As Rosemond Tuve puts it, "events connected by *entrelace-*

ment are not juxtaposed; they are interlaced [...]. We digress, or seem to, and then come back, not to precisely what we left but to something we understand differently because of what we have since seen" (362-63).

Obviously, *The Lord of the Rings* is not a result – as were these medieval romance cycles – of combining several separate tales into one. The motivation for interlacing several subplots is to be found here in the very development of action, or rather in the series of events which eventually result in the split of the Fellowship of the Ring into some smaller parties.

And so the first volume of *The Lord of the Rings* narrates a single course of events, the protagonists keeping together, travelling throughout Middle-earth towards their destination (even if there already appear suggestions of a possible split, as Boromir instead of destroying the Ring would rather take it to Minas Tirith and use it to save his country). The narrative simply consists in reporting the protagonists' travels from one place to another – through the Old Forest, Tom Bombadil's house, the Barrow Downs, Bree and the Ford to Rivendell, and, when the Company is formed, Khazad-dum, Lórien and Parth Galen, where eventually the members of the Fellowship take three different routes – the narrator's attention not concentrating merely on particular *loci*, as it would be in a chivalric romance (or in a fairy tale), but on the hardships of the journey itself:

> Telescoping of any of the travel stages in a formula typical of the fairy tale ("he rode and rode until he saw...") is absolutely out of question here. On the contrary [...] the attention drawn to details of the journey and to passing time tends to present the characters not only in their actions to overcome magic barriers, but also in their toil to cover the distance. (Zgorzelski 21)

But the events at Parth Galen initiate a different plot, consisting of three subplots, related to particular members of the Fellowship. The first two chapters comprise the search undertaken by Aragorn, Gimli and Legolas for the hobbits, Pippin and Merry, who have been abducted by the orcs. On their way they meet the Rohirrim, from whom they obtain at least some information concerning the band of their enemies. It is interesting that, while the three rescuers follow the orc troop, the reader knows as little about the real fate of the hobbits as they do (not to mention the fate of Frodo and Sam, to whom the narrator will return much later), and the relationship between cause and effect is reversed. The second chapter ends with an additional mystery – or rather two mysteries. An old man appears at night at the eaves of the forest and almost immediately disappears without a word, and the horses that the warriors borrowed from the Rohirrim disappear. Even if the old man is suspected to be Saruman (Éomer mentions him in his conversation with Aragorn), there are some doubts as to his identity: according to Éomer, Saruman "walks about like an old man hooded and cloaked" (*LotR* 432-33; see also 426), whereas the man they saw had "a hat not a hood" (433). Neither is it clear whether the nightly visitor was responsible for the escape of the horses. And at this moment the subplot is suspended. The next two chapters are devoted to Pippin and Merry. The narration goes back in time, so the initial events are more or less concurrent with those that opened Chapter 1. The tale follows the fates of the hobbits, first as captives among the orcs, and then, after Merry and Pippin's escape during the battle with the Riders, as guests of the ents. The narration returns to Aragorn, Gimli and Legolas, who are joined by Gandalf on their way to Meduseld. The narrative comprises the events at the Golden Hall, the exposing of Gríma's schemes and the healing of king Theoden, and finally the battle at Helm's Deep and the journey to Isengard. There the travellers meet the hobbits. Again the action goes back in time (even if it happens in the retrospective tale of Pippin and not in the main narration), the hobbits' subplot is continued where it was interrupted (or rather suspended) at the end of Chapter 4, and the narration again deals with the events concurrent with those which took place in Rohan and were presented in Chapters 5 to 8. The Company is together again (save Frodo and Sam) for some time, and then they part anew: Aragorn, Legolas, Gimli and Merry stay in Rohan, whereas Gandalf takes Pippin to Gondor. Book IV is entirely devoted to the adventures of Frodo and Sam, starting with their escape from Parth Galen and ending with Frodo falling into the hands of the Enemy's soldiers – so once more the narration goes back in time and covers the events parallel to those presented in the previous Book.

The interlacement is thus double-folded here. On the one hand there is Book IV, devoted entirely to the tedious journey of Frodo and Sam, accompanied by Gollum (the events being parallel to those which are presented in the first half of the volume), on the other – there is Book III which presents the interlacing subplots involving the rest of the Fellowship, who split twice: once when Merry and Pippin are captured by the orcs, and then when Gandalf takes Pippin to Gondor, leaving Aragorn and his companions behind. As Tolkien puts it himself in one of his letters: "The narrative now divides into two main branches: 1. Prime Action, the Ringbearers. 2. Subsidiary Action, the rest of the Company leading to the 'heroic' matter [...] totally different in tone and scenery" (*L* 275).

The next two books are organized according to the same principle, that is, Book V presents the interlacing fates of Merry, Aragorn, Gimli and Legolas on the one hand and Pippin and Gandalf on the other, with the further complication when Merry leaves the company with Éowyn. Here again we have some plots that are concurrent in the fictional world of the novel, and are presented as a bunch of interlacing tales. And so Chapter 1 of Book V is devoted to Gandalf and Pippin's ride to Minas Tirith and to the first day of their stay in the capital of Gondor. Chapter 2 takes up the subplot of the Rohirrim accompanied by Aragorn, Legolas, Gimli and Merry. It ends with another split of the Fellowship, when Aragorn and the Dunedains together with the elf and the dwarf lead the Grey Company to Pelargir, and Merry stays with King Theoden and the Riders. His adventures are continued in the next chapter, telling of the muster of Rohan and the beginning of the ride to Gondor. Chapter 4 returns to Pippin and Gandalf, telling us also about the return of Faramir to Minas Tirith, an event which links this subplot with that of Frodo and Sam (who met Denethor's younger son in the course of their journey). Chapter 5 continues with the account of Merry's fate exactly at the point it was interrupted two chapters before, and ends with the event closing the previous chapter – with the Riders' arrival at the Pelennor Fields in succour of Gondor. The battle on the Pelennor Fields brings all the parties (except Sam and Frodo) together, while the tale returns to the subplot of the Grey Company, which – like that of the siege of Isengard – is presented in a retrospective narrative. Book VI returns to the parallel plot of Frodo and Sam continuing their arduous march towards Mount Doom and comprises three chapters, the slowness of the progress being enhanced by the continuous tale – whereas the "heroic" plots (to use Tolkien's term) are full of turning points, the tempo of the events being stressed by the shifts of perspective and passing from one subplot to another. Only in the fourth chapter of Book VI are all the members of the Fellowship brought together, and the plot returns to its original linear mode.

"A temporal map" and links between plots

What is important in Tolkien's tale is the care taken to present the passing of time in a very precise way – also in the case of the interlaced subplots. The exact time of events is given – either suggested by dates or measured by the moon quarters. The narrator follows the rhythm of successive days and nights, even if nothing important happens; thus there are no elusive phrases like "after many days" or "some time passed". The reader is given enough data to reconstruct the detailed record of all the journeys and to compare the events occurring at various places but at the same time.[3] It seems that this is a *novum* in relation to the organization of time in the chivalric romances, where the adventures of the knights are not strictly regulated by the calendar (provided that there is any calendar at all in the romance world).

Such an exact observance of the passing of time constitutes a device which modifies the romance-like composition. Interlacement in Tolkien's text does not merely consist in telling various courses of events that take place simultaneously in a way that would stress the concurrent aspect of the plots, but in revealing relations between them, linking them into a pattern. The breaking of the chronological order of events by relating first a fragment of one subplot then a fragment of another going back in time, together with such a strict observance of the calendar, results in presenting the reader with episodes that seem to him as bewildering as they seem to the protagonist, and to have their true significance revealed only later.

Riddles and explanations

The relation between the subplots may be as obvious as in the case of the initial chapters of *The Two Towers*. Here we have Aragorn and his companions actually following the orcs' tracks, finding traces of both the orcs and the hobbits, which may at first seem enigmatic, but which are given full explanation later. As the exasperated Gimli says when they arrive at the battlefield

---

[3] Actually such a reconstruction has been proposed by Barbara Strachey in her book, where the author does not merely draw a map (or rather a series of maps) illustrating the travels of Frodo and his companions, but also provides the date of each stage of the journey. The drafts in the relevant volumes of the History of Middle-earth are also helpful in reconstructing the interlacement pattern in *The Lord of the Rings*.

in Rohan and find no traces of the hobbits: "We have been set many riddles since we came to Tol Brandir" (*LotR* 430). No doubt they have.

On the first night of the chase Aragorn, Legolas and Gimli come across a strange scene:

> Suddenly the Elf gave a cry and the others came running towards him.
>
> "We have already overtaken some of those that we are hunting," he said. "Look!" He pointed, and they saw that what they had first taken to be boulders lying at the foot of the slope were huddled bodies. Five dead Orcs lay there. They had been hewn with many cruel strokes, and two of them had been beheaded. The ground was red with their dark blood.
>
> "Here is another riddle!" said Gimli. "But it needs the light of day, and for that we cannot wait". (*LotR* 411-12)

The first riddle – that of the footprints found on the riverbank after Boromir's funeral – is solved both by Aragorn and by the reader. Aragorn quite rightly deduces what the reader already knows, being acquainted with the events closing Book II: these are the tracks left by Frodo and Sam who took their packs and went away by boat. But as to the riddle of the slaughtered orcs, the reader has to wait until the third chapter to get the proper explanation – a quarrel over the leadership resulting in a fight between two "races" of the orcs:

> Uglúk shouted, and a number of other Orcs of nearly his own size ran up. Then suddenly, without warning, Uglúk sprang forwards, and with two swift strokes swept the heads off two of his opponents, Grishnakh stepped aside and vanished into the shadows. The others gave way, and one stepped backwards and fell over Merry's prostrate form with a curse. Yet that probably saved his life, for Uglúk's followers leaped over him and cut down another with their broad-bladed swords. It was the yellow-fanged guard. His body fell right on top of Pippin, still clutching its long saw-edged knife.
>
> [...] The Orcs were getting ready to march again, but some of the Northerners were still unwilling, and the Isengarders slew two more before the rest were cowed. (*LotR* 437)

The number of the slain orcs, as well as the way they were killed, corresponds to the scene viewed by the rescue party two chapters earlier. The riddle is thus explained. And in the same way other riddles are given proper answers. What seems incomprehensible for the followers stops to be so when the parallel subplot is eventually narrated.

Thus the small footprints found on the second day of the chase find their equivalent in the episode of Pippin who, after the thongs on his legs have been removed by the orcs, deliberately runs aside to leave clear traces for the hoped-for rescuers. As far as the latter are concerned, it is not clear for them how the hobbit could leave the host even for a moment, and why he should do it. The same explanation is given to the leaf-shaped brooch found on the site, again left by Pippin on purpose to signal that the hobbits are still alive. The traces left by the hobbit are thus "read" properly, the signal given deciphered, but the reader has to wait for the more comprehensible report until the narrator takes up the other subplot.

Another riddle connected with the search for the hobbits comes when the companions eventually find the traces of the hobbits' meal – a mallorn-leaf with crumbs of lembas, and also pieces of cord together with an orc-knife, but no hobbit footprints. These tracks seem to make no sense at all. This is how Legolas comments upon them:

> Well, here is the strangest riddle that we have yet found! [...] A bound prisoner escapes both from the Orcs and from the surrounding horsemen. He then stops, while still in the open, and cuts his bonds with an orc-knife. But how and why? For if his legs were tied, how did he walk? And if his arms were tied, how did he use the knife? And if neither were tied, why did he cut the cords at all? Being pleased with his skill, he then sat down and quietly ate some waybread! [...] After that, I suppose, he turned his arms into wings and flew away singing into trees. It should be easy to find him: we only need wings ourselves! (*LotR* 478)

Even if Aragorn provides answers to some of the problems posed by his friend, other questions remain unanswered until their meeting with the hobbits at the gatehouse of Isengard. It is different with the reader, as the explanation of what seems puzzling to the elf can be found in the earlier chapters devoted to the fate of Pippin and Merry.

What is interesting is that it is not the hobbits themselves that provide the explanation to the puzzling signs and traces encountered during the chase (at least on the level of the narrator-narratee communication). When Pippin tells his tale, the narrator does not quote that part of it which refers to the days of captivity; he only states: "With that he [Pippin] plunged into an account of Boromir's last fight and the orc-march from Emyn Muil to the Forest. The others nodded as the various points were fitted with their guesses" (*LotR* 549), but which points these are, is not said. The task to make them agree with the listeners' guesses (or rather with the riddles they faced during the chase) is left mainly to the reader, who ought to compare the findings of Aragorn and his companions (presented in Chapter 1 and 2) with the fates of the hobbits (retold in the next two chapters).

Different points of view

Sometimes the events linking particular subplots are presented from different perspectives, with one group of characters seeing only some aspects of what constitutes the action proper for another group, and the full significance of the events is revealed in another part of the tale.

One such event which is given little notice, but which is fully explained when seen in connection with other subplots, is the episode at the beginning of Book III: Aragorn sees an eagle in the sky, and then sees it again on the following day. At first the presence of the bird seems incidental, a mere background for the main sequence of events. Only later – during the meeting with Gandalf – does the eagle turn out to be Gwaihir, who has been sent by the wizard "to watch the River and gather tidings" (*LotR* 484). Thus the anonymous bird, whose presence over the mountains could be interpreted as a natural occurrence, proves to be of importance to the course of the events (Gwaihir's role in the action is stressed by the Orthanc episode, when the eagle helped Gandalf escape from prison).

When Frodo with Sam and Gollum travel towards Mordor, three times they sense a Nazgûl passing over their heads. T. A. Shippey (146) writes:

> Across the whole breadth of the story, meanwhile, fly the Nazgûl. Frodo and Sam feel their presence three times as they wander across the Emyn Muil and the Dead Marshes [...] on the 29th February, 1st March and 4th March. Gollum feels sure this is no coincidence. "'Three times!' he whimpered. 'Three times is a threat. They feel us here, they feel the Precious. The Precious is their master. We cannot go further this way, no. It's no use, no use!'" What he says sounds plausible enough, but it's wrong. Three times *is* a coincidence, and actually we can guess each time what the Nazgûl are doing. The first was coming back from a fruitless wait for Grishnakh the orc, dead and burnt that same day, with the smoke from the burning "seen by many watchful eyes". The second was probing towards Rohan and Saruman. The third was heading for

Isengard, to alarm Pippin on its way with the thought that it had somehow been despatched for him.

Here the mistake committed by the characters is of a different kind – they interpret the events as "belonging" to another subplot concerning themselves and thus constituting a more or less immediate danger. But the principle is similar: particular subplots have shared elements that link them together.

On March 2nd when King Theoden's army is walking towards Helm's Deep, Éomer asks the keen-eyed Legolas to look towards Isengard. The elf says:

> I can see a darkness. There are shapes moving in it, great shapes far away upon the bank of the river, but what they are I cannot tell. It is not mist or cloud that defeats my eyes: there is a veiling shadow that some power lays upon the land, and it marches slowly down stream. It is as if twilight under endless trees were flowing downwards from the hills. (*LotR* 514-15)

Legolas is right with his guess. What he sees are the ents and huorns from Fangorn marching to conquer Isengard. But the elf does not know that yet, while the reader can guess the real significance of the marching shadows, knowing the ending of the fourth chapter.

Similarly strange may seem the relief brought to the defenders of Helm's Deep. When King Theoden rides out with his warriors to face the orc host, the landscape appears altered:

> The land had changed. Where before the green dale had lain, its grassy slopes lapping the ever-mounting hills, there now a forest loomed. Great trees, bare and silent, stood, rank on rank, with tangled bough and hoary head; their twisted roots were buried in the long green grass. Darkness was under them. Between the Dike and the eaves of that nameless wood only two open furlongs lay. There now cowered the proud hosts of Saruman, in terror of the king and in terror of the trees. (*LotR* 529)

Even if the reader may be as bewildered as the characters, knowing that the enthost marched to Isengard, and not to Rohan, there can be no doubts as to the origin of the strange wood. But the characters do not know even that, whereas Gandalf merely explains the strange relief by a riddle, to which Theoden can find no answer for the time being:

> Ere iron was found or tree was hewn,
> When young was mountain under moon;
> Ere ring was made, or wrought was woe,
> It walked the forests long ago. (*LotR* 531)

The next puzzling event – even for the reader – is the dry bed of the river Isen. According to Éomer it is the work of Saruman, but strangely enough after the huorn's return to Fangorn water starts to flow again. The full explanation of all these episodes is provided only in Pippin's tale in Chapter 9, when he tells us the events that followed the ents' departure from Fangorn.

Similar links bind the events on Emyn Muil which end with Boromir's death and the subplot of Frodo and Sam. Neither of the hobbits is aware of the fate of Denethor's son, but when they arrive at Henneth Annun they learn about it from Faramir, who first heard the sound of Boromir's horn (eleven days earlier) and then saw his brother dead in a boat going down the River.

> Then I saw, or it seemed I saw, a boat floating on the water, glimmering grey, a small boat of a strange fashion with a high prow, and there was none to row or steer it. [...] It waded deep, as if it were heavily burdened, and it seemed to me as it passed under my gaze that it was almost filled with clear water, from which came the light; and lapped in the water a warrior lay asleep.
>
> A broken sword was on his knee. I saw many wounds on him. It was Boromir, my brother, dead. I knew his gear, his sword, his beloved face. One thing only I missed: his horn. One thing only I knew not: a fair belt, as it were of linked golden leaves, about his waist. (*LotR* 651)

Thus the Faramir's vision links the subplot of Frodo and Sam with that of Aragorn and his companions as given in Book III.

The narrator's hints

Sometimes the narrator himself refers to the activities of the party in a parallel subplot. When Gollum offers to show Frodo another way to Mordor, the narrator comments upon the place mentioned, at the same time referring to the concurrent actions of other protagonists in other places:

> Its [i.e. of the pass into Mordor] name was Cirith Ungol, a name of dreadful rumour. Aragorn could perhaps have told them that name and its significance; Gandalf would have warned them. But they were alone, and Aragorn was far away, and Gandalf stood amid the ruin of Isengard and strove with Saruman, delayed by treason. (*LotR* 629)

Thus, the remark on the friends being far away is not a mere rhetorical device; it helps to localize the episode in time and to view it against simultaneous events, occurring elsewhere, in which other members of the Fellowship are involved. A similar function is fulfilled by the references to the shape of the moon or to the weather – as for example when the storm over Rohan is also perceived by Merry and Pippin travelling with the ents to Isengard, or the change of wind to an easterly direction is experienced both by the hobbits and Aragorn with his companions, even though both parties are in different places.

In Book V the time relations between particular subplots are made even more obvious. The reader is no more left to himself in reconstructing the parallel events, no matter how seemingly unrelated and distant in space. The initial sentence of the chapter brings the reader back to the episode that ended the previous Book – the departure of Gandalf: "Gandalf was gone, and the thudding hoofs of Shadowfax were lost in the night, when Merry came back to Aragorn" (*LotR* 756). The beginning of Chapter 3 again marks a precise spot on the "temporal map" drawn by the narrator: "And even as Pippin stood at the Great Gate of the City and saw the Prince of Dol Amroth ride in with his banners, the King of Rohan came down out of the hills" (*LotR* 774). A similar linking role is fulfilled by the endings of Chapter 5 and Chapter 6 of Book V – both present the same event, perceived from two different perspectives: that of Gondor and of the Riders. When there seems to be no hope for the defenders of Minas Tirith and the Black Riders gloat over the seemingly certain triumph of the forces of evil, something happens:

> Gandalf did not move. And in that very moment, away behind in some courtyard of the City, a cock crowed. Shrill and clear he crowed, recking nothing of wizardry or war, welcoming only the morning that in the sky far above the shadows of death was coming with the dawn.
>
> And as if in answer there came from far away another note. Horns, horns, horns. In dark Mindolluin's sides they dimly echoed. Great horns of the North wildly blowing. Rohan had come at last. (*LotR* 811)

The hope that the dawn carries and that is fulfilled in the sound of Rohan's horns finds its equivalent in the scene which ends the next chapter (and which – like the equivalent scene presented earlier – is preceded with a similar sense of doom experienced by the characters; it seems that the Riders came too late):

> [Theoden] seized a great horn from Guthláf his banner-bearer, and he blew such a blast upon it that it burst asunder. And straightway all the horns in the host were lifted up in music, and the blowing of the horns of Rohan was like a storm upon the plain and a thunder in the mountains. (*LotR* 820)

When it comes to the ending of the war (Chapter 3 and 4 of Book VI), the narrative becomes even more closely knit, with repetitions, parallel situations, and shifts of the scene that come more often than in the earlier part of the text.

As we can see, the subplots in *The Lord of the Rings* are interlaced in such a way that some common points are revealed, turning the plot into a network rather than a number of parallel "lines". What is important is that those common points are not merely the meetings of characters whose fates have been independent so far, but that one subplot contains traces of another: the traces being interpreted or – more often – misinterpreted by the characters, to find a complete explanation only later. The subplots which are concurrent in time are also linked in space, with common motifs or episodes.

A well-knit tapestry

As Eugene Vinaver (76) comments upon the interlacement technique of the chivalric romances:

> There is no single beginning and no single end [...] each initial adventure can be extended into the past and each final adventure into the future by a further lengthening of the narrative threads. Any [plot] can reappear after an interval so as to stretch the whole fabric still further until the reader loses any limitation in time and space.

Even if Tolkien's text takes over the compositional technique typical of the chivalric romance, its realization and its function for the compositional arrangement of the text seem different. In the earlier texts interlacement evidently functioned as a device allowing the author to broaden the presented reality, to insert new subplots, to introduce places and characters that are not related to each other, thus creating a versatile world and action with ramifications in various directions. Even if bringing together the various plots, with the recurrence of certain motifs, endows them with additional significance (see Vinaver 83), the openness of the romance world and the possibility of still enlarging it remains. In the case of *The Lord of the Rings*, the overall effect is unity and compactness of a single tale. "After all, *The Lord of the Rings* is just a novel telling about a single journey, even if consisting of multiple stages and multiple plots" (Zgorzelski 21). And certainly there is no chance for the reader to lose by "any limitation in time and space", on the contrary.

It seems that the way the subplots are interlaced and interconnected functions analogous to the maps and the map-like descriptions which are part of the narration. In the chivalric romances the topography consisted rather of *loci* "suspended" in space, whereas Tolkien has all his topographical points carefully interrelated and – rich as his world may be – woven into one whole. The same can be said about the subplots concerning various groups of characters. On the one hand they broaden reality, presenting a diversity of places, characters and sequences of events. But on the other hand this diverse and multifarious world appears to be closely knit, all its elements related to each other either in time or in space; particular events set in a way similar to particular places – with a map allowing immediately to perceive the whole pattern and not merely one part unrelated to others. Thus, the reality that is communicated in such a way reveals its nature as a complete world – complete as a tale, too, as contrasted to the "open" plot of the Arthurian cycle, where there is always room for another theme and another tale to be introduced and interwoven with the ones already present. But there seems to be more to it.

As a complete world with the time and space relations so precisely defined, Middle-earth reveals itself as an analogue (though not a reflection) of the extratextual reality. The same interlacement technique, which helps to achieve such compactness, foregrounds a tension suggested already in the introductory passages to *The Lord of the Rings*. The "Note on the Shire Records", on the one hand, assures the reader that the tale told in the book is history, not fiction, and that – from the perspective of the "author" – it is possible to trace back particular reports referring to the adventures of Frodo and others. On the other hand, there can be no doubt that – from the same perspective – the tale about the Ring is a literary and fictional text, similar to those that transform facts into a work of art and thus endowe them with additional value: that which is communicated by the very beauty of the utterance. The completeness of the world thus creates the illusion of reality, while the underlying patterns reveal the highly organized nature of an artistic text.

And something else is suggested, too – an analogy between reality and an artistic utterance. That analogy is most obvious in *The Silmarillion* when the world is presented as a polyphonic song turned into reality. It is also suggested by the diversity of literary texts about Middle-earth – *The Hobbit*, *The Lord of the Rings*, *The Adventures of Tom Bombadil* and *The Silmarillion* are rooted in different generic traditions, from a tale for children to heroic fantasy, a collection of poems, and a myth. But this, too, is suggested by the interlacement technique. It is a literary convention, a device to connect various plots into one whole; but it is also a fact in the textual reality, all the plots indeed being interrelated, and experienced by the characters as such, even if the connections are not immediately grasped and comprehended. Thus, the composition of the text foregrounds the underlying order of the presented universe.

Moreover, there is a tension between the characters' perspective and that of the implied reader which is enhanced by the interlacement pattern. The characters are so often lost not merely in space but also in the choices they have to make.[4] Yet, there is an overall pattern underlying the adventures of the characters which not only points to the textual composition but also to the order of reality which is communicated by it. What is obtained in the Arthurian romance due to the analogies and relations between particular plots on the textual level, as well as the intricate patterns of signs that particular elements of the presented reality turn into, is achieved in Tolkien's text by the modification of the interlacement technique to reveal the order also on the least abstract level of the tale – the level of the fictional world. And whereas the Arthurian characters may move

---

4 Aragorn so often repeats that all the choices he has made since Gandalf's (supposed) death seem to be wrong. But that is where he errs. His choices prove to be right, even if it may appear that they are incidentally so. They are in accordance with the overall pattern which in itself is a harmonious one. One is reminded here of Donald Swann's music to Tolkien's poem "The Road goes ever on". According to the composer's interpretation any "path" or "errand" chosen by the traveller eventually proves to be the Road (see Kokot 328). Thus, the interlacement technique may reveal the higher order of the universe which is only implied in *The Lord of the Rings* (West 86-88, Shippey 123-50).

in the world of signs (which perhaps finds its best realization in *The Quest of the Holy Grail*, where any object or episode may be ascribed additional meanings), the characters in *The Lord of the Rings* move in a world of facts – which is, however, no less full of sense and order.

Bibliography

The Death of King Arthur. Trans. James Cable. Harmondsworth: Penguin Books, 1971.

Kokot, Joanna. "Dynamics in Correlation. Words and Music in a Song by J.R.R. Tolkien and D. Swann." *Inklings. Jahrbuch für Literatur und Ästhetic* 5, 1987. 311-334.

Lewis, C. S. *The Discarded Image*. Cambridge: Cambridge University Press, 1964.

The Quest of the Holy Grail. Trans. P. M. Matarasco. Harmondsworth: Penguin, 1971.

Shippey, Tom A. *The Road to Middle-earth*. London: Grafton, 1992.

Strachey, Barbara. *Journeys of Frodo. An Atlas of J.R.R. Tolkien's The Lord of the Rings*. New York: Random House, 1981.

Tolkien, John Ronald Reuel. *Finn and Hengest. The Fragment and the Episode*. Ed. Allan Bliss. London: HarperCollins, 1998.

The Letters of J.R.R. Tolkien. Ed. Humphrey Carpenter. London: HarperCollins. 1995.

The Lord of the Rings. London: HarperCollins, 1995.

"Tree and Leaf". *The Tolkien Reader*. New York: Ballantine, 1966. 29-120.

Tuve, Rosemond. *Allegorical Imagery: Some Medieval Books and Their Posterity*. Princeton: Princeton University Press, 1966.

Vinaver, Eugene. *The Rise of Romance*. Oxford: Clarendon Press, 1971.

West, Richard C. "The Interlace Structure of *The Lord of the Rings*." *A Tolkien Compass*. Ed. Jared Lobdell. La Salle, IL: Open Court, 1975. 77-94.

Weston, Jessie. *From Ritual to Romance*. Garden City, New York: Doubleday Anchor Books, 1957.

Zgorzelski, Andrzej. "The Syncretic Nature of J.R.R. Tolkien's *The Lord of the Rings*." *Born of the Fantastic*. Gdańsk: Wydawnictwo Uniwersytetu Gdańskiego, 2004. 150-182.

About the author

JOANNA KOKOT is a professor of English literature at Warmia and Mazury University in Olsztyn. Her main field of research is English literature at the turn of the 19th and 20th centuries, especially the so called popular literature. She has authored a number of books in this area: *Tekst w tekście (Text within text*, 1992), *Gry z czytelnikiem w nowelistyce Rudyarda Kiplinga (Playing with the reader in Rudyard Kipling's short stories*, 1993), *Kronikarz z Baker Street. Strategie narracyjne w utworach Conan Doyle'a o Sherlocku Holmesie (The Baker Street chronicler. Narrative strategies in the Sherlock Holmes tales by Arthur Conan Doyle*, 1999), *"This Rough Magic". Studies in Popular Literature* (2004) and *W świetle gazowych latarni. O prozie gotyckiej przełomu XIX i XX wieku (Gaslights. On horror fiction of the turn of the 19*[th] *and 20*[th] *centuries*, in print). Some of her publications concern the literary output of J.R.R. Tolkien as well, the most important ones being: "Dynamics in Correlation. A Song by J.R.R. Tolkien and D. Swann" (*Inklings*, 1987), "Cultural Functions Motivating Art: Poems and Their Contexts in *The Lord of the Rings* by J.R.R. Tolkien" (*Inklings* 1992) and an essay on the Polish translations of proper names in *The Lord of the Rings*. She has translated into Polish Tolkien's essay "On Fairy-stories" as well as a number of scholarly studies on Tolkien, notably Tom Shippey's *The Road to Middle-earth* and *J. R. R. Tolkien. Author of the Century*, and Joseph Pearce's *Tolkien. Man and Myth* and *Tolkien. A Celebration*. Joanna Kokot is currently working on a book devoted to narrative strategies in the turn-of-the-19th-century fiction.

Bartomiej Błaszkiewicz

Orality and Literacy in Middle-earth

Abstract

The paper deals with the interplay of the cultural and literary traditions represented by the modes of orality and literacy in the secondary world created by J.R.R. Tolkien for *The Lord of the Rings*. The pursued argument stems from the standard methodology developed within the oral-formulaic theory in medieval studies. The theory is first applied to trace the interconnections between the oral and literate modes of social and cultural interaction in the culture of the Elves, and the paper presents the uniqueness of the elvish culture in this respect, which results mostly from the extreme longevity of the species. Subsequently the analysis focuses the influence of the culture of the various elvish tribes upon the other species inhabiting Middle-earth such as the Ents, who represent a culture of primary orality, through the humans (the people of Gondor as well as the Rohirrim), up to the Hobbits, whose largely literate culture incorporates elements of secondary orality. Finally, the paper discusses the question of oral literary composition and performance as practised in Middle-earth comparing the traditions represented by the various species to those known in the primary world.

The aim of the argument is to follow briefly the appearance and evolution of the modes of orality and literacy as these have functioned in the history of the peoples and races of Tolkien's Middle-earth and to outline the differences between Middle-earth and the primary world in this respect. Furthermore we will devote some close attention to the way in which the coexistence of these two respective modes conditioned the emergence and traditional practice of literature within the multifarious cultures which Tolkien made his world produce.

The first step in any such discussion must be to highlight those important divergences between Middle-earth and the primary universe which necessarily have an impact on the way in which orality and literacy will emerge as means of social interaction and artistic creativity in communities of intelligent beings.[1] Of such factors the following seem to be of particular importance:

- magic is, in Middle-earth, the way in which the spiritual penetrates the material; hence language in Middle-earth possesses objectively the features which the word-sign possesses in the world-view based on magic: this world-view is historically connected to human societies where social interaction is realised in primary orality;
- Middle-earth contains more than one kind of intelligent beings whose cultures partake of both oral and literate ways of social communication (whereas on Earth there currently exists one and, as far as can be ascertained, the only other comparable culture created by an intelligent species – that of Neanderthals – is now extinct and presumed to have never evolved beyond the state of pure primary orality);
- some of the species, such as the Ents or even some racially pure Men, enjoy a considerably longer average life span than the Earth's humans, while, crucially, all the different kinds of Elves are all immortal. This has a direct impact on the relationship between the communal and individual memory, which is one of the key factors in the evolution from orality to literacy;
- all of Middle-earth's species were created by Ilúvatar as instantly rational and capable of cultural interaction based on advanced forms of verbal communication, instead of arriving at such a state by a lengthy process of evolution and adaptation;
- some of the species of Middle-earth (primarily the Elves and through them the humans) have possessed the sense of unbroken cultural heritage and continuous tradition for a much longer period than any human civilisation in the primary world (where no civilisation could claim more than three thousand years of unbroken heritage compared to about seven thousand for the Men of Middle-earth, and much longer for the Elves).

---

1 The methodological framework of the argument is based on the research in oral-formulaic studies; for the classic oral-formulaic theory see Lord 1-46; for contemporary applications of it see Finnegan, *Literacy and Orality* 134- 169; Ong 31-75; Finnegan, *Oral Traditions* 25- 50; Finnegan, *Oral Poetry* 59-85; Foley, *How to Read* 22-57; Zumthor 13-31; for the medieval context of oral-ormulaic studies see Amodio, *New Directions* 1-32.

Thus all the species of Middle-earth come into being at a stage of advanced primary orality when the culture is mentally ready for the introduction of the literate forms of cultural expression (as it is intelligent and possesses a fully developed language), which means there are no psychological barriers at this point, and everything depends on the technical abilities to develop and propagate the literate forms of communication, by means of the written word or otherwise.[2]

In this context we shall need to look first at the Elves – the first rational species of Middle-earth to develop writing soon after its creation:

> Aulë it is who is named the friend of the Noldor, for of him they learned much in after days, and they are the most skilled of the Elves; and in their own fashion, according to the gifts which Ilúvatar gave to them, they added much to his teaching, delighting in tongues and in scripts, and in the figures of broidery, of drawing, and of carving. (S 35)

> Great became their knowledge and their skill; yet greater was their thirst for more knowledge, and in many things they soon surpassed their teachers. They were changeful in speech, for they had great love of words, and sought ever to find names more fit for all things that they knew or imagined. (S 63)

Thus the written word appears in the history of Middle-earth's Elves very early on and this can be taken, somewhat paradoxically perhaps, as proof that an advanced form of oral culture must have existed by that time among the Elves, as only advanced oral culture is able to prepare the language a community speaks for the introduction of the written word.[3] As may be furthermore observed from the above quotations the oral form of language, in a joint package with rationality, is Ilúvatar's gift to the Firstborn whereas the written form of language is something that has its origin in their love of the technical side of the art of writing and is developed due to their intellectual ingenuity rather than social necessity. Thus writing is here not something which helps a civilisation to develop and spread, but is rather created to

---

[2] Compare the argument about Tolkien's indebtedness to the heritage of the oral-derived genres in Sullivan 11-19.
[3] This is implicit in the definition of primary orality commonly accepted in oral-formulaic studies and of course it does not imply any disparagement of the notion of orality. Compare Amodio, *Writing* 4-5; Ong 10-11; Martin 10-11.

satisfy the aesthetic sophistication of a civilisation that is already flowering. In fact this element may be more closely observed in another passage from *The Silmarillion*:

> Now the Three Kindreds of the Eldar were gathered at last in Valinor, and Melkor was chained. This was the Noontide of the Blessed Realm, the fullness of its glory and its bliss, but in memory too brief. [...] Then it was that the Noldor first bethought them of letters, and Rumil of Tirion was the name of the loremaster who first achieved fitting signs for the recording of speech and song, some for graving upon metal or in stone, others for drawing with brush or with pen. (S 67)

Thus it is in the period of peace and prosperity that writing is ushered in to the culture of the Elves and it immediately produces results in terms of promoting a characteristically literate cast of mind in the elvish society. The obvious manifestation of this is to be found in the most symbolic example of recording the name of the individual who introduced the script, in a way which is historical and not mythical.

Nevertheless, the recording function of writing is far less crucial in a society made up of immortal beings, and where the linear one-way flow of history is a notion commonly understood and accepted from the culture's very beginning. Consequently the aim of oral poetry is the exultation of the moral sense of history rather than preserving the communal memory on which the society's sense of internal cohesion is based.

Thus if we were finally to define the elvish culture we would have to see it as one which is predominantly literate, but which relies on the actual use of the written word to an incomparably smaller extent than any literate culture of the primary world. It may be now seen that it is the fact that the species is immortal that makes their culture's communal memory resemble closely that of the Earth's literate civilisations, and it also, at the same time, allows the Elves to be less reliant on the use of the written word. This is because it was their retentive immortal memories which conditioned their culture to be primarily literate in character, whereas in the primary world this is a prolonged process of transition largely made possible through the use of writing.

Another crucial aspect to be observed at this stage is that the domination of the Noldor in terms of introducing and perfecting writing among the Elves. This highlights the inherently different pedigree and nature of the skill involved in creating the literate cultural environment and the skill of producing literature, as may become evident from the following passage in *The Silmarillion*:

> The Vanyar he loved best of all the Elves, and of him they received song and poetry; for poetry is the delight of Manwë, and the song of words is his music. (*S* 35)

Therefore the use of writing is emphatically not in kind with the art of poetic composition, for they remain the domains of different Valar and, consequently, different civilisations of the Elves excel in the skill needed for either. Furthermore, as one might suspect, the art of song-making is the nobler one as it is the domain of the chief of the Valar, and is consequently a matter of spirit rather than craft.

The outcome of all of this is that the Elves quickly evolve into the kind of civilisation where orally delivered poetry and the written literate chronicle exist side by side and become two different, but synchronically connected ways in which the elvish society celebrates its cultural heritage.[4] Since the elvish society does not forget, it does not need oral myth and oral literature to redefine its heritage periodically, as all human cultures have had to do in the primary world.

Consequently in the case of the Elves the strong sense of identification with the species' historical legacy is, in a way, doubly reinforced, and it becomes the norm in the history of Middle-earth that any race dissociating itself from the Quenya – the language most elevated in terms of cultural heritage – becomes sidetracked and ultimately declines in more or less dramatic fashion:

> For the Sindar [...] refused the tongue of the Noldor, [...] but the Exiles took the Sindarin tongue in all their daily uses, and the High Speech of the West was spoken only by the lords of the Noldor among themselves. Yet it lived ever as a language of lore [...]. (*S* 155)

Similarly the rejection of the elvish languages in Númenor around the year 2000, the Second Age marks the beginning of the kingdom's decline, since

---

4 In this context note the following quotations: "For as has been told and as is known to all, being written in lore and sung in many songs, Melkor slew the Trees [...]"; "in the north the Noldor built their dwellings and their towers, and many fair things they made in those days, and poems and histories and books of lore" (*S* 137).

the Elves' special status in Middle-earth marks them out as both custodians of the common heritage of all the intelligent species and teachers of the others as they consecutively appear.[5]

We begin now, chronologically, with the Ents. What we have just said may be confirmed by the crucial account given by Fangorn about the way his species was taught intelligent language by the Elves during the First Age:

> 'Some of my kin look just like trees now, and need something great to rouse them; and they speak only in whispers. But some of my trees are limb-lithe, and many can talk to me. Elves began it, of course, waking trees up and teaching them to speak and learning their tree-talk. They always wished to talk to everything, the old Elves did. But then the Great Darkness came, and they passed over the Sea, or fled far into the valleys, and hid themselves and made songs about days that would never come again.' (*LotR* 457)

Here we can see that the Elves taught the Ents language in its oral form. By doing so, the Ents, a species of extreme longevity, but, for all that, mortal succeeded in creating a culture of pure orality, which has survived in such an extreme, pristine form into the Third Age that it is to a large extent responsible for the species' isolation and decline. It is in this context that we need to consider the Ents' reliance on "old lists" for storing information, coupled with a ready acceptance of new-made variants which fit the traditional linguistic structures, as well as their profound belief in the significance of proper names and the need for the proper names to incorporate the true pedigree of the described object ("my name is like a story") and the names' magical function of providing an identity for the thing described by means of the inherent quality of the linguistic sign:

> '*Laurelindorenan*! That is what the Elves used to call it, but now they make the name shorter: *Lothlorien* they call it. Perhaps they are right: maybe it is fading, not growing. Land of the Valley of Singing Gold, that was it, once upon a time. Now it is the Dreamflower.' (*LotR* 456)

All of these features are fundamental in determining the world-view dominant in the situation of primary orality, and the Ents may in fact be the only kind of Middle-earth's creatures for whom this would be the natural element. Their example may be important for appreciating how different the Elves are,

---

5 Compare the argument concerning the role of the Elves in Chance, *Tolkien's Art* 111-140 and Shippey, *Road* 1-25.

by virtue of their immortality, from all the other creatures of Middle-earth, which has a direct bearing on their situation with respect to the oral-literate nexus. The Ents follow in this respect the earthly laws, while the Elves do not do so at all. Nevertheless, there is a clear link between the two cultures as the Ents' readiness to see all names as potentially conveying information about a given thing's character may, in all probability, be derived from the refined linguistic sensitivity of the Noldor, discernible, for instance, in the elaborate process of giving names to their children (as described in *MR* 214-217).

Later on, the Elves perform a corresponding role for the Edain, who, being mortal, seem not to be able initially to preserve their cultural continuity:

> But when he [Felagund of the Noldor] questioned him concerning the arising of Men and their journeys, Bëor would say little; and indeed he knew little, for the fathers of his people had told few tales of their past and a silence had fallen on their memory. (*S* 169)

We need to contrast the above passage with the later account of the Dunedain from around 400 Second Age to observe their development as a species and also the difference between their culture and that of the Elves with respect to orality and literacy:

> And the lore masters among them learned also the High Eldarin tongue of the Blessed Realm, in which much story and song was preserved from the beginning of the world; and they made letters and scrolls and books, and wrote in them many things of wisdom and wonder in the high tide of their realm, of which all is now forgot. (*S* 323)

Because a lot of knowledge which the humans of Middle-earth inherit is derived from the Elves, the Númenórean culture relies on the written word to a larger extent than did the kingdoms of the Elves. The literate character of such a culture is further reinforced by the fact that when the language, being essentially foreign, is abandoned by Ar-Pharazôn for nationalist reasons, the cultural heritage is irrevocably lost in the ensuing political turmoil.

Thus, we might say that, in the case of the humans of Middle-earth, the way to develop a cultural and spiritual awareness is through constructing a literate link with the Elves' oral culture. This can be seen in the Rohirrim, who did not, unlike the Dúnedain, stand in a close and direct cultural contact with any of the nations of the Elves, and who appear to have independently developed a culture based exclusively on primary orality. The outcome is that, while their uniqueness and many virtues contribute to the multicultural variety of Middle-earth, the Rohirrim do appear to fall behind their elder human allies in terms of their orientation in matters relating to spirituality (as can be inferred from Éomer's comment about Galadriel and his implied condemnation of "magic". His understanding of the notion of "magic" lags conspicuously behind the standard found among the Gondorian nobility).

In the closing years of the Third Age in *The Lord of the Rings* we encounter yet another intelligent species whose culture is a blend of oral and literate forms of social interaction, the Hobbits:[6]

> Of their original home the Hobbits in Bilbo's time preserved no knowledge. A love of learning (other than genealogical lore) was far form general among them, but there remained still a few in the older families who studied their own books, and gathered reports of old times and distant lands from Elves, Dwarves, and Men. (*LotR* 2)

The Hobbits, being a mortal race, seem to resemble the Men of Middle-earth in having never possessed a long cultural memory. Because they are much more removed from the culture of the Elves, as they have had no direct dealings with the immortal species, their culture has begun early on to rely on the written word to a far larger extent than that of the humans because of the obvious lack of any living tradition which would link their species with the Elves' historical heritage. This has allowed the Hobbits' literate habits of mind to become more deeply entrenched than has ever been the case among Men. Hence when the Hobbits suddenly enter the grand historical context at the time of the war with Sauron, the increase in their historical awareness actually incites the growth in the literate character of the culture and its reliance on the written word:

> By the end of the first century of the Fourth Age there were already to be found in the Shire several libraries that contained historical books and records. (*LotR* 14)

While it is worth noting that the evolution of the culture of the Hobbits follows the earthly norms in this respect, it seems that, in Middle-earth, such a level

---

6 Compare in this context the argument about the culture of the Shire in Curry 35-58.

of literacy as the Hobbits represent is more of a handicap than it is customary in the primary world. This is due to a number of factors:
- firstly, the culture of the Elves and men is, by the Third Age, much more oral than that of the Hobbits, and much that renders it unique cannot be conveyed by the written word;
- secondly, the high culture in the Shire is in fact highly elitist throughout the Third Age and remains so into the Fourth;
- thirdly, it seems that, in the case of the Hobbits, the biggest dangers of increased literacy (the danger of unduly limited access and the ensuing elitist bias of such a culture) combine with the biggest dangers of secondary orality (limiting orality to the lower classes and an exclusively "popular" culture).

Indeed the proof that this is precisely what has happened in the Shire may be found when we take a closer look at the books the Hobbits produced:

> The present selection is taken from the older pieces, mainly concerned with legends and jests of the Shire at the end of the Third Age, that appear to have been made by the Hobbits, especially Bilbo and his friends, or their immediate descendants. Their authorship is, however, seldom indicated. Those outside the narrative are in various hands, and were probably written down from oral tradition. (*ATB*, Preface, i-ii)

It is important to note fully the difference between *oral tradition* as practised by the Shire peasants and *oral tradition* as practised by the aristocracy of the Elves in order to appreciate the evidently disparaging ring of the expression in the quotation above. Here whatever is inferior about the literate culture of the Shire is to some significant extent caused by the fact that the Hobbits' literacy has no deeper basis in an aristocratic oral tradition where the link with the past would be most organically preserved, in Middle-earth as well as in the primary world. Because oral culture has, in the case of the Shire, been limited to the context of what may justifiably be termed "low social register", it does not provide the solid foundation on which literate culture may feed and develop. This is the reason why the song about Princess Mee included in Bilbo's archives contains a minute sparkle of the majesty and glamour of, say, Galadriel. It is, however, transformed out of recognition by the fact that the song has been composed among the peasant classes in a land which had no direct connection with the world of the real Elves and where knowledge about such things is restricted to a small group of the elite where literacy combines with sufficient erudition and refinement.

Indeed when one enters the Shire at the beginning of the Great Years of the Third Age the impression is one of, so to speak, extreme literacy, for the written word appears to be ubiquitous. Thus Bilbo invites everyone to his farewell party by means of written notes and attaches further notes to the presents (while Elrond does not seem to make use of any such devices to call the Rivendell council to debate the question of the ring); a written notice is nailed to the gate of Bag End to keep out folk not involved in the preparation of the event; a carefully phrased written document is needed to transfer Bag End onto Frodo (while none is necessary for Aragorn to second his claim to the throne of Gondor); and finally Frodo's claim made in Bree that he is writing a "tourist guide" causes interest but no awe. In fact it seems that, in Middle-earth, the culture based on the written word is, to an even greater degree than in the case of the primary world, a substitute for the lack of a direct link with the high culture represented within this framework by the Elves, which is still, to a defining degree, oral.[7]

It is against this context that one may now position the fact that in *The Lord of the Rings* the notion of the written word is very frequently given an ominously menacing or negative connotation frequently connected with the idea of forgetting.[8] Thus Butterbur's failure to deliver the written message from Gandalf nearly spoils Frodo's quest. Similarly, one recalls that the testimony of the ruin of Moria is to be reconstructed from a battered book recording the advance of the orcs and an inscription on the tomb of Balin (which itself echoes the prominence of inscription on the tomb of Túrin in *The Silmarillion*; and it is not to be forgotten that the introduction of writing among the Elves coincides with the first death – that of Melian). Finally, the ubiquitous written notices play a significant role in the introduction of Saruman's government in the Shire.

---

[7] In this context see also the remarks about Tolkien's understanding of the nature of living oral traditions in Shippey, "Indexing" 236-237 and Shippey, "Versions" 346-347.
[8] Compare the argument in Carruthers 1-79 about the role of memory in partly oral cultures.

Among similar examples none is, of course, more telling than the crucial scene when Gandalf receives the final proof of the true identity of Frodo's ring:

> 'Hold it up!' said Gandalf. 'And look closely!'
>
> As Frodo did so, he saw fine lines, finer than the finest pen-strokes, running along the ring, outside and inside: the lines of fire that seemed to form the letters of a flowing script. They shone piercingly bright, and yet remote, as if out of a great depth.
>
> 'I cannot read the fiery letters,' said Frodo in a quavering voice.
>
> 'No,' said Gandalf, 'but I can. The letters are Elvish, of an ancient mode, but the language is that of Mordor, which I will not utter here [...] It is two lines of a verse long known in Elven-lore.' (*LotR* 49)

The underlying menace of the scene is, of course, much enhanced by the fact that in a universe where the material world is penetrated by the spiritual in the form of magic, words are charged with an inherent objective spiritual power. This is the reason for Gandalf's refusal to read out aloud the inscription in the original (which he only undertakes in Rivendell, where the exceptionally positive magical qualities of the place may be counted on to counteract the risk).

It is, however, significant that evil is here able to infiltrate the peaceful land of the Hobbits through literacy because in a magical universe the sinister power of an evil spell exists objectively. Written down it may linger in a dormant form in a place where no one possesses the skill to read and thus awaken it. This is the special threat which an evil power operating through magic may pose and to which oral cultures are naturally more resistant. Here, as elsewhere in *The Lord of the Rings*, forgetting about the magic significance of written words, like forgetting the meaning of words which have been written down, may prove dangerous, hence writing, once invented, must be guarded by being understood.

In this context the scene must be linked with an even more disturbing report by Gandalf given at the council of Elrond. He tells the assembly that Denethor swore that there was no information to be found in the written scrolls stored at Minas Tirith that was not known to him. Here again the reason behind the loss of the crucial scroll made by Isildur and containing the description of the ring is also the ever present danger of literacy, the danger of forgetting without obliterating:

> 'Yet there lie in his hoards many records that few now can read, even of the lore-masters, for their scripts and tongues became dark to latter men.' (*LotR* 246)

In this way the existence of the written archives in Gondor, coupled with the steady decline of civilization and consequently of both literate learning and communal memory based on oral transmission,[9] allowed an enemy (Saruman) to benefit from the knowledge stored there without the people in charge being aware of the fact. This, of course, would not have been possible in an oral culture, and here the increase of responsibility which the introduction of the written word brings is clearly visible.

Now finally we may take a closer look at the way literature functions in Middle-earth in the specific context of the oral and the literate modes of social expression. In order to do so we shall take a closer look at the only surviving account of the literary habits of the Elves – the scene when during the feast Bilbo performs a song at the court of Elrond.

Here we face a situation which would be, to a significant degree, comparable to that of a European court during the High Medieval period.[10] The contact with literature at the elvish court is firmly oral at the node of reception and transmission, since, while Elrond's library contains "storied and figured maps and books of lore" (*LotR* 270), the only contact the Elves have with literature is in a situation of public oral delivery by minstrels (which has been an age-long tradition with the Elves, as king Thingol is said to have employed one).[11]

Nothing is said during the scene about the minstrels' exact mode of work, but we may possibly assume that when Bilbo performs his song there is no sense of him doing it in a way deviating from the standard of professional performers. Thus the Hobbit composes his song about Eärendil in a fixed form before its oral presentation, but he goes about it without resort to

---

9 For, to make matters worse, Boromir admits during the council that even the mere story of Isildur's end is not known to him: "If such a tale was told in the south it has been long forgotten" (*LotR* 237).
10 For the medieval perspective on oral delivery see Vitz 1-15.
11 This is the minstrel who betrays the love between Beren and Lúthien to the king as recounted in *S* 200.

writing, nor does he use any written prompts during his recitation, and "recitation" is precisely the word used by others in reference to what has just happened (*LotR* 230).

Thus, defining the situation more closely, we would have to say that we have here a case of oral reception and oral delivery, but literate composition. Thus the overall situation is not that of oral performance in the sense the term has in oral-formulaic studies as conducted in the primary world. This is because what is delivered by Bilbo is a fixed literate text. This text cannot be recreated in oral performance because it is not made in the oral-formulaic style, although it may be transmitted orally without losing its literate character. In other words it may be subject to oral transmission, but not to oral re-creation, because it is not made of orally modifiable material – thus all that will happen to it may be deterioration in a prolonged oral transmission (so Legolas complains, entering Lothlórien, of having forgotten much of the Song of Nimrodel – something he treats as a fixed, stable text which has never been written down and which may be not *re-created* once is has been composed, but which must be *recollected*).[12] It may be that Bilbo would create a new version of the song for another occasion if he were to forget the one that he has just made, but in this case the relation between the two would have to be diachronic (the new one would employ some of the material created for use in the original one – and the word "original" itself indicates literacy).

Of course, having stated the above we need to add that Bilbo's song does use some elements of oral style:
- first, it is composed in iambic tetrametre in what are essentially quatrains rhyming *abcb*, which may be treated as a formulaic metrical scheme for those Middle-earth species who use the Common Speech (here the proof may be that when in Lothlórien Frodo spontaneously composes verses commemorating Gandalf in almost identical verse form, Sam is able to improvise additional stanzas praising the wizard's skill at fireworks, although none of the songs shares any fixed phrases);
- secondly, although Aragorn helps Bilbo with the composition of the song about Eärendil, no one is able to distinguish who has contributed which

---

12 Compare the argument about the psychological aspects of oral transmission in Rubin 122-193.

particular lines, and this may be taken as proof of the highly conventional character of the verse, which is always a feature of oral style, although it is also typical of some definitively literate poetry.

As has been said, in its general outlines the practice of literature-making among the Elves of Middle-earth is similar to what may be found in human societies of the primary world which have possessed a corresponding social structure. The one clear point of difference here is the lack of oral *formulae* and formulaic narrative motifs in the text composed for oral delivery. The reason seems, once again, to be connected with the Elves' immortality. Customarily in earthly human societies, the conventions and *formulae* of traditional literature usually outlive not only the particular narratives, but the stories themselves because of the pattern of redefinition of the communal history which happens periodically in societies conditioned by orality. The Elves do not redefine the significance of the particular events of their past since they remember them first-hand. Therefore the need has never arisen to abstract an apparatus of formulaic devices for adapting a song to the new way in which the past is remodeled by a society made up of mortal beings, for whom remembering history is always something of a burden.

The feast at Rivendell may be thus seen as providing a glimpse of the most refined way in which the intelligent species of Middle-earth partake of literature. We may see here that the literature of the Elves is a product of a mixed oral/literate culture – one which is based on the oral transmission of a fixed text. If the same understanding of the principles of poetic composition permeates the rustic songs of Sam Gamgee of the Shire, this is testimony to the underlying cultural link between the various kinds of Ilúvatar's children who inhabit Middle-earth.

Bibliography

Amodio, Mark, ed. *New Directions in Oral Theory*. Tempe, Arizona: Arizona Center for Medieval and Renaissance Studies, 2005.

Writing the Oral Tradition. Oral Poetics and Literate Culture in Medieval England. Notre Dame, Indiana: University of Notre Dame Press, 2004.

Bradbury, Nancy Mason. *Writing Aloud: Storytelling in Late Medieval England*. Urbana: University of Illinois Press, 1998.

Carruthers, Mary. *The Book of Memory. A Study of Memory in Medieval Culture*. Cambridge: Cambridge UP, 1990.

Chance, Jane. *Tolkien's Art. A Mythology for England*. Kentucky: University of Kentucky Press, 2001.

ed. *Tolkien the Medievalist*. London and New York: Routledge, 2003.

Clark, George, and Daniel Timmons, eds. *J.R.R. Tolkien and His Literary Resonances. Views on Middle-Earth*. Westport CT: Greenwood Press, 2000.

Curry, Patrick. *Defending Middle-Earth. Tolkien: Myth and Modernity*. London: HarperCollins, 1997.

Finnegan, Ruth. *Literacy and Orality. Studies in the Technology of Communication*. Oxford and New York: Basil Blackwell, 1988.

Oral Poetry. Its Nature, Significance and Social Context. Bloomington and Indianapolis: Indiana UP, 1992.

Oral Traditions and the Verbal Arts. A Guide to Research Practices. London and New York: Routledge, 2001.

Foley, John Miles, ed. *Comparative Research on Oral Traditions: A Memorial for Milman Parry*. Columbus, Ohio: Slavica Publishers Inc., 1985.

ed. *Oral Tradition in Literature. Interpretation in Context*. Columbia: University of Missouri Press, 1986.

The Theory of Oral Composition. Bloomington and Indianapolis: Indiana University, 1988.

How to Read an Oral Poem. Urbana and Chicago: University of Illinois Press, 2002.

ed. *A Companion to the Ancient Epic*. Wiley-Blackwell: Oxford, 2009.

Havelock, Eric A. *The Muse Learns to Write. Reflections on Orality and Literacy from Antiquity to the Present*. Yale: Yale University Press, 1986.

LORD, Albert B. *The Singer of Tales*. Cambridge, MA and London: Harvard UP, 1960.

MARTIN, Richard P. "Epic as Genre." *A Companion to the Ancient Epic*. Ed. John Foley and John Miles. Wiley-Blackwell: Oxford, 2009. 9-19.

ONG, Walter J. *Orality and Literacy. The Technologizing of the Word*. London and New York: Routledge, 1995.

RUBIN, David C. *Memory in Oral Traditions. The Cognitive Psychology of Epics, Ballads and Counting-out Rhymes*. New York and Oxford: Oxford UP, 1995.

SHIPPEY, Tom A. *The Road to Middle-Earth*. London: HarperCollins, 1992.

"Indexing and Poetry in *The Lord of the Rings*." *Roots and Branches: Selected Papers on Tolkien by Tom Shippey*. Zurich and Berne: Walking Tree Publishers, 2007. 235-241.

"The Versions of *The Hoard*". *Roots and Branches: Selected Papers on Tolkien by Tom Shippey*. Zurich and Berne: Walking Tree Publishers, 2007. 341-349.

SULLIVAN III, C. W. "Tolkien the Bard: His Tale Grew in the Telling." *J.R.R. Tolkien and His Literary Resonances. Views on Middle-Earth*. Ed. George Clarke and Daniel Timmons. Westport CT: Greenwood Press, 2000. 11-19.

TOLKIEN John Ronald Reuel. *The Tolkien Reader*. New York: Ballantine Books, 1966.

The Silmarillion. New York: Ballantine Books, 1981.

Morgoth's Ring. London: HarperCollins, 1993.

The Lord of the Rings. London: HarperCollins, 1995.

The Adventures of Tom Bombadil. London: HarperCollins, 1995.

VITZ, Evelyn Birge et al., eds. *Performing Medieval Narrative*. Cambridge: D. S. Brewer, 2005.

ZUMTHOR, Paul. *Oral Poetry: An Introduction*. Minneapolis: University of Minnesota Press, 1990.

About the author

BARTŁOMIEJ BŁASZKIEWICZ is assistant professor in the Institute of English Studies, University of Warsaw and specializes in medieval literature. He received his doctoral degree in 2000 for a thesis on medieval and Renaissance modes of space perception in John Milton's *Paradise Lost*. In 2009 he published his post-doctoral dissertation on the role of oral-formulaic diction in selected Middle English verse romances. He is the author of over thirty academic articles on topics concerning the genres of the ballad and the romance, various aspects of oral culture in the Middle Ages, medieval space perception, the works of Chaucer, the *Gawain*-poet, and William Dunbar. He is also the author of articles on the works of J.R.R. Tolkien, George R.R. Martin, Terry Pratchett, Susanna Clarke, Neil Gaiman, and Douglas Adams in relation to the medieval heritage of the genre of fantasy. He has taught courses on the oral and literate ballad, medieval romance, John Milton, and contemporary fantasy literature, and has supervised over fifty MA thesises on medieval and fantasy literature.

Justyna Brzezińska

Rohan and the Social Codes of Heroic Epic and Chivalric Romance

Abstract

While writing *The Lord of the Rings* J.R.R. Tolkien drew inspiration from numerous literary and historical sources. The ideas for many of the characters and races he has created can be traced back to specific, mostly medieval, literary genres. A number of critics, among them such great authorities in the field of Tolkien studies as Tom Shippey, claim that the Rohirrim descend from the heroes of Anglo-Saxon poetry. I survey the arguments in favour of the Anglo-Saxon roots of the Rohirrim society, but I also point out that the Rohirrim are progressing from the heroic towards the chivalric model of society. I demonstrate that their culture incorporates many elements stemming from heroic culture which were later to become characteristic of the chivalric culture of the High Middle Ages, including the rituals of dubbing the knight and the office of the viceroy in place of an absent monarch. I suggest that, while still held together mainly by the values of kinship and honour, Rohan is a society in which a culture of the medieval chivalric type is also manifest. In the analysis of the heroes of Rohan special attention is given in the paper to the complexity of the character of Éowyn, particularly her inner conflict between duty towards her kin and people and the heroic desire for personal glory.

The Lord of the Rings presents the reader with a wide variety of races and cultures. There are, for example, the hobbits, who seem like a nineteenth-century middle class rural and small town population, and the elves, an ancient race of master artists and craftsmen, rich in the wisdom of bygone centuries; there are also the people of Gondor, with the castle-like fortress of Minas Tirith at the centre of their land and a social order bringing to mind the society of the High Middle Ages, where the knights constituting the upper class protect the country and the lower class consists predominantly of peasants and craftsmen. Though seemingly easy to identify, Tolkien's sources of inspiration are numerous and it may be interesting to look closely at least at some of them.

The Rohirrim, for example, on whom this essay focuses, can be seen as a multifaceted group, evoking on the one hand the Anglo-Saxon warriors of old epic poetry and on the other the later medieval knighthood governed by the chivalric code as presented in the romance genre. One must remember, though, that being a work of contemporary fiction *The Lord of the Rings* does not transfer verbatim into its plot the rules of conduct and models of life associated with these literary genres and types of society.[1]

To begin with it must be stated that the strongest and most commonly accepted model for the Rohirrim, as argued by numerous critics, is provided by the Anglo-Saxons. There are a number of arguments supporting this claim and I intend to present and discuss them in the following paragraphs. First let me turn to Tom Shippey, who in *The Road to Middle-Earth* as well as in *J.R.R. Tolkien: Author of the Century* thoroughly analyses all the connections between the Anglo-Saxons and the riders of Rohan. Beginning by discussing the possible etymology of the word *Mark*, used by the Rohirrim to refer to their country, he presents an analysis which proves that the word comes from the Old English words *mierce/ mearc*, the pronunciation of which, at least in the region of Mercia, would be 'mark'. Hence the conclusion is that the word *Mark*, alluding to Anglo-Saxon Mercia, underlies the name Riddermark.

Another interesting point is the banner of the Rohirrim bearing the image of a white horse on a field of green. Professor Shippey explains (*Tolkien* 119) that this had been inspired by the Uffington White Horse, a primitive carving in a chalk hill nearby a Neolithic long barrow called Wayland's Smithy, both of which are situated not far from Oxford. Further still, as observed by Shippey (*Tolkien* 119) and by Lee and Solopova (200), the names of the Riders and of their horses and weapons are also derived from the language of the Anglo-Saxons, more precisely its Mercian dialect; the names of the kings of Rohan, such as Théoden, Thengel, Fengel, and Folcwine are simply capitalized terms that mean 'king' or 'prince', while the name of the first ruler of Rohan, Eorl the Young, simply means 'earl' or 'warrior', the second meaning being rooted in times still before the idea of kingship gained prominence (Shippey, *Tolkien* 119-20). There is also a connection between the Rohirrim and the Goths, though. As opposed to the Anglo-Saxons, Gothic warriors fought on horseback, which makes the

---

[1] As Thomas Honegger also remarks, the Rohirrim "provide, structurally speaking, the heroic counterpart to the bucolic hobbits […] and the two peoples are complementary (and largely idealized) depictions of 'typically English' elements" (Honegger, "Rohirrim" 116).

Rohirrim exactly like them in this respect. What is more, when the Rohirrim, then referred to as the Éothéod, lived in the valley of the Upper Anduin, some of the names used among them, such as Vidugavia, Vidumavi and Vinithara, were clearly of Gothic origin.[2]

One of the most prominent Anglo-Saxon, or Old English, literary inspirations in Tolkien's literary construction of the culture of Rohan is derived from *Beowulf* and is clearly visible when it comes to the presentation of social customs and the behaviour of characters. This makes the Rohirrim a rendering of the Anglo-Saxons not only from the historical-linguistic but also from the historical-literary perspective. The way Legolas describes Meduseld, the hall of Théoden, is an echo of line 311 in *Beowulf*. The very name Meduseld, meaning simply 'mead-hall', comes from the poem as well and appears in line 3065.

Another aspect transferred directly and in detail from *Beowulf* into the chapter "The King of the Golden Hall" is the admittance procedure to which Gandalf, Aragorn, Legolas, and Gimli are subjected before being allowed to see king Théoden. Exactly like the Geats in the Old English epic confronted by the Danish guard at the beach a moment after their landing, the four travellers in *The Lord of the Rings* are first stopped by the guards at the gates of Edoras and subsequently by Háma, the Doorward, right before they enter Meduseld. Háma also asks them to leave behind their weapons, as they should not be admitted armed in front of the king. Here one can observe another close parallel with the text of *Beowulf*. During the meeting between the hero accompanied by his warriors and the guard posted on the coast, when the latter needs to decide whether to allow the strangers any further into the land he is supposed to watch, he says the following upon reaching a decision:

> "Anyone with gumption
> And a sharp mind will take the measure
> of two things: what's said and what's done.
> I believe what you have told me: that you are a troop
> loyal to our king. So come ahead
> with your arms and your gear, and I will guide you"
> (*Beowulf*, lines 287-90, trans. S. Heaney)

---

[2] For a more detailed discussion see Shippey, "Goths and Huns" 117-18 and Honegger, "Rohirrim" 123-24.

Similarly, when discussing their admittance into Meduseld and arguing about leaving the weapons, Háma finally decides to allow Gandalf to keep his staff and declares:

> 'The staff in the hand of a wizard may be more than a prop for age,' said Háma. He looked hard at the ash-staff on which Gandalf leaned. 'Yet in doubt a man of worth will trust his own wisdom. I believe you are friends and folk worthy of honour, who have no evil purpose. You may go in.'
> (*Two Towers* 135-36)

This situation also suggests, and again this is something Shippey points out (*Tolkien* 123-24), that the culture of the Rohirrim, although governed by certain rules and principles, is not yet a culture based on a written-down and thus fixed code of behaviour.

Even the structure of Edoras and its function in Rohirrim society brings to mind the reality of Anglo-Saxon communities. With Meduseld, the hall of the king, in its centre and being the only Rohirrim settlement, Edoras is also the focal stage of the country's social and political life. A vast majority of the men are Riders of Rohan, which means they do not have time for farming and the only animals important to their way of life seem to be their horses. It appears that the king possesses enough resources to be able to support his warriors,[3] whose major obligation in return is to support him in any military conflict and protect the land and its people. In line with the critical comments summarised above, this is how Tolkien first characterises the Riders through Aragorn's description of them for Legolas and Gimli: "'They are proud and wilful, but they are true-hearted, generous in thought and deed; bold but not cruel; wise but unlearned, writing no books but singing songs, after the manner of the children of Men before the Dark Years'" (*Two Towers* 28).

Having briefly enumerated the similarities and connections between the Anglo-Saxons and the Rohirrim, it may now be worthwhile to take a closer look at the development of knighthood and its governing set of principles forming the so-called 'chivalric code', the defining ethos of this social group, to which it initially strongly adhered. Although the quotation below alludes to the genre of romance as the place of formation of the chivalric code, literature may only

---

3 For more information see Shippey, *Road* 150-54 and Lee and Solopova 200-1.

have helped to unify and cement the knightly ethos, but, it is often assumed, the qualities or characteristics forming it came into the romances as a reflection of real life. Still, it may have been the other way round, i.e. that the romance genre motivated members of the audience to emulate the idealized behaviour presented in the texts in their real lives.

> From a very early stage we find the romantic authors habitually associating together certain qualities which they clearly regarded as the classic virtues of good knighthood: *prouesse, loyauté, largesse* (generosity), *courtoisie*, and *franchise* (the free and frank bearing that is visible testimony to the combination of good birth with virtue). The association of these qualities in chivalry is already established in the romances of Chrétien de Troyes (written c. 1165 – c. 1185), and from his time on to the end of the Middle Ages their combination remains the stereotype of chivalrous distinction. (Keen 2)

Most aspects of chivalry became very quickly formalized and developed their ritual-like character. This was exactly the case with the ceremony of dubbing. As Keen writes in *Chivalry* as early as 1250 there appeared a poem entitled *Ordene de chevalrie* presenting a full description of a conventionalised dubbing of a knight. One of the most important aspects of the ceremony came towards its end, when the future knight was presented with a sword which served to remind its bearer, with its two sharp edges, of the duty to defend the poor from their oppressors (Keen 7).

The presentation with the sword was central and crucial to the ceremony of knighting. Its significance was rooted in the times when it was exclusively part of the crowning ritual. It is known that when in 791 Charlemagne crowned Louis the Pious king of Aquitaine, he girded him with a sword. This later became incorporated into the liturgical elements of coronation and transferred on to the knighting ceremony.

> The girding of the aspirant with his sword was clearly a very central element in the secular ritual of making a knight, older and more basic to it than the *collée* or *paumée*... But the earliest references that offer any details of an elaborate girding ceremony – something more than the mere delivery of arms – concern not knights, but kings. [...] The liturgy of making a knight seems therefore to have a whole series of very close connections with the coronation rite. (Keen 72)

Another work discussed by Keen and providing valuable information as to the duties of a knight is Ramon Lull's *Libre del ordre de cavayleria*, the first and most important of them being the defence of the Christian faith against the infidels. The service a knight could offer was not only due to his temporal lord, but also to all those considered weak: women, children, and the old. To be able to fulfil the two earlier commandments every knight was supposed to exercise and practise his skills both in hunting and in tournament. The service offered to his lord was not limited only to the time of war. In time of peace a knight was supposed to undertake the duties of a judge and of supervising the landowner sin the lands given him by the overlord. While performing all the duties listed above a knight was also supposed to take care to develop his virtues, such as wisdom, charity, loyalty, and most importantly courage.

"Chivalrous" virtues, such as *largesse, prouesse*, and loyalty quickly came to be considered typical, if not stereotypical, features of noble character. Much the same qualities were clearly present even considerably earlier in Germanic, Anglo-Saxon literature.

> Liberality, loyalty and courage are the principal virtues in the warrior society depicted in the Anglo-Saxon epic of *Beowulf* (which may have been written as early as the eighth century). Already present too in that poem is the view of youth as a testing time, in which the young warrior seeks to prove himself in the service of foreign lords and far from home. (Keen 52)

Texts such as *Beowulf* or *The Battle of Maldon*[4] show that characteristics such as loyalty and courage already held a principal place among the ideals of the warrior group in Anglo-Saxon times.

Having presented the knightly characteristics, it is time to identify examples of this pattern of behaviour in some of the central characters in *The Lord of the Rings*. The most prominent warrior characters that easily come to mind and are certainly worth inspection in the light of the information given above concerning the chivalric code and both the historical and literary idea of knighthood are Aragorn, Boromir, and Faramir.

---

4 The poem tells how a local English army, led by Earl Beorhtnoth of Essex, faces a host of Viking invaders. The Earl is killed and many of his followers run away. Yet his personal retainers follow the traditional Germanic warrior code, which states that after the death of the leader they ought to continue the fight until victory or glorious death. The decision is supported by numerous declarations of loyalty and courage, the most famous one being: "Courage shall grow the harder, heart the keener, / Spirit the greater, as our strength lessens." For more information on the poem and its inspirational influence on Tolkien's work see Holmes, Honegger "Homecoming" and Ruud 478-79.

The character of Aragorn can be seen changing and developing throughout the plot of the novel from a simple Ranger referred to as Strider, through a valiant warrior uniting in his person both knightly features and characteristics of an epic warrior, to finally become the noble kingly figure he was always destined to be.[5]

Boromir and Faramir both come from the noble line of the Stewards of Gondor – they are, one might say, born to become knights of their homeland. The society and culture of Gondor,[6] especially when compared to Rohan, is definitely meant to be interpreted as one corresponding to the High rather than the Early Middle Ages. Gondor's society is more complex in its organization, the written culture is well developed, which can be easily seen when Gandalf repeatedly visits Minas Tirith to read old scrolls, and the people themselves, though undeniably valiant, are not as fierce and rash as the Rohirrim. Even though Boromir fails to resist the temptation of the Ring, he nevertheless remains a strong, brave and noble character to his very end, dying heroically during an attempt to save Merry and Pippin from being kidnapped by the Orcs.[7] His younger brother, Faramir, a skilled leader of men and a brave warrior, is no less ready and willing to oppose the Enemy and his forces.[8]

Comparing the ways in which Pippin and Merry offer their services to Denethor and Théoden, respectively, gives the reader a clear impression of how different Gondor is from Rohan. When Pippin is brought to Minas Tirith by Gandalf and confronted with the Steward, to whom he is to describe the circumstances pertaining to the death of Boromir, Denethor's first-born son, the hobbit feels he is being blamed and, at least partially, held responsible for the warrior's death. It may be said that Denethor, well aware that Pippin owes his life to Boromir, and working through this sense of gratitude as well as the hobbit's pride and honour, manipulates him to pledge his service to the Steward of Gondor. The pledge is long and elaborate and it is obvious that its wording is following a fixed pattern:

---

5 For a more detailed discussion of Aragorn see Ruud 292-93 and Armstrong.
6 For more information on Gondor see Ruud 501-3 and Straubhaar.
7 For further portrayal of Boromir see Ruud 294-95 and Davis.
8 More information on Faramir can be found in Ruud 297-98 and Thomas.

> 'Here do I swear fealty and service to Gondor, and to the Lord and Steward of the realm, to speak and be silent, to do and to let be, to come and to go, in need or plenty, in peace or war, in living and dying, from this hour henceforth, until my lord release me, or death take me, or the world end. So say I, Peregrin son of Paladin of the Shire of the Halflings.'
>
> 'And so this do I hear, Denethor son of Ecthelion, Lord of Gondor, Steward of the High King, and I will not forget it, nor fail to reward that which is given: fealty with love, valour with honour, oath-breaking with vengeance.' Then Pippin received back his sword and put it in its sheath.
> (*Return of the King* 17-18)

It seems very probable that a written version of this ritualised dialogue could be found somewhere within the annals of Gondor.

A similar scene with Merry and Théoden as participants involves quite a different kind of emotion. The king of Rohan understands the hobbit's need to participate in the current events, even if he is not a grand warrior, and offers him the place of his squire. Instead of solemn, ceremonial vows, there is love and devotion, feelings commonly shared by close kinsmen. There is no complex system of dependencies, no power play, the king of Rohan wishes only to bless Merry and hopes he will find good fortune in the fighting to come, which is precisely what motivates Merry to lay his sword at Théoden's feet:

> 'I have a sword,' said Merry, climbing from his seat, and drawing from its black sheath his small bright blade. Filled suddenly with love for this old man, he knelt on one knee, and took his hand and kissed it. 'May I lay the sword of Meriadoc of the Shire on your lap, Théoden King?' he cried. 'Receive my service, if you will!'
>
> 'Gladly will I take it,' said the king; and laying his long old hands upon the brown hair of the hobbit, he blessed him. 'Rise now. Meriadoc, esquire of Rohan of the household of Meduseld!' he said. 'Take your sword and bear it unto good fortune!'
>
> 'As a father you shall be to me,' said Merry.
> (*Return of the King* 46)

It can be fully appreciated now how relevant the heroic, and soon to become chivalrous, qualities are to Tolkien's presentation of the Rohirrim. One of these traits was certainly loyalty to the king. Even though their king is old, ailing and ill-advised by Wormtongue, Éomer often stresses, and he can certainly be seen as one speaking for all of the Rohirrim, that it is his utmost priority to serve the king and carry out his orders, but not blindly so.

The Rohirrim are also generous, another heroic quality which was easily incorporated into the later knightly ideal. When meeting Aragorn, Legolas, and Gimli as they are crossing the plains of Rohan in pursuit of the Orc host that kidnapped Merry and Pippin, Éomer, though preoccupied with war and wishing very much to remain cautious with unexpected trespassers, nevertheless ultimately provides these ones with a precious gift of horses. It is true that the horses are borrowed on the condition that the travellers return with them to Edoras; still, after Gandalf's supposed stealing of the most precious horse in the Mark, Shadowfax, Éomer is generous enough to trust in the travellers' honour and grant them this precious gift.[9]

There is also the ceremoniousness of certain situations pointing to the fact that the relationships in the Rohirrim society are governed by the heroic code. The scene of Éomer offering Théoden his sword in an act of submission to his rule, or the moment when Éowyn is presented with a sword and corselet before the door to Meduseld, are just two examples of the ceremonial gestures of the kind that had become increasingly popular since very early in the Middle Ages and continued to be so through the High Middle Ages, and which can be seen in the earliest literature, particularly heroic epic poems, *chansons de gestes*, and romances.[10] It is worth noting that characteristics such as pride and honour, honesty and generosity, or some pertaining in particular to military exploits, like courage and prowess, are common to both systems of values, the Anglo-Saxon and the Anglo-Norman one. It needs to be borne in mind that the core concepts in the code were present from the very beginning and then only modified, improved upon and embellished as time passed and society changed.

Having already quoted a brief, general description of the Riders, focusing mostly on their character, let me now concentrate on their external appearance. Tolkien tells us that they were "tall and long-limbed; their hair flaxen-pale, flowed under their light helms, and streamed in long braids behind them; their faces were stern and keen"; describing their equipment, the narrator adds that "in their

---

9   For a full description of the meeting between Éomer and the travellers see *Two Towers* 29-40.
10 For full descriptions of these ceremonial gestures see *Two Towers* 143, 151.

hands were tall spears of ash, painted shields were slung at their backs, long swords were at their belts, their burnished shirts of mail hung down upon their knees" (*Two Towers* 29). The painted shields and ashen spears clearly bring to mind Beowulf and his companions heading to Heorot to rid Hrothgar of his bane. In those times the warriors' wooden shields were often decorated with intricate paintings so that the adversary would not be able to see the pattern of the rings and to hit the shield so as to split it easily.

It may prove worthwhile to look more closely at the first encounter between Éomer and the party consisting of Aragorn, Legolas, and Gimli. When Aragorn wishes to know with whom the loyalty of the Rohirrim lies, Éomer replies like a gallant knight: "I serve only the Lord of the Mark, Théoden King son of Thengel" (*Two Towers* 31). This sounds like a typical statement of loyalty to one's kinsman and leader known from medieval court poetry. This kind of loyalty based on personal relations, on knowing and respecting one's ruler, makes the Rohirrim wish to follow Éomer and to serve him. Along with the two different oaths of allegiance made by Pippin and Merry, this episode shows clearly how the sense of fellowship and devotion to the leader constitutes the driving force in the community of Rohan, whereas following and obedience are institutionalized in Gondor.

Despite being a devoted subject of Théoden, Éomer nevertheless also exhibits traits of character typical of an epic hero of the ancient past when he declares: "Indeed in this riding north I went without the king's leave" (*Two Towers* 36). Obviously, on that occasion Éomer broke the knightly rules of conduct which include, most importantly, being true to one's liege-lord and fulfilling his orders. Like Éowyn, as we shall see later, he is a type of heroic character that is far too independent and wilful to always obey the orders of an overlord. Furthermore, having heard of the distance the three friends had covered and the speed they did it with in order to overtake the Orcs, Éomer offers the following comment: "This deed of the three friends should be sung in many a hall" (*Two Towers* 35). This clearly alludes to a tradition preceding medieval romances and brings to mind the poets singing about heroic deeds in such texts as *Beowulf*, or the even earlier *The Iliad* and *The Odyssey*. Thus, the Rohirrim appear to embody a combination of features that connect them both with the codes of heroic epic poetry and with medieval romances and their respective cultural backgrounds.

The only significant difference between the Rohirrim and the Anglo-Saxons is the attitude to horse riding and horses in general. As Shippey notes (*Tolkien* 120-21) texts such as *The Battle of Maldon* and *The Anglo-Saxon Chronicle* demonstrate the Anglo-Saxon wariness when it comes to horses and fighting on horseback. The very first lines of *The Battle of Maldon* (lines 1-2) call for the warriors to abandon their mounts and proceed to confront the enemy on foot. In Rohan, however, horses are greatly respected and clearly considered companions important in battle. It was a common practice for epic heroes and famous warriors to name their horses, thus we know that Alexander the Great rode Bucephalus and Roland's horse was called Veillantif. That is why, as it was already mentioned above in the context of generosity, it is a very noble gesture on the part of Éomer to lend the travellers two of the precious horses. Aragorn, himself a heroic figure and future king, promises to return the borrowed horses and at the same time visit the king in his capital. As both leaders adhere to the principle of honesty, which was a prominent value already in the warrior society, and they would never break a promise, Éomer may allow himself to act on the knightly virtue of *largesse*.

When after Gandalf's intervention Théoden is freed from the influence of Wormtongue, it turns out that Éomer has been imprisoned for disobeying the king's orders. When the young Marshall is released from prison, he is also given back his sword and thus comes armed before the king: "Éomer was there. No helm was on his head, no mail was on his breast, but in his hand he held a drawn sword; and as he knelt he offered the hilt to his master" (*Two Towers* 143). Such gesture of obedience and fealty is exactly what one would expect of a knight. It also ought to be borne in mind that Éomer was Théoden's sister's son and even the first epics explore such relationships as strong and special, even stronger than the bond between father and son. Even though he lost his only son and heir, Théoden appreciates and cultivates the bond between himself and his nephew, knowing that Éomer is the leader the Rohirrim will follow gladly. Family relationships in Gondor are, by contrast, far more strained. Thus, Denethor sees Faramir more as a captain who owns him absolute obedience precisely because they are related, rather than as a son who wishes to please his father, fulfil his duty towards his country and people and, at least to some extent, fill the gap left after the death of his older brother, Boromir.

A common practice, taking its beginning in the old tribal cultures, was that a woman remained part of her own clan or family even after getting married. To ensure the loyalty of her children, most importantly the firstborn son, a young child was, as a rule, sent to the house of its maternal uncle to be brought up there. That is how the strong bond between the uncle and the maternal nephew, commonly used as a stock motif in heroic and romance literature, came into being. One of the best known examples must be the relationship between Roland and Charlemagne, the former being the latter's sister's son, and while it is true that the Celts were the people who particularly prioritized the tie between the mother's brother and the sister's son, giving an account of the ancient Germanic culture Tacitus writes the following: "the sons of sisters are as highly honoured by their uncles as by their own fathers. Some tribes even consider the former tie the closer and more sacred" (Miller 93).

Despite being offered Éomer's sword[11] Théoden firmly requests his own to be found. Soon the faithful guardsman Háma presents it to his king. "Háma knelt and presented to Théoden a long sword in a scabbard clasped with gold and set with green gems. 'Here, lord, is Herugrim, your ancient blade', he said" (*Two Towers* 145). The most important aspect of this scene is the fact that the blade bears a name. Just like Roland wielded Durendal, so king Théoden has his Herugrim. It was an indispensable feature of the epic to give the hero a weapon that would not only bear a name but also have a noble history of previous wielders. Because of the glory it had accumulated over years and through its previous owners, such a weapon served not only in battle but was also a means of having its current owner participate in the splendour of the heroes of the past.

Soon enough the reader also learns that the role awaiting Éowyn is that of a vassal protecting the people in the name of the king. Upon setting out towards Helm's Deep, Théoden needs to leave his people under the rule of a universally respected leader. This is when Háma suggests that the people's trust lies in the members of the royal family. At first Théoden passes Éowyn

---

11 As the reader learns later on, during the description of the battle of Helm's Deep, Éomer's sword is not some nameless piece of steel. When the young Marshall attacks the enemies, he screams a battle cry worthy of a valiant knight or an epic hero: 'Gúthwinë!' cried Éomer. 'Gúthwinë for the Mark!' (*Two Towers* 164).

over completely and does not consider her as a potential leader. The idea appears only when Háma voices it: "There is Éowyn, daughter of Éomund, his sister. She is fearless and high-hearted. All love her. Let her be as lord to the Eorlingas, while we are gone" (*Two Towers* 151). The opinion expressed by an experienced guardsman may be taken as representing both the army's and the people's stand concerning who is to govern the kingdom. Clearly, Éowyn was considered appropriate for the position of the leader of her people in time of war. An interesting analogy from Anglo-Saxon history to look at in this context would be Æthelflæd,[12] born around year 870 AD, and declared the Lady of the Mercians around 911 AD. She was the eldest child of King Alfred the Great, ruler of the West Saxons. Educated at her father's court alongside her brother, who was later to become King Edward the Elder, she received also a military education. Married to Ethelred, lord of the Mercians, she not only strengthened the ties between Essex and Mercia, but also took an active part in fortifying the lands belonging to her and her husband and in confronting the Danes who kept threatening the area at that time.

Éowyn was chosen not because, being a woman, she would make a good caretaker for her countrymen. It is clearly stated that she is seen as one of the house of Eorl, without any indication that it was her sex that determined the task she was assigned by Théoden. Not only is she described by Háma as fearless and high-hearted, with epithets that could be easily applied to a knight. She is also said to be staying with her people as their overlord's representative, which would be perfectly understandable in the context. The use of the term *lord*[13] underlines the fact that Éowyn is perceived as equal to any man the king could have possibly assigned the task of protecting the more vulnerable part of the population.

Furthermore, after Théoden orders the heralds to proclaim to the people that they are going to be led by Éowyn during his absence, there is also a little ceremony in which one might see the symbolic transfer of power and responsibility: "Then the king sat upon a seat before his doors, and Éowyn knelt before

---

12 For more information on Æthelflæd see the studies by Jane Wolfe and Guida M. Jackson.
13 The etymology of the word 'lord' suggests that, before it was associated with exercising power over people, the word's strongest connotations were with caring for the subjects' welfare and providing them with food – see http://www.merriam-webster.com/dictionary/lord and http://www.etymonline.com/index.php?term=lord.

him and received from him a sword and a fair corselet" (*Two Towers* 151). The episode can be seen as a very early stage of development for the ceremony of dubbing a knight, so important for the chivalric culture. Éowyn was born to the noblest family in Rohan, but when presenting her ceremonially with the insignia of military rule the king makes sure all know it is his authority that stands behind her and her actions and decisions. Whoever doubts and questions her as the overlord questions the king's rule and his wisdom. Leslie A. Donovan offers the following comment pertaining to this situation:

> As with other valkyrie-identified women, Éowyn's female identity does not preclude her from wielding power, regardless of whether Tolkien presents her character gendered as a courtly princess or as an armoured warrior. Gifts suitable for a warrior rather than a courtly woman, Éowyn's arms are awarded to her by her king. [...] Eowyn's training for battle grants her the authority to lead her people, govern them and provide for their welfare in the absence of Théoden. [...] Although her desire physically to engage in battle is rejected by Théoden, Éowyn has the valkyrie's personal power and social obligation to take up arms herself as a means of protecting her people. When some critics view Éowyn's character as either reflective of the powerlessness inherent of her rejection of femininity through her warrior trappings, Hama's words indicate instead her authority to be simultaneously a woman and a warrior. (Donovan 122)

Upon accepting the sword and corselet, Éowyn also dons the duties corresponding to those of a vassal in medieval feudal society.

While Éowyn acts out of love for her uncle and not in exchange for material security or land, she disregards her personal desire to participate in the war and sacrifices that for keeping her people safe under a universally respected rule. As the reader learns later, Éowyn fails in her duties. Though in the end the breach proves a blessing for her kingdom and deals Sauron's forces a major blow, it needs to be borne in mind that a retainer who disobeys his lord stains his honour and gives people reason to doubt the truthfulness of his vows and pledges. Even if Éowyn simply knows what is expected of her without having to receive orders from the king, and there are no elaborate oaths to be broken by her leaving Dunharrow for the Fields of Pelennor, it can still be assumed that her uncle wanted for her to remain with their people, maybe as much as he wanted her to be safe, away from the fighting, for as long as possible. It is worth bearing in mind, though, that one of the basic characteristics of a heroic personality involves attitudinal problems when it comes to simply following orders without questioning them. The struggle between the heroic and the kingly principles has been perfectly summed up by Miller: "More essentially still, the sovereign, at least in the myth-borne and perfect pattern, aims to guide and balance his realm with an eye to the gains of fruitful peace, while the warrior hero's obsessive concern is nearly always with confrontation, force, war and the trial and judgement of blood" (Miller 140).

When the battle of Helm's Deep is resolved, and Aragorn decides to travel through the Paths of the Dead, he stops at Dunharrow where Éowyn has led her people for cover and brings her the news of victory. It becomes evident that Éowyn admires him and is drawn to him. She sees in him the proud heir of an ancient dynasty of kings and an exceptional leader of men, by whose side she would love to ride into battle and even die. Taking pride in the military achievements of one's countrymen and thinking it imperative not to watch the war from a safe distance but participate in it as actively as possible are all typical traits of a model hero. That is why Éowyn, brought up amongst people adhering to such values, feels an urge to follow her kin and countrymen into battle. It is dishonourable for a warrior to know there are others fighting for one's country while one can only watch. Even a responsible task assigned by the overlord cannot blot out the shame entirely.

Admiring Aragorn as a unique leader of men and knowing she is unable to persuade him to change his plans, Éowyn decides to accompany him to the Paths of the Dead. She comes to ask him whether she could ride with him for he is her perfect liege-lord and she wishes to be his bravest and most faithful vassal. When Aragorn tries to explain that she has no "errand" in the South, she makes one last effort pointing out that his other companions do not have any other reason for accompanying him than their feeling of love and loyalty towards him: "They go only because they would not be parted from thee – because they love thee" (*Return of the King* 55). Obviously, she tries to convey to Aragorn that she also loves him, but contrary to how most readers, including the infamous director of *The Lord of the Rings* trilogy, seem to interpret Éowyn's words, her love is not that of an infatuated girl but, rather, the love of a vassal towards his overlord. Arargorn possesses all the assets that Éowyn has seen lacking in her uncle over the years: he is old enough to be experienced but young enough to have the strength to lead a company of men into and through peril to victory; working towards regaining his noble heritage, he nevertheless does not fear to risk his life in performing all the valiant deeds people would expect from the future king of Gondor; finally, he commands great loyalty and seems to be able to effortlessly bind to himself everyone with whom fate brings him together even for a short time. Éowyn implores: "Lord, [...] if you must go, then let me ride in your following. For I am weary of skulking in the hills, and wish to face peril and battle" (*Return of the King* 54).

Éowyn's declaration that she would like to prove herself in battle, a clear proof of her courage befitting an exceptional hero, would be highly admirable if it were not for the fact that it totally undermines her faithfulness to her king, overlord and uncle, Théoden. As his kin, left in protection of her own people, Éowyn should be proud of the king's trust and understand that her countrymen see her as equal to all the men in the royal family without her needing to prove herself any more. Aragorn, well aware of the supreme duties of kingship, or simply lordship, needs only one sentence to express what for him is crucial and self-evident, while Éowyn still needs time to comprehend and accept it: "Your duty is with your people," he answers (*Return of the King* 54). Éowyn is unable to see that she has been elected the country's lord protector because of her personal courage and nobility, the most admirable traits of character for the people of the House of Eorl; and that because everybody knows that she does not fear pain, death and fighting till the bitter end, they entrust to her their lives. When finally asked what it is she fears most, she answers: "A cage, [...] to stay behind bars, until use and old age accept them, and all chance of doing great deeds is gone beyond recall or desire" (Tolkien, *The Return of the King* 55).

It is easy to misinterpret Éowyn's words. Most readers readily assume that she feels constrained by the fact that she is a woman and considers her womanhood to be the main reason for assigning her the role she performs in the name of her king, and that the cage stands, therefore, for the household and its duties. I would, however, venture to argue that the cage Éowyn is talking about stands for all the duties of an overlord she is supposed to take over since king Théoden leaves her behind to "govern the folk in his stead" (*Return of the King* 77). It is easy to guess that Éowyn will seize any chance to fight beside her beloved uncle and her brother, even if it be against the explicit command of the king. When morning dawns on the day of Aragorn's departure, she approaches the company leaving for the Paths of the Dead dressed as a rider and bearing a parting cup. Her manners would not allow her to let the party leave without saying their farewells. It was a ritual present already in heroic culture, and preserved in the knightly one, to drink for the safe journey of the departing guests, and it was the host who was supposed to offer the parting drink to his friends, thus sending them on their way with a blessing. Éowyn does not neglect this duty but uses the opportunity to once again try to divert Aragorn from the road he has chosen, or at least to make him include her into his company.[14]

Éowyn's overwhelming desire to fight has both positive and negative repercussions. On the one hand, it is extremely immature and results in leaving the Rohirrim in a position where they are liable to losing all members of the reigning family in one sweep. From the point of view of the feudal code, the decision must be seen as an inexcusable neglect of one's responsibilities towards one's people. Éowyn not only broke her word as a vassal and representative of the king, but she also disappointed the trust set in her. Both her brother and uncle believed her mature enough to understand that a representative of the house of Eorl must stay with the Rohirrim and lead them till the end. Éowyn's presence assured a greater degree of peace and calm amongst her people because they would never want to disobey her. More importantly, should Éowyn get caught by the forces of the enemy, she could be used as a great bargaining card, which would cause Théoden and Éomer a lot of trouble and add to their pain.

On the other hand, as readers subsequently learn, Éowyn had to be on the Pelennor Fields at the same time as the king of the Nazgûl and destroy him, albeit with some help from Merry. The extremely important role she had to play in the course of not only that particular battle but the war in general required her to disobey orders so she could further the fate of Middle-earth by her act of bravery. Moreover, as she is clearly presented as a Germanic kind of warrior-heroine, I believe it would not be a far-fetched interpretation if one assumed

---

14 For an interesting reading of Éowyn and her relationship with Aragorn see the paper by Melissa McRory Hatcher. See Honegger, "Dangers of Drink", for an in-depth analysis of the "parting cup" scene.

that her decision concerning going into battle was also heavily influenced by the code of behaviour centred on "that view of true honour which obligated the follower not to survive his leader fallen in battle" (Miller 41). Because of the importance of the outcome of her actions, it is difficult to criticize Éowyn. The best possible solution is to draw two conclusions, each concerning one aspect of the situation: as a tool guided by destiny, Éowyn fulfilled her task perfectly, but she failed as a vassal and proved herself immature by not obeying her king's orders and putting her personal desires before the responsibilities to her people. Still it ought to be noted that, being a brave warrior, she was not afraid to bear the consequences of her decisions.

Clearly, Éowyn's personal desire to fight for her lord and land must be seen as connected in the prophecy concerning the lord of the Nazgûl. Glorfindel, one of the elves of Rivendell, prophesied that no living man would ever defeat the Nazgûl king. At the point of the confrontation Éowyn discloses her true identity, claiming that being a woman she will certainly achieve the deed. What Éowyn will perform on the Fields of Pelennor will be a feat worthy of an epic hero. At this moment she becomes as magnificent a hero as Roland defending Charlemagne and his army at the Roncevaux Pass. Just as that legendary nephew did not want to disappoint his uncle so Éowyn rushes to protect hers. Despite the threats of the Nazgûl, she firmly states that as long as she lives nobody, be it man or undead creature, shall touch Théoden: "You stand between me and my lord and kin. Begone if you be not deathless! For living or dark undead, I will smite you, if you touch him," and though "the winged creature screamed at her", yet "the Ringwraith made no answer, and was silent, as if suddenly in doubt" (*Return of the King* 129). Éowyn's unyielding courage is truly something one would expect from a knight as magnificent as Roland. Even though she broke her vows and pledges of fealty towards Théoden, she did it not so much for selfish reasons but rather because she could not imagine deserting her loved ones in the hour of the confrontation with a superior enemy and not protecting them at the cost of her own life. She considered it unthinkable that the uncle, whom she had come to love as a father, could die on some faraway battlefield without her at least trying to save him.

It is interesting to take a closer look at the scene of Éowyn's encounter with the Nazgûl and think about the actual injuries suffered by the heroine. Then it becomes clear that the Nazgûl had not actually even wounded Éowyn. The only harm she suffered came about as an aftermath of the blow she dealt the enemy. In this she is once again similar to Roland. He also did not die of any wounds inflicted on him by the enemy, but it was the effort of the fight and the desperate blowing of his horn that caused his brain to start leaking out through his ears. Similarly, when it comes to Éowyn, the fact that she mightily struck such a fell creature as the Nazgûl results not only in the breaking of her arm, but also makes her fall under the deadly influence of the shadow. During the confrontation with the Nazgûl Éowyn almost achieves the goal to which all epic heroes aspire – dying a glorious death on the battlefield. Miller underscores the difference between the normative, civilized view of a good death as "a death in peaceful circumstances at a 'ripe old age', in which the dying one tranquilly undergoes a nearly organic (even vegetative) transmutation after the arc of his life is complete" and a heroic individual's demand of "his own violent and early end" (326-27).

Conversation over Éowyn's sickbed reveals that Aragorn himself thought her interest in him the fruit of her longing for freedom: "but in me she loves only a shadow and a thought: a hope of glory and great deeds, and lands far away from the fields of Rohan" (*Return of the King* 163). Aragorn understands perfectly well that Éowyn wished not so much for him as for all that he stood for: freedom, possibility of proving oneself in battle and finally the glory to be won by heroic deeds. Soon Éowyn recuperates and wishes to be discharged from the Houses of Healing so she could join the forces fighting against Sauron: "I cannot lie in sloth, idle, caged. I looked for death in battle. But I have not died, and battle still goes on" (Tolkien, *The Return of the King* 285). Here once again she uses the cage metaphor and repeatedly refers to idleness and sloth. Evidently, these are her obsessive thoughts concerning the evaluation of her involvement in the events of the war. She once again openly admits to simply wanting to die in battle, her desire to die being surprisingly strong. Her control breaks when Faramir refuses her wish: "But I do not desire healing [...] I wish to ride to war like my brother Éomer, or better like Théoden the king, for he died and has both honour and peace" (*Return of the King* 285). It is not merely the desire for glory and renown; rather, Éowyn seems to be too scared of performing the same duties day after day and wishes to die and have it over with.

Having carefully looked at the society of Rohan and analysed its most important characters as well as the key events in the development of the plot concerning them, it is certain that the members of the royal house of Rohan may be seen as nobility, evoking two kinds of medieval aristocracy. On the one hand, when looking at the characters of Éomer, Éowyn and Théoden and their attitude towards gaining renown through combat, it is difficult not to think of wild epic warriors, still waiting to be tempered and refined into the knighthood depicted in medieval romances. Just like Siegfried, Beowulf or, in the case of Éowyn, Brunhild, they also wish to prove their prowess in battle and it is obvious they believe dying with a sword in hand is much nobler than living your life in peace till the end of your days. They bear the mark of early medieval warriors for whom heroic death was the only acceptable way of leaving this world. On the other hand, if one considers the ceremonial gesture accompanying the pledge of allegiance Éomer swears to Théoden, or the manner in which Éowyn is presented by her uncle with a sword and corselet, resembling the dubbing ceremony, or the way she is designated by the king to be an overlord for the Rohirrim during his absence, these actions seem to be governed by much more elaborate rules of conduct, associated with the later medieval code of chivalry. As Tom Shippey has put it, "Professor Tolkien no doubt did not believe in the real prehistoric existence of his 'Riders'. However, he may very well have believed in the existence of something very like them" ("Goths and Huns" 118). What is more, the idea of Éowyn becoming a 'knight' is something that transgresses the conventions of any code of conduct actually existing in the distant past. Thus, the creation of the Rohirrim society and the rules they live by is not only an interesting mix of the early and late medieval social codes but also a genuine product of the author's imagination.

Bibliography

ARMSTRONG, Helen. "Aragorn." *J.R.R. Tolkien Encyclopaedia: Scholarship and Critical Assessment*. Ed. Michael D.C. Drout. London: Routledge, 2006. 22-24.

The Battle of Maldon. 14 June 2012. <http://www.battleofmaldon.org.uk/ >.

DAVIS, Alex. "Boromir." *J.R.R. Tolkien Encyclopaedia: Scholarship and Critical Assessment*. Ed. Michael D.C. Drout. London: Routledge, 2006. 74-75.

DONOVAN, Leslie A. "The Valkyrie Reflex in J.R.R. Tolkien's *The Lord of the Rings*; Galadriel, Shelob, Éowyn and Arwen." *Tolkien the Medievalist*. Ed. Jane Chance. London, New York: Routledge, 2003. 106-132.

DROUT, Michael D. C. *J.R.R. Tolkien Encyclopaedia: Scholarship and Critical Assessment*. London: Routledge, 2006.

HEANEY, Seamus, trans. *Beowulf: A New Verse Translation*. London: W.W. Norton, 2000.

HATCHER, Melissa McRory. "Finding Woman's Role in *The Lord of the Rings*." *Mythlore* 25.3-4, Spring/Summer 2007.

HOLMES, John R. "Battle of Maldon, The." *J.R.R. Tolkien Encyclopaedia: Scholarship and Critical Assessment*. Ed. Michael D.C. Drout. London: Routledge, 2006. 52-54.

HONEGGER, Thomas. "Éowyn, Aragorn and the Hidden Dangers of Drink." *Inklings – Jahrbuch für Literatur und Ästhetik* 17. Moers: Brendow, 1999. 217-225.

"'The Homecoming of Beorhtnoth': Philology and the Literary Muse." *Tolkien Studies* 4, 2007. 191-201.

"The Rohirrim: 'Anglo-Saxons on Horseback'? An Inquiry into Tolkien's Use of Sources." *Tolkien and the Study of His Sources: Critical Essays*. Ed. Jason Fisher. Jefferson, North Carolina and London: McFarland, 2011. 116-132.

JACKSON, Guida M. *Women Rulers throughout the Ages: An Illustrated Guide*. Santa Barbara, CA: ABC-CLIO, 1999.

KEEN, Maurice. *Chivalry*. Yale: Yale University Press, 1984.

KOCHER, Paul H. *Master of Middle-Earth: The Fiction of J.R.R. Tolkien*. New York: Ballantine Books, 2003.

LEE, Stuart D., and Elizabeth Solopova. *The Keys to Middle Earth: Discovering Medieval Literature Through the Fiction of J.R.R. Tolkien*. Palgrave Macmillan, 2006.

MILLER, Dean A. *The Epic Hero*. Baltimore: The Johns Hopkins University Press, 2002.

Ruud, Jay. *Critical Companion to J.R.R. Tolkien*. New York: Facts on File, 2011.

Shippey, Tom A. *The Road to Middle-earth*. Boston and New York: Houghton Mifflin, 2003 [1982].

J.R.R. Tolkien: Author of the Century. London: HarperCollins, 2000.

"Goths and Huns: The Rediscovery of the Northern Cultures in the Nineteenth Century." *Roots and Branches: Selected Papers on Tolkien by Tom Shippey*. Zurich and Jena: Walking Tree Publishers, 2007. 115-136.

Straubhaar, Sandra Ballif. "Gondor." *J.R.R. Tolkien Encyclopaedia: Scholarship and Critical Assessment*. Ed. Michael D.C. Drout. London: Routledge, 2006. 248-249.

Thomas, Paul Edmund. "Faramir." *J.R.R. Tolkien Encyclopaedia: Scholarship and Critical Assessment*. Ed. Michael D.C. Drout. London: Routledge, 2006. 196-197.

Tolkien, John Ronald Reuel. *The Letters of J. R. R. Tolkien*. Ed. Humphrey Carpenter with the assistance of Christopher Tolkien. London: HarperCollins, 1995.

The Lord of the Rings: The Fellowship of the Ring (I), The Two Towers (II), The Return of the King (III). London: HarperCollins, 1999.

Wolfe, Jane. *Aethelflaed: Royal Lady, War Lady*. Chester: Fenris Press, 2001

About the author

Justyna Brzezińska is a doctoral student in the Institute of English Studies at the University of Warsaw. She defended her M. A. thesis in the same Institute in 2009 and in 2010 returned to the Institute to begin her doctoral studies. Her research focuses on the medieval heritage of modern fantasy literature.

Maria Błaszkiewicz

Tolkien's Queen-Women in *The Lord of the Rings*

Abstract

The paper explores the possibility of accounting for the alleged absence and/or insignificance of women in *The Lord of the Rings*. Starting from the full admission of the fact that women in *The Lord of the Rings* are almost absent, the paper endeavours to view this absence neither as a sign of the author's prejudice nor his failure as a writer, but as a conscious design the purpose of which is not to diminish the importance of the female element but, on the contrary, to glorify it. This task is attempted on the basis of the analysis of the significance of the figure of the queen, especially in the context of the fertility myth, for the overall pattern and meaning of Tolkien's literary output based on the relevant epic *topoi* including the omphalic space and heroic intrusion. As a result, the spatial and thematic connection between the presence or absence of a female figure and evil is revealed, placing *The Lord of the Rings* in a unique position among Tolkien's works where such a design, although hinted at, is never repeated in this form.

The purpose of the present paper is to explore the possibility of accounting for the alleged absence and/or insignificance of women in *The Lord of the Rings*. This issue has often been raised, sometimes in serious academic publications, but more often in either popular, or embarrassingly unscholarly ones (cf. Leibiger 710-712; Ringel 159-171; Otty 154-178, Partridge 179-198). A variety of attempts at defence were raised, some very interesting, some quite desperate, and most of them quite unsuccessful. The apologies usually centred round the prominence of the figure of Galadriel, often compared to Virgin Mary (Maher 225-236; Pearce 111), or stressed the unseen though extremely important presence of Arwen as one of the crucial objectives of Aragorn's quest (West, "Her Choice" 317-327). The reason why those arguments, indisputable and interesting as they were, did not seem to dispel the doubts was that it is impossible to deny that women are very scarce in *The Lord of the Rings* and their absence is very strongly felt. Indeed, paradoxically, this very absence pointedly highlights those solitary female figures that do appear within more than a thousand pages of Tolkien's work.

My argument will be based on this palpable fact that women in *The Lord of the Rings* are almost absent, but this absence will be viewed neither as the sign of the author's prejudice or his failure as a writer, but as a conscious design which aims not to diminish the importance of the female element but, on the contrary, to glorify it. This will be attempted on the basis of the analysis of the significance of the figure of the queen for the overall pattern and meaning of Tolkien's literary output.

Even a very cursory glance at *The Hobbit* and the *legendarium* shows dramatic differences in their treatment of female characters. *The Hobbit* is strikingly devoid of them as the only important reference to a female is the fact that it is Bilbo's dead mother's genes that urge him to long for a less respectable and dull life. The shadow of Belladonna Took, however important for the meaning of the story, does not alter the fact that it is almost obsessively male-oriented. The fact has been duly noted, of course, but what has been overlooked is the possibility of including it in an overall interpretation of this puzzling little book in terms of an academic joke made by a learned medievalist. The comic dimension of *The Hobbit* is fully realised only if one takes into account its meta-textual and mock-heroic character. In this context, the lack of female characters is one of the chief factors leading to the text's deviation from the traditional ending of romance or fairly-tale quest (the hero can marry no princess because there aren't any) which seems implied by the deceptively conventional structure of the narrative. Bilbo the bachelor, with his anachronistic language, opinions and environment (Shippey 55-134), is further juxtaposed against the generic assumptions the tale apparently refers to by his wanderings in the world whose conventionality is compromised further and further as the story progresses (note the clashes resulting from the introduction of fairy-tale-like creatures and, on the other side, the dark political and psychological meandering of the final part, with its purely superficial alliances and moral labelling of the Battle of the Five Armies, not to mention the mock-heroic character of the tale in which one seeks to recover the dragon hoard by employing a burglar).

The *legendarium* seems to address the problem of female characters from a completely different angle. Modelled on traditional narratives like myth, epic and saga, the stories consequently seem to employ conventional gender roles characteristic of those genres,[1] although a strong bias towards the courtly notion of female superiority permeates the whole (Hopkins 365; Leibiger 710; Sturgis 301), regardless how far a particular episode departs from the romance paradigm (West, "Real World Myth" 261). Quite uncharacteristically, though, this superiority is mostly evident in the case of married couples, which frees the presentation of women from a purely mechanical and often perfunctory rhetoric of courtship and renders it more significant and deep-rooted. Starting from the power and significance of Varda, the most revered of all the Valar and the wife of the supreme ruler of Arda, Manwë, Eru's viceroy, the catalogue of married couples includes Melian and Thingol, Lúthien and Beren, Idril and Tuor, Aredhel and Eöl, and Míriel Ar-Zimraphel and Ar-Pharazôn. Significantly, a purely social difference of status often coupled with moral or intellectual perfection can in Tolkien's world be underlined by actual ontological superiority as his world combines vertical hierarchy with a diversity of intelligent species. Female characters in the *legendarium*, although admittedly fewer than their male counterparts, are nevertheless significant and numerous enough to become most prominent, actually to an extent often surpassing the standard established in the European epic tradition (cf. Felson & Slatkin 91-114; Foley 105-118). It is not a coincidence that the literary unfolding of Tolkien's idea of Middle-earth started with the story of Beren and Lúthien, in which the female character is not only in the centre as the actual goal of the quest but also plays a very active part in the adventure episodes of the story (cf. West, "Real World Myth" 265). In one of his oldest legends, the story of the children of Húrin, the female element is very dramatically presented as a tragic and pivotal factor in the characters' fates.

Viewed against this background, the situation of *The Lord of the Rings* cannot be simply attributed to prejudice, or ignorance. As has already been stressed, women are scarcely present in the great expanse of Middle-earth described in this work. Apart from the Shire episodes with the three most prominent female

---

1 This has also met with heavy disapproval (Mains 43; Ringel 159). It is, however, not the aim of my paper to either defend or discuss this aspect of Tolkien's world.

hobbits, Lobelia Sackville-Baggins, Mrs Maggot, and Rose Cotton, where both the number and significance of women differs considerably from the rest of the text, there are actually only six living female characters referred to by name, Goldberry, Arwen, Galadriel, Éowyn, Yoreth, and Shelob. To these we may add seven historical ones, one of which represents a large group of departed and presumably long dead Entwives, and, last but not least, Varda Elbereth, the only Valar named explicitly – apart from Morgoth, who is usually referred to as "the Great Enemy".

Further scrutiny demonstrates also a strange spatial distribution of those few females. The portion of Middle-earth featuring in *The Lord of the Rings* maps can be divided into four distinctive parts. The first division, between west and east, is naturally confined by the Great River marking the boundary between the western lands, which enjoy different degrees of freedom from Sauron's domain, and the desolation and waste of the east, which finds its culmination in its southern extreme, Mordor. This eastern area is literally devoid of women or in fact of habitation as such, being moreover a probable site of the past dwindling and presumed extinction of the Entwives. In the south, on the western border of Mordor, dwells the book's sole evil female, Shelob the spider. The western part of Middle-earth in the course of the narrative becomes distinctly divided into the troubled south, paradoxically a seat of old kingdoms (Gondor and Rohan) and thus perceived by its inhabitants as the civilised region though at present torn and ruined by war, and the north, mysterious, obscure, more scantily populated, but sheltering the hidden sources of vitality and beneficial power, Lórien, Rivendell, and the Shire. This region is a homeland of all female characters save Éowyn and Yoreth, the book's only women south of Lórien and west of the River mentioned by name.

Both the number and distribution of female characters is combined with the overall image of desolation that slowly unfolds as the hobbits embarking on a quest traverse the lands, finally coming to the extreme south to face different aspects of the palpable fact that, to put it bluntly, Middle-earth is dying. The hobbits enter a world that is distinctly different from their homeland, not only because it is vast and dangerous but, even more strikingly, because it is desolate, empty, and in extreme cases corrupted seemingly beyond repair (cf. Dickerson & Evans 185-192). Their quest leads them through vast empty spaces not because they want to avoid settlements but because it seems that there aren't any. The lands they cross have names, for they used to be inhabited, and the deplorable present is thus contrasted with glimpses of the glorious past. Interestingly, in those glimpses female characters are given special prominence as if to stress the contemporary unnatural masculinity of the world. Apart from the stories about Sauron's past treachery, the Last Alliance, and the victorious war, the dominant legends from the past are, first of all, the story of Beren and Lúthien and the song of Nimrodel. Even the images of war in the adventure with the Barrow-wight are counterbalanced by Bombadil's remembrances of the past:

> He chose for himself from the pile a brooch set with blue stones, many-shaped like flax-flowers or the wings of blue butterflies. He looked long at it, as if stirred by some memory, shaking his head, and saying at last:
>
> 'Here is a pretty toy for Tom and his lady! Fair was she who long ago wore this on her shoulder. Goldberry shall wear it now, and we will not forget her!' (*LotR* 145)

Now, the predominant image is that of emptiness, barrow-downs, and ruins. The continuous references to the past, usually obscure for the hobbits (and for many readers), are made not only to provide historical depth,[2] but also, or especially, in order to stress the present desolation and emptiness:

> we have reached the borders of the country that Men call Hollin; many Elves lived here in happier days, when Eregion was its name. […] the trees and the grass do not now remember them. Only I hear the stones lament them: *deep they delved us, fair they wrought us, high they builded us; but they are gone.* (*LotR* 275-76)

The same imagery will also dominate many places which are still inhabited. When the Fellowship approach Edoras, they pass the burial mounds of the kings of the Rohirrim in front of the royal seat. Moreover, considering the fact that the son of the present king is dead, his nephew imprisoned, and his niece, reflecting the predicament of the land, is denied the possibility of development and fruition, the line of the royal barrows is not likely to extend much further. Instead, the whole of the Mark hovers on the brink of destruction, which is

---

[2] In his famous essay, "*Beowulf*: The Monsters and the Critics", Tolkien stresses the predominant function of historical references for the creation of historical depth (16). This seems also the leading function of the historical references in *The Hobbit*. Interestingly, *The Lord of the Rings*, while repeating Bilbo's route, does not imitate this design. Here, historical references, however obscure they may seem at first, play different, often especially important roles for the overall design, meaning, and interpretative possibilities of the book.

likely to turn the entire country into one huge graveyard. The culture that draws its strength from the memory of the past, a fact symbolised by the flowers of *simbelmynë* on the mounds, is likely to disappear as no one will be left to remember it. Two other settlements of the Rohirrim presented in *The Lord of the Rings* are mere strongholds to provide refuge in times of war.

Gondor with the city of Minas Tirith, one of the two initial destinations of the quest, is presented even more pronouncedly as a dying place. The travellers notice that regardless of the additional threat of the ensuing siege, the mighty race has already been dwindling for some time:

> Yet it was in truth falling year by year into decay; and already it lacked half the men that could have dwelt at ease there. In every street they passed some great house or court over whose doors and arched gates were carved many fair letters of strange and ancient shapes: names Pippin guessed of great men and kindreds that had once dwelt there; and yet now they were silent, and no footsteps rang on their wide pavements nor voice was heard in their halls, nor any face looked out from door or empty window. (*LotR* 736)

The dominating image of Gondor, in an ironical contrast to the banner of the kings, is the dead White Tree in front of the sombre and sepulchral palace encasing an empty throne:

> A sweet fountain played there in the morning sun, and a sward of bright green lay about it; but in the midst, drooping over the pool, stood a dead tree, and the falling drops dripped sadly from its barren and broken branches back into the clear water. (*LotR* 736)

The most obvious reason for this state of things is the devastating and long lasting struggle with Sauron's power. Contrary to the past, when the might of the Dark Lord was matched and forestalled by the kings of Elves and Men, now the odds have drastically changed and it seems that the long centuries of interregnum in the divided kingdoms of the Númenórean exiles will swiftly come to an end with Sauron's final offensive, especially if combined with the impending migration of the Elves. This natural devastation as a sign of war is enhanced by Tolkien's persistent nature imagery in his presentation of evil. Its operations are invariably and inseparably linked with the destruction of the environment. That Sauron's influence brings death could not be more emphatically conveyed than by the description of the lands he has already dominated and which have long ceased to resemble anything but an industrial waste-land.

There is, however, another important reason for the depiction of Middle-earth as a dying place. The governing principle of Tolkien's world is the mythical understanding of kingship. His idea of a theocratic chain of command expresses itself also in nature which needs to be ruled, and actually to be wed to the rightful king (Kipling 237). The desolation of Middle-earth can only be healed by the combination of two equally important events: the final deposition of the tyrant, and the restoration of the true king. This concept of kingship entails the importance of the fertility myth and the epic omphalic space. Epic space, from its Homeric beginnings, mirrors the top-to-bottom structure of society through the vertical construction of the city crowned with the halls of the king, often placed in the central tower, and the horizontal division between the centre, with the *axis mundi,* and the chaotic outside (Cook 5-35). This is most obviously expressed in *The Lord of the Rings* by the construction of Gondor's present capital as a vertical structure crowned with an empty throne. Aragorn's ascent to this throne is a necessary condition for the restoration of life and fertility in Middle-earth, but, quite interestingly, his full enthronement is made absolutely impossible without his marriage. Elrond presents him with the sceptre of Annúminas, the final element of his regalia, when he arrives in Gondor escorting the king's bride. This significant aspect of the royal marriage and thus the importance of the figure of the queen is by no means Tolkien's invention, as it can be found in traditional coronation rites and royal myths all over the world (Hocart 101-104). However, the construction of his imaginary world provides Tolkien with an opportunity to specially enhance this feature. Aragorn is therefore able to marry Arwen only after a specific set of signs and portends is fulfilled, the most important one being the finding of the sapling of the White Tree, a blatant fertility symbol. Thus the king, having demonstrated his legitimacy not just by winning the war, but also by his healing powers, is blessed with the new White Tree and consequently with the sceptre and the hand of the queen.[3] A strikingly similar set of requirements is actually fulfilled by Sam, who, after marrying Rose and restoring the Shire's natural beauty with

---

3 I discussed the special significance of Aragorn's enthronement and the solar myth in *The Lord of the Rings* in my articles: "Kingship and the Solar Myth in J.R.R. Tolkien's *The Lord of the Rings*" (*PASE Papers in Literature, Language and Culture, Part One*, ed. G. Bystydzieńska, E. Harris, and P. Lyons, Warszawa: Uniwersytet Warszawski, 2005. 34-39) and "*Now come the days of the King!*: The Significance of the Coronation Scene in J.R.R. Tolkien's *The Lord of the Rings*" (*Anglica* 16, 2007: 37-52).

the help of the Gift of Galadriel, becomes Mayor, the Shire's equivalent of a monarch (cf. Rosebury 138). In this way the Shire, the only fully independent part of Middle-earth by the decree of King Aragorn, becomes a miniature Gondor, completing the fertility imagery of the revived land.[4]

Tolkien uses the quest motif in combination with such epic conventions as heroic intrusion and omphalic space, notably in the variants closely connected with the figure of the queen (familiar from *The Odyssey* and *The Aeneid*). The function of quest helpers (and in a different way, obstacles) typical of the fairy tale quest story is also employed (Auden 35-36). Thus, the quest route starting from the still intact north-western quarter of Middle-earth and leading into both the ultimately mutilated south-east and the practically barren south west, crosses the territories inhabited by all the book's female characters, who are in most cases stationary and inseparably connected with their dwellings. If one considers the friendly places on the map, they seem to divide into mere resting places where one is not safe, and sometimes it is the task of the quest hero to restore order or suggest a right way through the impending danger (Bree, Rohan, Fangorn, Gondor, Henneth Annûn), and virtual sanctuaries, where evil does not dare to enter. One cannot fail to notice that while women are usually absent in the first category of places, a female figure emerges as an important or leading character in each place of the second type (Maggot's Farm, the House of Tom Bombadil, Rivendell, Lórien). Farmer Maggot has a very resolute wife, while Tom Bombadil's house is ruled by the mysterious and semi-divine Goldberry, and in Rivendell the hobbits meet Arwen. The next, and most powerful, place of their refuge is Lórien, with its majestic ruler, Galadriel.

Those sanctuaries are, quite understandably, associated primarily with such comforts as the heroes most immediately need, that is, safety, nourishment, warmth, and rest. Later, there appear equally if not so immediately indispensable needs for spiritual consolation and (if possible) comfort, advice, and help. Most of these values have always been associated with the family, and therefore with the harmonious co-existence of male and female principles, so it is quite natural that such imagery should dominate Tolkien's places of refuge. The ef-

---

[4] Sam's heroic and royal dimension has been discussed in "Samwise the Great" (*Aiglos* Special Issue 2, Summer 2012).

fect is especially striking when compared to the aforesaid palpable absence of women and the imagery of desolation dominating the rest of Middle-earth.

The first place of refuge, Farmer Maggot's house, is especially strongly seen as a family dwelling:

> Two of Maggot's sons and his three daughters came in, and a generous supper was laid on the large table. The kitchen was lit with candles and the fire was mended. Mrs. Maggot bustled in and out. [...] In a short while fourteen sat down to eat. There was beer in plenty, and a mighty dish of mushrooms and bacon, besides much other solid farmhouse fare. The dogs lay by the fire and gnawed rinds and cracked bones. (*LotR* 93)

By means of the imagery stressing the classical oppositions between darkness and light, the scene produces an overpowering impression of the contrast between the hostile and dark outside infested with the menace of the Black Riders and the safe inside, brimful of life and harmony, cheerful and stable. Thus the omphalic model of space that will dominate the book's presentation of sanctuaries is already introduced in this homely scene together with the insistence on the presence of the female ruler figure in position of the highest authority. It is worth noting that because Maggot Farm is still part of the Shire, the family imagery might not seem as striking as it is for, contrary to the rest of Middle-earth, the Shire as a whole is still practically untouched by Sauron's destructive influence. However, and very significantly, this is the first time a family dwelling is presented in the novel, since Bag End was a bachelor's residence. The Farm is therefore both a place of refuge and an image of the world the hobbits are leaving behind.

Interestingly, the same imagery is used in the presentation of the next sanctuary, the House of Tom Bombadil. The sense of safety is even more palpably felt here as the contrast characteristic of the omphalic space is provided by the Old Forest and the nightmarish adventure of the Old Man Willow. The effect is further augmented by Tom's welcome as he invites the heroes to partake of a feast at once noble and rustic, consisting of "yellow cream and honeycomb, and white bread, and butter; milk, cheese, and green herbs and ripe berries gathered" (*LotR* 122). The figure of the lady of the house is, however, distinctly different from the robust and authoritative Mrs. Maggot; although no servants are mentioned and Goldberry first appears busying herself "about the table"

(*LotR* 125), she can hardly be expected to "bustle around" as both Tom's introductory verses and his welcoming speech place her rather in the class of queens: "here's my Goldberry clothed all in silver-green with flowers in her girdle!" (*LotR* 124). She is the mysterious River-daughter, and the verses describing her first meeting with Tom Bombadil, himself a puzzle, stress her unspecified origin, semi-divine or at least fairy-like. This, together with Goldberry's most courtly relationship with her husband, transforms the simple fare on the table into an image of natural harmony, at once pastoral and royal.

Contrary to the traditional omphalic distinction between the chaotic outside and the peaceful centre, Tolkien's post-Romantic environmental vision does not class the uncultivated wilderness as inherently evil – on the contrary, however dangerous, it is usually the source of goodness (Curry 59-98; Dickerson & Evans 71-144). This is modified in the scenes combining the old idea of *omphalos* with the image of the queen, in which the outside is always hostile. The Shire around Maggot's farm is sinister because of the intrusion of the Black Riders into its otherwise safe and peaceful space. In the Goldberry episode, in turn, the forest is presented as ominous. However, the Old Forest is evil not because it is a forest but because it retains the corruption of Morgoth, being one of the few places where old Darkness still lurks. Hence the nightmarish quality of the place: "they all began to feel that all this country was unreal, and that they were stumbling through an ominous dream that led to no awakening" (*LotR* 121). This feature of the chaotic outside is counterbalanced by the dream imagery permeating the hobbits' stay in Bombadil's house. The prophetic character of Frodo's dream is intermingled with fear which is a major quality of the visions of his friends. All are forestalled by the voice of Goldberry who is apparently able to guard the household even from oneiric evil influence. "Have peace now [...] until the morning! Heed no nightly noises! For nothing passes doors or windows here save moonlight and starlight and the wind off the hill-top" (*LotR* 125). This motif returns in the Lórien episode, where Galadriel declares firmly and authoritatively: "do not let your hearts be troubled [...] tonight you shall sleep in peace" (*LotR* 357).

It is interesting that the larger cultivated space surrounding the House of Tom Bombadil is clearly contrasted with the forest full of "mist and tree shadows and deep water, and untame things" (*LotR* 123), and subsequently contracts to create a sharper division between things inside and outside, reminiscent in fact of the Maggot episode. The insistent contrast between light and darkness is here enriched with two ancient epic tropes, the threshold and the hearth. Those places are persistently used in connection with omphalic symbolism both in Homer (especially in *The Odyssey*) and, obsessively, in *The Aeneid* with an additional insistence on the repetitive use of the word *moenia* literally meaning "walls" (Cook 22-24; 36-40). In the House of Tom Bombadil those aspects of the epic chronotope, already present earlier ("they went into the farmer's kitchen and sat by the wide fire-place. Mrs. Maggot brought out beer in a huge jug, and filled four large mugs. It was a good brew,"[5] *LotR* 93), are combined with another, the evocation of water inside the *omphalos*, which is again reminiscent of Homer and the epic queen of the sanctuary, Arete.

> The four hobbits stepped over the wide stone threshold [...].
>
> In a chair, at the far side of the room facing the outer door, sat a woman. Her long yellow hair rippled down her shoulders, her gown was green, green as young reeds, shot with silver like beads of dew; and her belt was of gold, shaped like a chain of flag-lilies set with the pale-blue eyes of forget-me-nots. About her feet in wide vessels of green and brown earthenware, white water-lilies were floating, so that she seemed to be enthroned in the midst of a pool.
>
> [...] They [...] began to bow low, feeling strangely surprised and awkward, like folk that, knocking at a cottage door to beg for a drink of water, have been answered by a fair young elf-queen clad in living flowers. (*LotR* 123)

This royal imagery surrounding Goldberry foreshadows the future impact the queen figures will have on the Fellowship, especially on Frodo.

Each such encounter includes establishing a special inner bond through eye-contact: "the hobbits looked at her in wonder; and she looked at each of them and smiled. 'Fair lady Goldberry!' said Frodo at last, feeling his heart moved with a joy that he did not understand" (*LotR* 123). Frodo senses that Gooldberry wields a power different from the one he remembers from his former contact with the Elves: "less keen and lofty was the delight, but deeper and nearer to mortal heart; marvellous and yet not strange" (*LotR* 123). In

---

5 The unifying character of the scenes presenting the female characters in *The Lord of the Rings* as drink dispensers has been very interestingly interpreted by Leslie Donovan in terms of their connection with the Valkyrie figure. Unfortunately this similarity is stretched too far. I am sincerely thankful to Dr. Olga Hołownia for consulting Icelandic scholars and confirming my doubts about this interpretation.

this sense, the scene parallels Frodo's two meetings with the Elvish queenly figures. The silent, mysterious, and courteous encounter with Arwen in Rivendell, when "suddenly it seemed to Frodo that Arwen turned towards him, and the light of her eyes fell on him from afar and pierced his heart" (*LotR* 238), is followed by the more challenging test of Galadriel's eyes: "the Lady [...] said no word but looked long upon his face. [...] And with that word she held them with her eyes, and in silence looked searchingly at each of them in turn. None save Legolas and Aragorn could long endure her glance (*LotR* 356-357). Similarly, Goldberry's majestic beauty corresponds with that of the other two queen figures, of which Arwen shall be discussed first:

> In the middle of the table, against the woven cloth upon the wall, there was a chair under a canopy, and there sat a lady fair to look upon [...] Young she was and yet not so. The braids of her dark hair were touched by no frost; her white arms and clear face were flawless and smooth, and the light of stars was in her bright eyes, grey as cloudless night; yet queenly she looked, and thought and knowledge were in her glance, as of one who has known many things that the years bring. Above her brow her head was covered with a cap of silver lace netted with small gems, glittering white, but her soft grey raiment had no ornament save a girdle of leaves wrought in silver. (*LotR* 227)

And then Galadriel is described as "very tall", looking "grave and beautiful", and "clad wholly in white", with hair "of deep gold", with "no sign of age" upon her, unless it were in the depths of her eyes, which "were keen as lances in the starlight, and yet profound, the wells of deep memory" (*LotR* 354).

The prominence of the doorstep as a final border between safety and danger can also be seen in the Maggot episode, where the Rider comes to the very door of the house but no further. Goldberry as queen faces the darkness outside the door, encircled with light and water, and contrasts it with the "deep waters" of the wild, and actually completes the closure of the sanctuary with an almost ritual gesture: "then lightly she passed them and closing the door she turned her back to it, with her white arms spread out across it. 'Let us shut out the night! [...] Fear nothing! For tonight you are under the roof of Tom Bombadil'" (*LotR* 123). Waking up from his prophetic nightmare, Frodo wonders "if he would ever again have the courage to leave the safety of these stone walls" (*LotR* 134).

The same motif will underlie the presentation of Lothlórien as a realm guarded by Galadriel's special powers. Here, the actual doorstep is no longer a real but rather a metaphorical one, as the protective spells encircle the whole realm, reminiscent of the Girdle of Melian. Interestingly, when the Goldberry and Galadriel episodes are analysed in sequence, a pattern not unlike an incremental repetition may be discerned in the insistence on similar and yet gradually enriched elements. The simple water symbolism is transferred into the scene in which the Mirror of Galadriel becomes a vehicle of prophetic vision. Later, the same water in the Phial will become a most formidable weapon. Similarly, the food offered in Lórien is not only nourishment for the weary travellers, but the lembas they are given for the road also have special qualities of sustaining not only physical but also spiritual needs.[6] In the same way Galadriel's protection of the extended threshold is not just passive. She is actually portrayed as an active opponent of Sauron:

> Do not be afraid! But do not think that only by singing amid the trees, nor even by the slender arrows of elven-bows, is this land of Lothlórien maintained and defended against its Enemy. I say to you, Frodo, that even as I speak to you, I perceive the Dark Lord and know his mind, or all of his mind that concerns the Elves. And he gropes ever to see me and my thought. But still the door is closed! (*LotR* 364-365)

The omphalic space in Galadriel episode is expressed both in its horizontal aspect (the Girdle) and the vertical dimension (Caras Galadhon). Interestingly, Lórien is a place where the old distinction between cultivated and uncultivated space, thus the garden and the forest, so palpably present even in the Goldberry episode, is finally abolished. The kingdom is actually one great, golden wood encircled by the barren wilderness, whose western and eastern borders are rivers. Without breaking this uniformity, the capital Caras Galadhon, the City of the Trees, is both sylvan and vertical and boasts all the important features of a most ancient idea of *omphalos*:

> There was a wide treeless space before them, running in a great circle [...]. Beyond it was a deep fosse [...]. Upon the further side there rose to a great height a green wall encircling a green hill thronged with mallorn-trees taller than any they had yet seen in all the land. Their height could not

---

[6] Hence some even tried to compare it with Eucharist, a notion all the more tempting considering Tolkien's devout and conscious Catholicism (cf. *L* 288). On 'Lembas' see the entry by Honegger in Drout's *Encyclopedia*.

> be guessed, but they stood up in the twilight like living towers. [...]
> They went along many paths and climbed many stairs, until they came to the high places [...] where stood the mightiest of all the trees; its great smooth bole gleaming like grey silk and up it towered, until its first branches, far above, opened their huge limbs under shadowy clouds of leaves. Beside it a broad white ladder stood [...]. (*LotR* 353-354)

The mighty tree on top of the hill links this passage with its numerous epic counterparts, and adds a new element to the natural harmony of this sylvan *omphalos*, a union between civilisation and nature which was Tolkien's ideal. The huge chamber at the top of the tree is the seat of the royal pair, "side by side" on "two chairs beneath the bole of the tree and canopied by living boughs" (*LotR* 354). Even their unusual height might be here interpreted in epic terms as the same tendency to value verticality associated with "rule and grandeur on the personal scale" (Cook 8).

This insistence on the vertical axis interestingly corresponds with all the other queen episodes. In the case of Goldberry, although the House is situated on rising ground (*LotR* 121), the cultivation of the land around it and its "wide stone threshold" (*LotR* 123) put greater emphasis on the horizontal axis. Additionally, an interesting inversion of the epic verticality is added in the inclusion of a low stone room overlooking the river, which augments the feeling of safety for the hobbits, used to subterranean dwellings. Here this effect of cosiness and safety evoked by the replacement of the unfamiliar evil outside with the familiar inside still links the House of Tom Bombadil with the Shire, and thus with Farmer Maggot.

Although Rivendell is vertical enough (not to mention the sharp contrast between safety it offers and the hostile wilderness that surrounds Elrond's small domain), the figure of Arwen, whom the Fellowship meet there for the first time, does not seem to contribute directly to this element of the epic chronotope. Silent and mysterious, she no longer belongs to Rivendell from the point of view of the book's ideology, however strong her ties with her father. It is Minas Tirith after the war that will become her domain and there her significance as an epic queen will shine most brightly. On the other hand, her presence in Rivendell, apart from the narrative necessity of introducing her character early in the story, seems, in the light of the overall pattern of the book, to be absolutely indispensable as an indicator that this place is also a sanctuary, and as such blessed by a queen figure.

The very construction of Minas Tirith, with an almost vertiginous insistence on verticality, stresses the city's significance as a true centre for the newly-revived Middle-earth, the *axis mundi* in its most ancient significance, connecting the created world with the divine level. This is made possible not only by the figure of Aragorn as the lawful king, but also by the figure of the queen Arwen, the wife and the future mother. This role is foreshadowed in the final image of Minas Tirith in *The Lord of the Rings*, where Frodo meets the royal pair by the fountain and the new White Tree, at the top of the citadel: "and Frodo went to the King as he was sitting with the Queen Arwen by the fountain, and she sang a song of Valinor, while the Tree grew and blossomed" (*LotR* 974).

The figure of Arwen as a symbol of Middle-earth's future, particularly Gondor, is contrasted with that of Yoreth, who clearly stands for Gondor as it was before the defeat of Sauron. On the one hand, as an old crone she represents the barrenness and decline, on the other, it is her remembrance of old sayings that facilitates the recognition of Aragorn as the Healer King. No matter how ridiculous and irritating she might be, her role as a repository of old wisdom and therefore a guardian of tradition cannot be ignored, especially if combined with her function of being Arwen's foil.

Apart from Yoreth, who appears in a very short if important episode, the only female figure the Gondor-bound part of the Fellowship encounter after leaving the area of the sanctuaries is Éowyn.[7] Even this isolation contributes to the presentation of this perhaps most curious of Tolkien's women. Loneliness forms one of the most important features of the princess of the Rohirrim. Another is futility. The fates of her family and country reduce her role and actually deprive her of the right to the central position her gender entitles her to in Tolkien's work.

---

7 In the course of many years I have discussed some of the notions presented here with my students attending a seminar and a course on Tolkien. Those classes proved fruitful for both sides, which I gratefully remember, and feel obliged to mention the names of Dominika Bojanowska, Karolina Sofulak, Agata Staszewska, Wioletta Skorupska and especially Justyna Brzezińska, who actually later wrote her M. A. thesis partly about the figure of Éowyn and, while this book was in progress, her article "Éowyn – the Misunderstood Lady of Rohan" was published in *Aiglos* (Special Issue 2, Summer 2012: 59-74). I feel therefore obliged to stress that any similarity between our views results from this connection and not any unlawful borrowing.

She, alone of all the females, does not rule. Even Yoreth symbolically presides over the memories of her nation. Éowyn is placed in the centre of Meduseld, which, however close to the epic *omphalos*, is no longer a sanctuary. Evil has penetrated the country's heart, the king is dwindling slowly under its poisonous influence, and his son and heir is dead. Éowyn's function at Théoden's side, which seems to her "more ignoble than that of the staff he leaned on" (*LotR* 867), is not that of a queen but of a nurse unable to help or protect her uncle from the evil influences of those who have already crossed the threshold of the dark hall, which has ceased to be a shelter and is now a cage. Although clad in white, tall, straight, and golden-haired, Éowyn is no Galadriel. Her eye contact with the principal hero of the Fellowship has shattering consequences for herself; the only moment water is mentioned in Meduseld has nothing to do with her; and she is not only unable to guard her guests from nightmares, but herself suffers agonies of despair in her nightly vigils: "who knows what she spoke to the darkness, alone, in the bitter watches of the night, when all her life seemed shrinking, and walls of her bower closing in about her, a hutch to trammel some wild thing in?" (*LotR* 867). Similarly, the fertility imagery is used to show Éowyn's predicament in the world tainted with evil:

> When I first looked on her and perceived her unhappiness, it seemed to me that I saw a white flower standing straight and proud, shapely as a lily, and yet knew that it was hard, as if wrought by elf-wrights out of steel. Or was it, maybe, a frost that had turned its sap to ice, and so it stood, bitter-sweet, still fair to see, but stricken, soon to fall and die? (*LotR* 866)

The extent of the blemish on Éowyn's nature becomes evident when, asked to become the viceroy and to protect the Rohirrim who seek refuge in Dunharrow, she is actually unable to do her duty. Incidentally, her duty is not in any way circumscribed here within the traditional scope of female activities. A popular critical opinion that she "defies attempts to domesticate her and goes to battle [...] also out of despair at her being relegated to the home" in a "rejection of female domesticity" (Leibiger 711) is a gross misconception. The cage she fears is not a home, as nobody thinks of marrying her (except for Gríma in his vile dreams, which only strengthens my point), but it is inaction and powerlessness resulting from the predicament of Rohan. When the healed king goes to war, the Rohirrim declare that they trust the House of Eorl. Éowyn is therefore left in Rohan as any younger child of the king would be, regardless of gender, and it is obvious that in the (most probable) eventuality of the death of Théoden and Éomer (her *elder* brother) she would rule. In the scene where she begs Aragorn to let her accompany him to Gondor she is wearing armour not because she has already resolved to impersonate a male warrior, but because her role in Rohan requires her to do so. Her inability to rise to the occasion is redeemed later, not only by her crucial role during the battle on the Fields of Pelennor, but also through her recognition of her fault. In her encounter with Faramir, Éowyn sees herself as "merely wayward, like a child that has not the firmness of mind to go on with a dull task to the end" (*LotR* 959-960). The plight of Middle-earth has made it impossible for her to grow up, and her attempt to change identity is actually not aimed at changing the gender, but at finding death in battle. This death wish is finally replaced with the self-awareness and maturation, and ultimate fulfilment facilitated by the victory over Sauron, and in personal terms, her love for Faramir. This transformation is presented in Éowyn's own words, when she has finally become a fully conscious and independent adult:

> Then the heart of Éowyn changed, or else at last she understood it. And suddenly her winter passed, and the sun shone on her.
>
> 'I stand in Minas Anor, the Tower of the Sun', she said, 'and behold! The Shadow has departed! I will be a shieldmaiden no longer, nor vie with the great riders, nor take joy in the songs of slaying. I will be a healer, and love all things that grow and are not barren.' (*LotR* 964-965)

Although the speech ends with the declaration "No longer do I desire to be a queen", clearly signifying the renunciation of her fascination with Aragorn, paradoxically this is the moment when Éowyn becomes a queen in the Tolkienian understanding of the term. This will later be confirmed by her becoming the princess of the blighted Ithilien, which under her and Faramir's rule will become a fertile garden.

This perspective provides a most interesting explanation of the fact that it is only fairly late in the design of the story that Arwen replaces Éowyn as Aragorn's bride. After all "the author could have done worse than to arrange a match with a woman capable of leading her people" and "slaying the Lord of the Nazgûl in single combat", and the final decision not only provided Aragorn with "a much more complex and mythologically richer relationship" (West, "Her Choice"

318) but also enabled Tolkien to use the character of Éowyn in a different and extremely significant context.

Only one female featuring in *The Lord of the Rings* remains to be discussed. This is Shelob, the anti-queen of her anti-*omphalos*. The only evil female, and one of only three evil females in Tolkien's *opus*, the spider is presented with the conscious use of reversed imagery uniformly employed in the portrayal of Tolkien's queens. Her subterranean lair, as such reversing the vertical axis of the *omphalos*, situated on the horizontal plane surrounded by deadly webs, embodies an 'anti-omphalic' spatial organisation, namely the labyrinth (Dufau 114). Far from being a sanctuary, it is clearly a deadly trap, its "queen" interested in killing and devouring her guests. A clear-cut distinction between darkness and light also creates a reversal of the established pattern. Shelob's Lair is filled with the kind of "darkness visible" in the *legendarium* associated with Ungoliant, Shelob's monstrous and mighty great-great-great grandmother. The light is not only brought by the hero, but also very successfully used in the fight as a weapon. Likewise, Shelob's monstrous ugliness, "the most loathly shape that he had ever beheld, horrible beyond the horror of an evil dream", is set against the consistent beauty of the other female characters:

> Most like a spider she was, but huger than the great hunting beasts, and more terrible than they because of the evil purpose in her remorseless eyes [...]. [She had a] huge swollen body, a vast bloated bag, swaying and sagging between her legs, its great bulk was black, blotched with livid marks, but the belly underneath was pale and luminous and gave forth a stench. Her legs were bent, with great knobbed joints high above her back and hairs that stuck out like steel spines, and at each leg's end there was a claw. (*LotR* 725)

The significance of this figure does not end here. Most notably only Shelob and Ungoliant are female and evil as well as important. The third of Tolkien's evil females, Thuringwethil, features only in one episode of the story of Beren and Lúthien (*S* 214-18), and apart from her role as an obstacle in their quest, is not significant in any way. Her gender is also practically accidental for the meaning of the story, perhaps apart from the fact that she provides a female opponent for Lúthien. Apart from those three, Tolkien's evil is male. This startling fact cannot be omitted from the present analysis since it strengthens Tolkien's clear stance upon the lack of the feminine principle being an evil in itself, leading inevitably to death. Not only are his Dark Lords male, but it seems that so are practically all their supernatural supporters. In the *legendarium*, Melkor as a twin brother of Manwë and his obvious opposite is also the one who is alone, contrary to his happily married brother.[8] The fact that Melkor hates Varda is not very surprising as this is his attitude towards virtually all creation, though she is also, interestingly, the feared one. This fact acquires an even deeper meaning when confronted with his relationship with another powerful female, Ungoliant, actually an anti-Varda figure (*S* 86).

Ungoliant is a most exceptional character, being the only female follower of Melkor. She is also another character whom Melkor fears with a less metaphysical and more animalistic corporeal fear. She hates light (and thus Varda) but does not fear it. Her stance makes her actually a figure potentially more powerful and fearsome than Melkor,[9] though her personality makes her less dangerous as her ambitions are as if implosive.[10] Her hatred of the light does not stop her from desiring it in an organic sense. Her lust is defined as appetite (not necessarily devoid of sexual undertones, as she is said to have behaved in a spidery fashion, killing and devouring her mates). Shelob, although strikingly similar in her appetites and her quasi-independent position towards Sauron, is nevertheless incomparably weaker than her predecessor. Her powers are local, and although she is really dangerous within the confines of her domain, she does not desire to expand, in her utmost egotism she rather expects the world to come to her:

> But still she was there, who was there before Sauron, [...] and she served none but herself, drinking the blood of Elves and Men, bloated and grown fat with endless brooding on her feasts, weaving webs of shadow, for all living things were her food, and her vomit darkness [...] little she knew of or cared for towers, or rings, or anything devised by mind or hand, who only desired death for

---

8   The *Valaquenta* mentions that he was once rejected by Varda, but it is not specified in what sense, whether he was her suitor or whether she simply rejected him as a rebel and destroyer. Indeed the very principles these two stand for are naturally opposed, she being the goddess of light, he in his ultimate choice, of eternal darkness. Varda's decision to join Manwë is presented in the context of her rejection of everything Melkor began to stand for. "In the light is her power and her joy. Out of the deeps of Eä she came to the aid of Manwë, for Melkor she knew from before the making of the Music and rejected him, and he hated her, and feared her more than all others whom Eru made" (*S* 28).

9   "[Ungoliant] swelled to a shape so vast and hideous that Melkor was afraid" (*S* 89). "She rose against him, and her cloud closed about him; and she enmeshed him in a web of clinging thongs to strangle him. Then Morgoth sent forth a terrible cry [...] the greatest and most dreadful that was ever heard in the northern world" (*S* 94).

10 "Of the fate of Ungoliant no tale tells. Yet some have said that she ended long ago, when in her uttermost famine she devoured herself at last" (*S* 95).

all others, mind and body, and for herself a glut of life, alone, swollen till the mountain could no longer hold her up and the darkness could not contain her. But that desire was yet far away, and long now had she been hungry, lurking in her den while the power of Sauron grew. (*LotR* 723-724)

This diminishing of the significance of the evil female spider signifies that the type of evil represented by the male has already prevailed. Interestingly, a situation in which this militant type might be taken over by a woman is suggested in the scene of the temptation of Galadriel. The most powerful of all Queens, she contemplates her conversion into a Ring Wielder in terms which suggest that the result would be much more horrible and probably final in its invincible mixture of despair and love, beauty and admiration, the qualities male evil lacks.

> 'In place of the Dark Lord you will set up a Queen. And I shall not be dark, but beautiful and terrible as the Morning and the Night! Fair as the Sea and the Sun and the Snow upon the Mountain! Dreadful as the Storm and the Lightning! Stronger than the foundations of the earth. All shall love me and despair!'
>
> She lifted up her hand and from the ring that she wore there issued a great light that illumined her alone and left all else dark. She stood before Frodo seeming now tall beyond measurement, and beautiful beyond enduring, terrible and worshipful. Then she let her hand fall and the light faded, and suddenly she laughed again [...] 'I pass the test' she said. (*LotR* 366)

Significantly, the figures of female characters in *The Lord of the Rings* are so carefully structured and their presentation is so obviously and consciously linked together by a network of symbols, recurrent images, and even incremental repetition that this becomes clearly distinct from the techniques Tolkien employs in the handling of male characters, varied and lacking any overall pattern. This observation inevitably leads to the conclusion that Tolkien's design in *The Lord of the Rings* has been to highlight the exceptional and royal function of a woman, a source of life in all its senses.

Bibliography

AUDEN, W. H. "The Quest Hero." *Understanding The Lord of the Rings. The Best of Tolkien Criticism.* Ed. Rose A. Zimbardo and Neil D. Isaacs. Boston and New York: Houghton Mifflin, 2004. 31-51.

COOK, Patrick J. *Milton, Spenser and the Epic Tradition.* Aldershot: Ashgate, 1999.

CURRY, Patrick. *Defending Middle-earth. Tolkien: Myth & Modernity.* London: HarperCollins, 1998.

DICKERSON, Matthew, and Jonathan Evans. *Ents, Elves, and Eriador. The Environmental Vision of J.R.R. Tolkien.* Lexington: University Press of Kentucky, 2006.

DONOVAN, Leslie. "The Valkyrie Reflex in J.R.R. Tolkien's *The Lord of the Rings*: Galadriel, Shelob, Éowyn and Arwen." *Tolkien the Medievalist.* Ed. Jane Chance. London and New York: Routledge, 2003. 106-132.

DUFAU, Jean-Christophe. "Mythic Space in Tolkien's Work (*The Lord of the Rings, The Hobbit* and *The Silmarillion*)." *Reconsidering Tolkien.* Ed. Thomas Honegger. Zurich and Berne: Walking Tree Publishers, 2005. 107-128.

FELSON, Nancy, and Laura Slatkin. "Gender and Homeric Epic." *The Cambridge Companion to Homer.* Ed. Robert Fowler. Cambridge UP: Cambridge, 2004. 91-114.

FOLEY, Helene P. "Women in Ancient Epic." *A Companion to Ancient Epic.* Ed. John Miles Foley. Oxford: Wiley-Blackwell, 2009. 104-118.

HOCART, Arthur Maurice. *Kingship.* London: Humphrey Milford; Oxford UP, 1927.

HONEGGER, Thomas. "Lembas." *J.R.R. Tolkien Encyclopedia. Scholarship and Critical Assessment.* Ed. Michael D.C. Drout. New York and London: Routledge, 2007. 353-354.

HOPKINS, Lisa. "Female Authority Figures in the Works of Tolkien, C. S. Lewis and Charles Williams." *The Proceedings of the Tolkien Centenary Conference.* Ed. Patricia Reynolds and Glen GoodKnight. Milton Keynes and Altadena: The Tolkien Society and The Mythopoeic Society, 1996. 364-366.

KIPLING, Gordon. *Enter the King. Theatre, Liturgy and Ritual in the Medieval Civic Triumph.* Oxford: Clarendon Press, 1998.

LEIBIGER, Carol A. "Women in Tolkien's Works." *J.R.R. Tolkien Encyclopedia. Scholarship and Critical Assessment.* Ed. Michael D.C. Drout. New York and London: Routledge, 2007. 710-712.

MAHER, Michael W., S. J. "'A land without stain': Medieval Images of Mary and Their Use in the Characterization of Galadriel." *Tolkien the Medievalist.* Ed. Jane Chance. London and New York: Routledge, 2003. 225-236.

MAINS, Christine. "Fantasy, 1900-1959 – Novels and Short Fiction." *Women in Science Fiction and Fantasy.* Vol. 1. Ed. Robin Anne Reid. Westport: Greenwood Press, 2009. 34-44.

OTTY, Nick. "The Structuralist's Guide to Middle-earth." *J.R.R. Tolkien: This Far Land.* Ed. Robert Giddings. London: Vision and Barnes & Noble, 1984. 154-178.

PARTRIDGE, Brenda. "No Sex Please – We're Hobbits: The Construction of Female Sexuality in *The Lord of the Rings.*" *J.R.R. Tolkien: This Far Land.* Ed. Robert Giddings. London: Vision and Barnes & Noble, 1984. 179-198.

PEARCE, Joseph. *Tolkien: Man and Myth. A Literary Life.* London: HarperCollins, 1998.

RINGEL, Faye. "Women Fantasists: In the Shadow of the Ring." *J.R.R. Tolkien and His Literary Resonances. Views of Middle-earth.* Ed. George Clarke and Daniel Timmons. Westport CT and London: Greenwood Press, 2000. 159-172.

ROSEBURY, Brian. *Tolkien: A Cultural Phenomenon.* New York: Palgrave Macmillan. 2003.

SHIPPEY, Tom. *The Road to Middle-earth. How J.R.R. Tolkien Created a New Mythology.* Boston and New York: Houghton Mifflin, 2003.

STURGIS, Amy H. "Tolkien, J.R.R. (1892-1873)." *Women in Science Fiction and Fantasy.* Vol. 2. Ed. Robin Anne Reid. Westport CT: Greenwood Press, 2009. 301-303.

TOLKIEN, J.R.R. *The Silmarillion.* Ed. Christopher Tolkien. London: Unwin Paperbacks, 1983.

The Monsters and the Critics and Other Essays. Ed. Christopher Tolkien. London: George Allen and Unwin, 1983.

The Letters of J.R.R. Tolkien. Ed. Humphrey Carpenter with the assistance of Christopher Tolkien. London: George Allen and Unwin, 1981.

The Lord of the Rings. Boston and New York: Houghton Mifflin, 2004.

WEST, Richard C. "Real-world Myth in a Secondary World: Mythological Aspects in the Story of Beren and Lúthien." *Tolkien the Medievalist.* Ed. Jane Chance. London and New York: Routledge, 2003. 259-267.

"'Her Choice was made and Her Doom Appointed': Tragedy and Divine Comedy in the Tale of Aragorn and Arwen." *The Lord of the Rings 1954-2004: Scholarship in Honor of Richard Blackwelder.* Ed. Wayne G. Hammond and Christina Scull. Milwaukee, Wisconsin: Marquette UP, 2006. 317-330.

About the author

MARIA BŁASZKIEWICZ (neé Wójcicka) completed her Ph.D. dissertation entitled "Behold the King! Kingship and Epic Heroism in the Literary Works of J.R.R. Tolkien" in 2003. Her research interests concentrate on a diachronic study of the epic, also in the context of the fantastic. Her published articles on J.R.R. Tolkien include: "Tolkien's Evil Kings", "The Theme of Heroic Intrusion in J.R.R. Tolkien's *The Lord of the Rings*", "The Theme of Heroic Intrusion in J.R.R. Tolkien's *The Hobbit*", "Enter the Hobbit – the Hobbits and the Theme of Heroic Intrusion in *The Lord of the Rings*", "The Great Chain of Writing: Tolkien's Story of Beren and Lúthien and the Epic Tradition", "*Done is a batell on the dragon blak.* The Theme of the Fight with the Monster in the Literary Works of J.R.R. Tolkien", "Tolkien's Warrior-kings", and "*Who are you, and what are you doing in this land?* A Different Way of Looking at Known Things: An Epic Reading of *The Lord of the Rings*". She also published articles on Chaucer, Milton, Händel, Dickens, the Gothic tradition, C.S. Lewis, Terry Pratchett, and Susanna Clarke. Currently she is working on a book about the vicissitudes of epic in the first half of the 18th century, particularly in the libretti of Händel's oratorios. Like her husband Bartłomiej she teaches the literature in English of Britain and Ireland at the Institute of English Studies at the University of Warsaw.

Barbara Kowalik

Elbereth the Star-Queen Seen in the Light of Medieval Marian Devotion

Abstract

Even though the Catholic tinge of Middle-earth has been recognized by critics like Joseph Pearce and acknowledged by Tolkien himself, the affinity of Varda/Elbereth with Mary has not been explored, and this is, therefore, what this paper purports to do, particularly in the context of Tolkien's medievalist background, for the 'interpretatio mediaevalia' is inevitably connected with the 'interpretatio catholica' or 'interpretatio christiana', as Thomas Honegger points out (50). The heroes of Tolkien's trilogy repeatedly invoke Elbereth at various pivotal points of their anti-quest of the Ring, so Elbereth's role of supernatural aide and patroness of Middle-earth, strikingly parallel to the protective guidance of the Virgin Mary in medieval Christendom, is clearly underlined. The paper embraces the simplest and most plausible explanation of Elbereth's position, linking it to Tolkien's personal Marian devotion, which in turn must have been coloured and reinforced by his immersion in medieval literature. In the following discussion references are made to medieval liturgy, theology, and poetry, including a variety of literary genres, such as Old English metrical charms and Middle English lyrics, romances, *gestes*, and miracles of the Virgin.

Readers naturally bring into a text their own experiences, interests, and literary competence, which often results in readings quite disparate from the responses of the interpretative community at large. While imbibing the atmosphere diffused over the world of *The Lord of the Rings*, I have always had a strong impression of entering a space guarded by an invisible and benevolent female presence akin to that of the Holy Virgin Mary in medieval Christendom, a feeling which, I suppose, would not be readily shared by the majority of Tolkien enthusiasts. Still, in his memories of J.R.R. Tolkien, his friend George Sayer emphasises the writer's ardent, old-style Catholicism, conforming to the pre-Second Vatican Council mode, whose reforms Tolkien did not applaud.[1] Sayer stresses, among other things, Tolkien's deep veneration

---

1 Tolkien's Polish friend Przemysław Mroczkowski remembered that during English Mass J.R.R. Tolkien prayed from a Latin missal (see Fiałkowski).

of the Virgin Mary. He mentions a letter he received from Tolkien in which the author attributed whatever was beautiful in his works to Mary's influence, affirming it to be the greatest influence upon his life (Sayer 10-11, 13-14). Similarly, as Joseph Pearce observes, in a letter to another friend, Father Robert Murray, Tolkien stated that he owed his conception of beauty, in its majesty and simplicity, to the Virgin Mary, and conceded that *The Lord of the Rings* was a principally religious and Catholic work (Pearce 103).

Marian devotion being a salient feature of traditional Roman Catholicism, it is natural that critics have attempted to identify the exact sources for the Marian inspiration in *The Lord of the Rings*.[2] Most of all, the figure of Galadriel has been associated with the Virgin Mary, starting with Father Murray's comment in the aforementioned letter upon Galadriel's resemblance to the Holy Virgin (*L* 171-172). Charles A. Coulombe, in turn, has suggested that the nature of Mary is far more clearly visible in the figure of Elbereth (58).[3] Tolkien himself seems to have been pleased with Father Murray's association of his work as a whole with the state of grace, and of Galadriel with Mary in particular, yet his reply to his friend's letter suggests, as well, that he thought of Mary's influence upon his literary output in more general terms of overall inspiration (Pearce 103). On another occasion, Tolkien once again guardedly admitted that he owed much of the character of Galadriel to "Christian and Catholic teaching and imagination about Mary"; at the same time, though, he pointed out that "Galadriel was a penitent", and "in her youth a leader in the rebellion against the Valar" (Duriez 100), which, implicitly, firmly differentiated her from Mary of Nazareth.

In addition, the critical argument about the Elven queen's similarity to the valkyries of Norse mythology (Donovan 106-132) places Galadriel in a non-Christian context and reveals her potential for a variety of interpretations. Unlike Galadriel, and very much like the medieval Heavenly Queen, Varda/Elbereth belongs to a much earlier, legendary and mythical stage of Middle-earth's history and now reigns from a transcendent space, which corresponds

---

2 Christopher Clausen claims that in making Galadriel remarkably reminiscent of the Virgin Mary Tolkien was inspired by G. K. Chesterton's poem "The Ballad of the White Horse" (10-16).
3 After I finished writing this paper I came across an article that argues for the affinity of Mary and Elbereth in the context of liturgical prayer. Cf. Marcin Morawski, "The Rivendell Hymnal and Tenebrae – Tolkien, Elves and the Roman Liturgy," *Aiglos*, Special Issue 2 (2012), 103-109.

to Mary's Assumption, that is, being taken body and soul to her Son's kingdom in heaven at the end of her earthly life and reigning from there.[4] Like Elbereth in Tolkien's Middle-earth, Mary did not walk upon the medieval *middle-earth*, synonymous with this world as opposed to afterlife, but was accessible to its inhabitants through stories, icons, relics, prayers, and songs. Galadriel, on the other hand, is the actual, personally accessible queen of the Elves, belonging to the contemporary historical plane of the Elves, hobbits, and other races. Thus, although a case has been made for Galadriel's association with medieval images of Mary (Maher 225-36), Varda's affinity with the Holy Virgin seems closer. Furthermore, the Loreto Litany on which Maher's argument rests is, strictly speaking, a post-medieval product: historical documents first mention it in 1531; the Pope recognised it officially in 1587; and it has remained the only official Marian litany in the Catholic Church since 1601, being since then a remarkably fixed and stable text, with only a few additions made over the subsequent centuries.[5]

In fact, an increase in the Litany's popularity throughout the sixteenth century coincided with a decline in typically medieval Marian piety, which was epitomised by the Hours of the Virgin, a sequence of prayers to the Mother of God that, ideally, were recited in the course of the day hour by hour and, unlike the Breviary, chiefly by the laity. Children's elementary school books, usually containing the Hours of the Virgin, were called, from the hour of prime, primers in England: the child protagonist of Chaucer's Prioress's Tale was sitting at school at such a primer when he heard older children sing the Latin Marian antiphon, *Alma redemptoris mater*; he was so enraptured with the melody and the words that he learnt the song by heart, for he had special devotion to Mary, always saying *Ave Maria* as he went on his way; the daily singing of the antiphon ensures the protagonist of this tale Mary's favour, typically of the genre of the miracle of the Virgin (lines 1692-1740). The Books of Hours were often lavishly and beautifully illustrated, and sometimes contained private prayers with pictures and names of their owners, exemplifying an individualisation of

---

4 Tolkien reflected upon Mary's Assumption in one of his letters (*L* 286).
5 To illustrate the Litany's stability: one invocation, Queen conceived without original sin, was added in 1854, when the dogma of the Immaculate Conception was officially introduced, while another one was introduced in 1917, in the aftermath of war, when Mary started to be officially called Queen of Peace. For a detailed study of the Loreto Litany see Kútnik.

religious devotion. On the whole, medieval Books of Hours enabled ordinary people direct, democratic, uncensored and potentially continuous contact with Christ, the Holy Virgin, and the saints. The Books started to disappear when the Council of Trent (1545-63) recommended prayer directly to God. In 1568 Pope Pius V removed the general obligation on the part of the clergy to say the Hours of the Virgin as part of their Divine Office. The subsequent process of marginalisation culminated in the 1960s, when the Second Vatican Council entirely eliminated the Hours of the Virgin from the Church's new official prayer book, *The Liturgy of the Hours*.

Admittedly, the Loreto Litany grew out of the earlier traditions. Its content was shaped by the medieval practice of describing Mary by means of metaphors and symbolic images, such as the Gate of Heaven or the Morning Star (both appearing in the *Alma redemptoris mater* antiphon). The Litany's form derived, in turn, from the kind of prayers favoured already in the early Byzantine Church, where a leader uttered a series of short petitions and a group followed each supplication with a specific response. Still, the Loreto Litany gives only a partial idea of the wealth, variety, democracy, and spontaneity of actual medieval Marian devotion. It is the latter, I contend, that is more closely paralleled by the hobbits' ejaculations to Elbereth uttered at various critical points of their journey.

Elbereth was one of the names given in the Sindarin language of the Elves to Varda, who was said to have been the greatest and most revered of the Valier, the female Valar. Her different names in Tolkien's *œuvre* correspond, as far as the principle of plurality of names is concerned, to a variety of names by which Mary was known in the medieval Church. The crucial text of the Elven devotion to Elbereth in *The Lord of the Rings* is not a litany but a hymn, a form highly characteristic of medieval Western Marian devotion. The first situation in which Elbereth is evoked in the story is when Frodo, Pippin, and Sam, threatened by a Black Rider, meet Elves in the Woody End of the Shire. The hobbits are frightened and Frodo feels an overwhelming desire to slip on the Ring.

> But at that moment there came a sound like mingled song and laughter. Clear voices rose and fell in the starlit air. The black shadow straightened up and retreated. It climbed on to the shadowy horse and seemed to vanish across the lane into the darkness on the other side. Frodo breathed again. (*LotR* I 104)

The hobbits enthusiastically recognise the Elves, and Frodo explicitly refers to the power of their "songs of the Blessed Realm", particularly their hymn in praise of Elbereth. He describes to his companions the effect the singing of the hymn had on the Black Rider: "You did not see, but that Black Rider stopped just here and was actually crawling towards us when the song began. As soon as he heard the voices, he slipped away" (*LotR* I 104). Elbereth's power over the agents of darkness corresponds with Mary's power over Satan, foreshadowed already in the first biblical Book of Genesis, where woman is given the power to bruise the serpent's head (Gen. 3.15), whereas in the prophetic Book of Revelation closing the New Testament a woman successfully escapes from the great dragon symbolizing Satan (Rev. 12.1-9).[6]

Thus, the hobbits' first experience of the Elves is formed by the incredibly beautiful and joyful Elven song performed collectively on the road in adoration of Elbereth. The lyrics are translated and quoted at length in the novel. Tolkien makes it plain that it is the power of the Elves' united praise of Elbereth that has driven the forces of evil and darkness away. Frodo then speaks to the leader of the Elves, Gildor, and greets him in the ancient language of the High Elves: "*Elen sila lumen omentielvo*" ("a star shines on the hour of our meeting", *LotR* I 107), acknowledging thereby the spiritual presence and assistance of Elbereth, whose name means "the Star-Queen". Mary is likewise associated with stars in the biblical Book of Revelation, where the woman in heaven clothed with the sun and bearing a crown of twelve stars has traditionally received a Marian interpretation (Rev. 12.1); in medieval hymns and lyrics Mary is praised as the star of the sea: *Ave maris stella*. In return for Frodo's appropriate greeting, Gildor bestows upon the hobbits a good-bye blessing: "May Elbereth protect you!" (*LotR* I 112). The whole situation reminds one of Marian formulas used in medieval literature (including popular romances)[7] for greetings and farewells. The first meeting between the hobbits and the Elves is marked by Elbereth's spiritual presence and becomes a foundational experience of the hobbits' faith in the power of the Star-Queen.

---

6 In Tolkien's mythology, Melkor, associated with eternal darkness, hates and fears Varda/Elbereth and is rejected by her (*S* 28), while he is in league with Ungoliant, a hideous, light-hating female (*S* 86, 89, 94, 95). One is reminded of the apocalyptic great dragon and great whore, at war with the sun-clothed and star-crowned woman (cf. Rev. 12; 17).

7 In the opening of *The King of Tars*, for example, the minstrel narrator greets his audience by reference to Mary, "For Marie loue, þat swete þing" (line 2), and at the end of *Octavian* the eponymous hero's success is attributed to "the grace of Mary free" (line 1845).

From that time on the hobbits instinctively turn to Elbereth in moments of danger. Thus, when the dreadful Lord of the Nazgûl attacks Frodo, the latter spontaneously cries out the opening invocation of the Elven hymn: "*O Elbereth! Gilthoniel!*" (*LotR* I 258). This exclamation, similar to a battle cry, empowers Frodo to fight: "At the same time he struck at the feet of his enemy. A shrill cry rang out in the night [...]" (*LotR* I 258). Commenting upon the fight, Strider explains that the name of Elbereth was more deadly to the Enemy than the stroke of Frodo's sword (*LotR* I 260). This belief corresponds to the magical power names were imbued with in early medieval culture, including that of Anglo-Saxon England. Generally, in a magical worldview words appropriately arrayed are invested with great power and this is the case of the Elven hymn to Elbereth.

Soon enough the Ring-bearer finds himself threatened by the Black Riders again and utters an oath against them: "By Elbereth [...] you shall have neither the Ring nor me!", and a miracle occurs; the river separating Frodo from the Black Riders rises and some of them are drowned "under angry foam", while the others are chased away by "small shadowy forms waving flames", led by "a shining figure of white light" (*LotR* I 282). The situation illustrates the world seen as an arena of struggle between forces of good and evil, which is characteristic of medieval allegorical literature. One is reminded of Old English metrical charms as well. In Charm 4, in particular, "Against a Sudden Stitch", shots are envisaged as delivered by violent women riding over the hill and the land, suggesting witchcraft and black magic. Tolkien, on the other hand, shows the combative power of the forces of good, the shining figure of white light and her agents waving flames, reminiscent of Mary and her angels. Following the Old English incantations, directions were often given to pray to the Christian God and the saints, for example, to say three *pater nosters* and three *aves*. Furthermore, in Charm 1, "For Unfruitful Land", Saint Mary is invoked not only along with Our Lord and the Holy Cross but also, and most powerfully, along with Mother Earth, *Erce*, whose name is hailed three times.[8] This illustrates how the early Christian church accommodated pagan magic.[9]

---

8 For texts of Old English charms see Dobbie.
9 For further argument of this kind see Flint.

Also in the exegetical tradition and liturgy of the Church Mary was attributed the power to fight the enemy: two Old Testament heroines, Esther and Judith, both of whom saved God's people from destruction, were seen as prefiguring Mary. Mary's militant character is retained in the oldest medieval tradition. For example, Nennius in Chapter 56 of the early ninth-century *History of the Britons*, while describing one of King Arthur's battles, says that Arthur carried the image of the holy Mary ever virgin on his shoulders and the pagans were put to flight on that day. Also, the most valiant of Arthur's knights, Sir Gawain, has an image of Mary painted on the inner side of his shield in the romance of *Sir Gawain and the Green Knight*.

In Rivendell, the hobbits once again have an opportunity to listen to the Elves singing together. This time the singing takes place in the Hall of Fire and appears to be a communal ritual. Frodo "stood enchanted, while the sweet syllables of the elvish song fell like clear jewels of blended word and melody. 'It is a song of Elbereth,' said Bilbo. 'They will sing that and other songs of the Blessed Realm many times tonight'" (*LotR* I 312). Tolkien again emphasises the enchanting beauty of the songs, which are not translated this time, a fact that enhances their ritual and aesthetic functions. It is also in Rivendell that Bilbo enjoys looking at what he calls "the stars of Elbereth" (*LotR* I 312) in an act resembling mystical contemplation. If we interpret Elbereth as Mary's fictional counterpart, Bilbo's contemplation is not merely aesthetic for Christian liturgy identifies Mary with God's wisdom, which in the Old Testament takes the personal form of a woman (compare, for example, Proverbs 8.22-31, which has been a scriptural reading in Marian votive masses).

Elbereth readily comes to the assistance of Legolas the Elf as well, when he calls upon her name, "*Elbereth Gilthoniel!*" (*LotR* I 508), while he is about to shoot an arrow from his great bow, and accordingly his arrow brings down the black shape. One may recall that in medieval ballads Robin Hood depended on the help of "Our dere lady" and loved her "all ther moste" (*A Gest of Robyn Hode*, lines 35-36). Most memorably, though, Elbereth empowers Sam to defeat Shelob. When Sam cries the words of the Elven hymn to Elbereth, his true identity and indomitable spirit are recovered, even though he speaks in a language he does not know. The hymn has stayed in Sam's mind since the first meeting with the Elves in the Shire, and his memory of it was reinforced in Rivendell. Facing Shelob, Sam first turns to Galadriel, and his mental picture of the Elven queen leads him further on to recall the hymn sung by the Elves in honour of Elbereth. Interestingly, it is only when Sam spontaneously repeats the words of the hymn and pronounces Elbereth's name that the powers in Galadriel's phial become activated. Thus, it is not Galadriel but Elbereth and the power of calling upon her that is the ultimate source of the phial's power:

> 'Galadriel!' he said faintly, and then he heard voices far off but clear: the crying of the Elves as they walked under the stars in the beloved shadows of the Shire, and the music of the Elves as it came through his sleep in the Hall of Fire in the house of Elrond.
>
> *Gilthoniel A Elbereth!*
>
> And his tongue was loosed and his voice cried in a language he did not know:
>
> *A Elbereth Gilthoniel*
> *O menel palan-diriel,*
> *Le nallon si di'nguruthos!*
> *A tiro min, Fanuilos!*
>
> And with that he staggered to his feet and was Samwise the hobbit, Hamfast's son, again.
>
> 'Now come, you filth!' he cried. 'You've hurt my master, you brute, and you'll pay for it. We're going on; but we'll settle with you first. Come on, and taste it again!'
>
> As if his indomitable spirit had set its potency in motion, the glass blazed suddenly like a white torch in his hand. It flamed like a star that leaping from the firmament sears the dark air with intolerable light. No such terror out of heaven had ever burned in Shelob's face before. (*LotR* II 422)

As we can see, the terror came ultimately *out of heaven*. The mirror's blinding light was put into effect by supernatural power. One is reminded of Arthur's magical sword, which he "had by myracle", and which Merlin told him to draw from its scabbard only when it came to the worst: thus, at a battle's critical point Arthur "drewe his swerd Excalibur, but it was so bryght in his enemyes eyen that it gaf light lyke thirty torchys, and therwith he put hem on bak" (Malory 12-13).

Like the Latin liturgical and paraliturgical prayers of the Catholic Church, or the medieval macaronic lyrics which mixed English with Latin or French – "Of on that is so fayr and bright, / *Velud maris stella*" (Duncan 105); "Mayden moder milde / *oiez cel oreysoun*; / from shome þou me shilde" (Brown, *Lyrics of the XIIIth Century* 155), or like the spiritual gift of *glossolalia*, speaking in tongues, Sam's exclamation in a language unknown to him is immediately effective. It works a bit like a magical incantation. Tolkien the medievalist knew that in the early English Church prayers used by Anglo-Saxons replaced and, in the process, amalgamated with their pagan counterparts, as in the case of the Old English charms, the performance of which was often accompanied with the use of objects like amulets, plants hung or placed in a special place, potions, or brews. Sam's call upon Elbereth, combined with the use of Galadriel's phial, parallels the operation of the Old English charms. George Sayer recalls a walk with Tolkien when the writer told him a little story about celandine (*Chelidonium maius*): while gathering this plant people were supposed to recite a combination of *Ave Maria* and *Pater noster*, which replaced runic charms uttered on such occasions in olden times (5). On the same walk Tolkien told Sayer about the properties of the herb called bennet (*Geum*): the English, he explained, refer to it as the herb of St. Benedict, believing that it is blessed because it protects one against the devil; "if it is put into a house 'the devil can do nothing, and if a man carries it about with him no venomous beast will come within scent of it'" (Sayer 5). Once again one is reminded of Old English charms, this time the "Charm of Nine Herbs".

In the encounter with the orcs Sam chooses the word *Elbereth* to be a password between his master and himself for he realises that "No orc would say that" (*LotR* III 222) – Sam's belief not only reflects the magical power of words but also reminds one of St. Paul's conviction that "no man can say that Jesus is the Lord, but by the Holy Ghost" (I Cor. 12.3). On the same occasion during the hobbits' anti-quest, the Phial of Galadriel proves to be an extremely effective weapon again, readily responding to Sam's faithful and courageous spirit, enflamed by his sincere call upon Elbereth.

> Sam drew out the elven-glass of Galadriel again. As if to do honour to his hardihood and to grace with splendour his faithful brown hobbit-hand that had done such deeds, the phial blazed forth suddenly, so that all the shadowy court was lit with a dazzling radiance like lightning; but it remained steady and did not pass.
>
> '*Gilthoniel, A Elbereth*!' Sam cried.

> For, why he did not know, his thought sprang back suddenly to the Elves in the Shire, and the song that drove away the Black Rider in the trees.
> *'Aiya elenion ancalima!'* cried Frodo again behind him.
> The will of the watchers was broken with a suddenness like the snapping of a cord, and Frodo and Sam stumbled forward. Then they ran. (LotR III 225)

Tolkien once again emphasises the effectiveness not of the glass by itself but in combination with the invocation of Elbereth. Moreover, in this crucial battle, it is the perfect agreement between the two hobbits' intentions that is decisive in their victory over the forces of evil. It reminds one of Christ's assurance that "if two of you shall agree on earth as touching anything that they shall ask, it shall be done for them" (Matthew 18:19). Accordingly, Sam and Frodo's synchronised ejaculations to Elbereth empower the two hobbits and make them prevail against the evil will of the watchers. The hobbits' personal courage and well-tried mutual friendship are of course vital for their victory but the decisive factor is the external supernatural aid brought by their united call. It is worth recalling that Tolkien viewed life in terms of a cosmic war between the forces of good and evil, God and Satan. George Sayer remembers, for instance, that when the famous writer received an early model of a tape recorder as a gift, he "first recorded the Lord's Prayer in Gothic to cast out the devil that was sure to be in it since it was a machine" (Sayer 8). Likewise, Tolkien was convinced that the sacraments protected a believer from the bondage of evil. He made the following observation about Ireland, "it is as if the earth there is cursed, it exudes an evil that is held in check only by Christian practice and the power of prayer", and in his view even land could be involved in the cosmic struggle between good and evil (Sayer 13). Stratford Caldecott (31-32) interprets Tolkien's belief that without help from outside it is impossible to renounce the Ring and be rid of the hold it has over us, like it does over Frodo and Sam, in terms of the concept of grace in Christian theology.

All the aforementioned episodes from *The Lord of the Rings* illustrate the power of such external spiritual help as the Christian religion identifies with the power of prayer, which in the medieval Catholic Church was associated with the figure of Mary. The variety and effectiveness of prayer tacitly present in *The Lord of the Rings* is truly astounding: from the collective singing on the road, similar to the songs of medieval crusaders and pilgrims, through the communal ritual worship in the Hall of Fire, reminiscent of the singing of the divine office in the monasteries, to the individual miracle-working petitions and acts of solitary mystical contemplation. In addition, there are greetings, blessings, oaths, and powerful names. There is, finally, unanimous supplication of the two perfectly united minds of Frodo and Sam. A similar diversity and centrality of prayer can be found in medieval literature, not only in religious texts, such as hagiography, miracles of the Virgin, or the *exempla* told by preachers, but in secular ones as well. In chivalric romances, in particular, those medieval adventure stories that closely parallel Tolkien's work, the protagonists repeatedly call upon and refer to saints, who in return come to their aid. Among those, the Blessed Virgin Mary had the reputation of being the most trusted and powerful intercessor. Thus, Sir Gawain of the alliterative romance *Sir Gawain and the Green Knight*, which Tolkien had edited together with E.V. Gordon in 1925, and which he had translated into modern English, was Mary's devout knight. Tolkien's characters, likewise, address themselves to a female spiritual supporter, Elbereth, especially in moments of desperation.

Like the Elven hymn to Elbereth, medieval Marian lyrics consisted of words and melody and, like the Elven hymn, they were, as a rule, originally composed and performed in Latin and only later translated into vernaculars. The panorama of languages in Anglo-Saxon England parallels that of Tolkien's Middle-earth, Latin possibly corresponding with Quenya, or the High-elven, "an ancient tongue of Eldamar beyond the Sea, the first to be recorded in writing"; it was "no longer a birth-tongue, but had become, as it were, an 'Elven-latin', still used for ceremony, and for high matters of love and song, by the High Elves" (*LotR* III, Appendix F 507). The hobbits first hear the hymn to Elbereth sung by the High Elves in Sindarin, a language that evolved from Quenya. They barely understand the hymn, like the majority of medieval populace that was ignorant of Latin. The Westron, in turn, the language of both hobbits and men, may be taken to correspond to English in its many dialects, such as West Saxon. Tolkien explains that the language spoken in Middle-earth used to have many varieties but the differences between them have lessened as it has turned into the Common Speech (*LotR* III, Appendix F 509), a process that may be seen as analogous to a gradual standardization of English.

Translating some of the High-elven songs into the Common Speech, Frodo acts like a medieval translator of Latin songs. He is an educated hobbit that, unlike Sam, understands the Elven-latin a little and can interpret it. Tolkien conveys Frodo's delight in hearing an alien, exotic-sounding tongue combined with a beautiful melody. The impression made by the hymn to Elbereth upon the hobbit parallels what medieval English people must have felt when hearing Latin liturgical chants.[10]

> The singing drew nearer. One clear voice rose now above the others. It was singing in the fair elven-tongue, of which Frodo knew only a little, and the others knew nothing. Yet the sound blending with the melody seemed to shape itself in their thought into words which they only partly understood [...] The song ended. 'These are High Elves! They spoke the name of Elbereth!' said Frodo in amazement. (*LotR* I 105)

The High Elves are recognised by the fact that they use the name of Elbereth, and are not unlike medieval Christians who are defined by their devotion to Mary. When Frodo listens to an elegy sung by Galadriel, Tolkien provides both the original High-elven text and the hobbit's translation of it into the Common Speech (cf. *LotR* I 495-496). The manuscripts with medieval Marian lyrics likewise often provide, side by side, the original Latin version and a Middle English translation (cf. e.g. the Latin hymn *Gaude virgo mater Christi*, translated as "Glade us maiden, moder milde" in the Trinity College, Cambridge MS. 323). Moreover, different translations of the same song existed in different dialects. There was no single, authorised version just as there was no one standard, official language, and the renderings were not literally faithful, rather they approximated the original, just as Frodo's interpretations approximate the Elven songs.

Elbereth's high position in Middle-earth corresponds with Mary's place in the medieval world. The Elves hail Elbereth as "Queen beyond the Western Seas!" (*LotR* I 105), which corresponds with Mary's title of the Heavenly Queen –

---

10 For example, in the twelfth-century chronicle of Ely King Cnut is said to have been greatly impressed by the chanting of the monks, heard from a distance while on a journey by water to Ely, and subsequently the king composed verses on the subject in English: "Merie sungen ðe muneches binnen Ely [...]" (Wilson 159).

compare, for example, the thirteenth-century Middle English lyric, *Edi beo þu, heuene quene* (Duncan 106). The name Varda signifies "The Exalted" and "The Lofty" (*S* Index 428), and parallels Mary's elevation above all beings as Queen of Heaven, Lady of this World, and Empress of Hell (cf. e.g. Brown, *Religious Lyrics of the XVth Century* 23-24). Like Mary, the addressee of many prayers and songs of adoration (cf. e.g. Brown, *Religious Lyrics of the XVth Century* 25-78), Varda/Elbereth is a powerful intercessor: "Of all the Great Ones who dwell in this world the Elves hold Varda most in reverence and love. Elbereth they name her, and they call upon her name out of the shadows of Middle-earth, and uplift it in song at the rising of the stars" (*S* 16-17).

The Elves call upon Varda particularly in the evening and through the night. The hobbits first hear the Elven hymn to Elbereth at twilight, when the world is falling gently into dusk and after a star comes out in the darkening East (cf. *LotR* I 102), like the star that appeared on the eve of Jesus' birth and guided the Magi. In both cases, the stars represent guidance, protection, joy, and the forces of good against those of evil and darkness. In Rivendell, the Elves sing their songs of the Blessed Realm long into the night (cf. *LotR* I 311). There is a clear parallel with medieval Christian liturgy. Already in the early Byzantine Church the evening was a favourite time of day for the singing of litanies and similar forms of prayer, interweaving a single voice with group responses. Throughout the Middle Ages, not only in the twelfth and succeeding centuries, when the Marian devotion had its heyday, but already in Anglo-Saxon England, particularly in the period of the Benedictine Reform, there flourished the cult of the Virgin Mary, as richly documented by Mary Clayton. The most solemn and widely observed Hours of the Virgin were twilight, the time of Vespers-cum-Compline, and dawn, the time of Matins-cum-Lauds. Matins was prayed at night or upon rising, and was in an important sense a night Office, its prayers being called nocturns. Similarly, Tolkien, writing about calendars in Middle-earth, states that the Eldar paid special attention to the twilight and dawn as the times of star-opening and star-fading (cf. *LotR* III, Appendix D 485).

From early on, Mary was a central figure in medieval daily liturgy. The Eastern Church celebrated the Eucharist "in honour and memory of our most highly blessed and glorious Lady Theotokos [the Bearer of God] and ever virgin Mary, through whose prayers do You, O Lord, receive this sacrifice upon your altar in heaven" (Constantelos 119). In Western parishes the daily bell-ringing announced the major canonical Hours and particularly their concluding prayers to the Virgin for peace (Helander 183). As the songs of Elbereth stand out in the Elven singing in the Hall of Fire, so did Marian songs form the culmination of the medieval Hours, each of which consisted mainly of Psalms, with varying combinations of hymns, prayers, lessons, and antiphons. Although the Psalms do not mention Mary, those sung during the Hours were given a mystical interpretation pertaining to her (Wieck 492-94). The most frequently sung prayers to the Virgin included the *Ave Maria* and the four great independent Marian votive antiphons: *Salve Regina* (Hail, Holy Queen), *Alma Redemptoris Mater* (Gracious Mother of the Redeemer), *Regina Caeli* (Queen of Heaven), and *Ave Regina Caelorum* (Hail, Queen of the Heavens). Each of these antiphons had a single familiar melody. At the climax of Vespers, or Evensong, as the altar was incensed, the standing community chanted the Magnificat, the Canticle of Mary.

In the medieval world, the daily liturgy, with its scriptural readings, music, poetry, images, incense, colours, and vestments, had remarkable poetic qualities and indeed was a kind of poem. The same pertains to the elvish ritual in the Hall of Fire, focalized through Frodo's perception:

> At first the beauty of the melodies and the interwoven words in elven tongues, even though he understood them little, held him in a spell, as soon as he began to attend to them. Almost it seemed that the words took shape, and visions of far lands and bright things that he had never yet imagined opened out before him; and the firelit hall became like a golden mist above seas of foam that sighed upon the margins of the world. Then the enchantment became more and more dreamlike, until he felt that an endless river of swelling gold was flowing over him, too multitudinous for its pattern to be comprehended; it became part of the throbbing air about him, and it drenched and drowned him. Swiftly he sank under its shining weight into a deep realm of sleep. (*LotR* I 306)

The music transports Frodo into an unknown realm. The way Tolkien describes it is strongly reminiscent of the vision of New Jerusalem in the Middle English *Pearl*, a poem he knew very well for he translated it into Modern English. In both visions there is a significant amalgamation of sound, voice, music, colour, light, jewellery, flowing movement, tremor of the air, and dreaming. Moreover, just as the exquisite poetry of the *Pearl*-poet conveys the reader/listener into the heavenly land so does the singing of the Elves transfer Frodo to a beautiful realm of his imagination. In both cases, the creative power of poetry is at work. Bilbo notes the insatiable "elvish appetite for music and poetry and tales" (*LotR* I 311). But in both cases the poetry is connected with ritual as well, a major social event, filling up the vacuum between spiritual and material realities. Tolkien describes the elvish ritual in the Hall of Fire as a principal social gathering, in which all the folk of Rivendell participate. Some of them perform the music and some listen to it intently. Everybody can come into the Hall or leave it at any time during a seemingly interminable service. As Frodo and Bilbo leave the Hall of Fire, they can hear a single clear voice rising in song. It is a song to Elbereth.

The centrality of liturgy in the medieval world and the crucial place of Mary therein are beautifully conveyed in Dante's *Divine Comedy*, in which liturgy, in its broad sense of adoration, connects earth with afterlife.[11] While the Church sacraments do not have place in heaven, souls in purgatory and paradise continuously sing hymns and anthems, both in Latin and in the vernacular tongue. The same idea is suggested by the *Pearl*-poet's description of the heavenly city, filled with adoration but lacking a church building. In Dante's *Commedia* praise of Mary is a recurrent motif, introduced in Canto VII of *Purgatory*, where souls at rest at the end of the day sing *Salve Regina*, which was often sung at the close of Vespers or Compline. Dante shows that, at the falling of darkness, the souls pray for God's care throughout the night and protection against disturbing dreams and the Evil One. As they pray, two angels, bearing flaming swords, come to guard them. We have seen that Tolkien describes the circumstances and effects of the elvish song to Elbereth in the Shire in a similar fashion. In paradise, many of the joyful hymns of praise are directed to Mary. In Canto XXIII, for instance, Dante sees white fires, spirits of the blessed, each of which possesses a deep devotion to and love for Mary. The poet is deeply moved by their tender singing of *Regina Caeli*, which fills him with prolonged delight. Dante's impressions parallel Frodo's response to the elvish singing.

Medieval devotion to Mary can be observed in numerous invocations and lyrics of adoration of the Glorious Queen, composed in the vernacular as well as

---

11 For the role of liturgy in medieval vernacular literature, including Dante, see Vitz (551-618).

Latin. They include Anglo-Norman lyrics, Italian lauds, the Spanish *Cantigas de Santa Maria*, vernacular translations of Latin hymns and amplifications of *Ave Maria* (Vitz 570-75). For example, an Italian *lauda*, "song of praise", exalts Mary as "Heavenly light of great splendour", "star of the sea that is never concealed", "divine light", and "lady most fair in the image of God" (Vitz 570). Mary is repeatedly associated with light and brightness in those poems. "O ladye, þat arte so bright / As is þe sunne in þe firmament", says the speaker of a Middle English lyric, and repeats, "O lovely lady bright and sheene", while another poet hails Mary as queen of heaven and star of bliss (Brown, *Religious Lyrics of the XVth Century* 25, 37). In our context one particularly interesting motif is the recurrent theme of *Ave maris stella*, which occurs in the form of either translations or poems loosely inspired by the Latin hymn under the same title. In these lyrics Mary is invoked as "se-stoerre bryht" (Brown, *Religious Lyrics of the XIVth Century* 20), "ster of se", "ster of day", and "wyndow of hewen mirth" (Brown, *Religious Lyrics of the XIVth Century* 55-56), and "sterne on þe se so bright" that brings "liht vn-to þe blind" and whose shining brilliance surpasses that of all our jewels (Brown, *Religious Lyrics of the XIVth Century* 58). The speakers implore the Queen of Heaven to pray for them to her Son (Brown, *Religious Lyrics of the XVth Century* 35-37), shield them from shame (Brown, *Religious Lyrics of the XIVth Century* 20), and save them from folly (Brown, *Religious Lyrics of the XVth Century* 35). One speaker prays, "O Sterne so brycht, þat gyfes lycht / til hewyne and haly kyrk, / þi help, þi mycht grant ws ful rycht"; he asks the fair lady to "ostend", unveil, her face, and contrasts her light with the dark clouds coming from hell (Brown, *Religious Lyrics of the XVth Century* 36-37).

The prominence of the imagery of light in the medieval Marian lyrics finds an analogy in Tolkien's evocations of Elbereth in terms of light and especially starlight. The Elven hymn invokes her as "Lady clear" and "Light to us that wander here", refers to her "clear eyes", "bright breath" and shining hand that has sown stars, her "silver blossom", "in the Sunless Year", so that now "windy fields" are "bright and clear" (*LotR* I 105). In *The Silmarillion* this poetic imagery is explained as referring to the myth that tells of Varda/Elbereth as the female counterpart of Manwë, one of the seven Lords of the Valar, whom Men have often called "gods" (15): "With Manwë dwells Varda,

Lady of the Stars, who knows all the regions of Eä. Too great is her beauty to be declared in the words of Men or of Elves; for the light of Ilúvatar lives still in her face. In light is her power and her joy" (16). Varda has perfect sight and is revered as the mother of stars. The Elves name her Elbereth or Elentári, both terms signifying "Star-Queen". They also call her Gilthoniel or Tintalle, "star-kindler".

The principle of light underlying Tolkien's created world parallels the medieval metaphysics of light as unfolded by the English Franciscan scholar, Robert Grosseteste in his treatise *On Light*.[12] In Tolkien's mythology, creation has its origin in and happens through light: the light of Ilúvatar, the One, who "made visible the song of the Ainur", and "they beheld it as light in the darkness" and "therefore Ilúvatar gave to their vision Being" (*S* 16). This primary light is reflected in the face of Varda, the Star-Queen. The Elves, especially the high and noble ones, reflect her starlight in their own turn, particularly when they praise her. Thus, when the hobbits first come upon High Elves in the Shire, they can see "the starlight glimmering on their hair and in their eyes", and "a shimmer, like the light of the moon above the rim of the hills before it rises" falling about their feet (*LotR* I 106). When the song of Elbereth is being sung in the Hall of Fire, Frodo observes Aragorn standing by Lady Arwen: he "seemed to be clad in elven-mail, and a star shone on his breast", and "Arwen turned towards him and the light of her eyes fell on him from afar and pierced his heart" (*LotR* I 312). The head of Legolas appears to Frodo to be "crowned with sharp white stars that glittered in the black pools of the sky behind" (*LotR* I 508). The last meeting with the Elves takes place when it is evening, and the stars are glimmering in the eastern sky: the Elves are singing of Elbereth and as they approach, Frodo and Sam first see a shimmer; Elrond has "a star upon his forehead", Galadriel seems "to shine with a soft light", and the ring on her finger bears "a single white stone flickering like a frosty star" (*LotR* III 374-375).

---

12 The importance of light to Tolkien and to the Elves has been elucidated in *Splintered Light*, a fine study by Verlyn Flieger, who has shown Tolkien's indebtedness to Owen Barfield's metaphor of splintered and refracted light for the fragmentation of meaning in language and argued that the same principle underlies Tolkien's conception of the languages, peoples, and history of Middle-earth. Nevertheless, medieval theories of light like Grosseteste's also seem to be reflected in Tolkien's subcreated world.

Although the association of Elves with beauty and light is already present in the *liosalfar* of the Eddas, Tolkien raises the importance of natural light to a metaphysical principle in a manner that is fully comparable only with the medieval philosophy and theology of light. Also his invented languages reflect this principle. The key word of the Elven-latin, *êl*, means "star", and in Tolkien's mythological explanation of the origin of the Elven language it is associated with vision or sight: "According to Elvish legend, *ele* was a primitive exclamation 'behold!' made by the Elves when they first saw the stars. From this origin derived the ancient words *êl* and *elen*, meaning 'stars', and the adjectives *elda* and *elena*, meaning 'of the stars'. These elements appear in a great many names" (*S* 434). For example, the name Elendil, Aragorn's ancestor, means "star-lover", and it can also be translated as "elf-friend". Some of the Elves have epithets that connect them with stars: Arwen is called Undómiel, "Evenstar", while Eärendil is not only called "the Evening Star", most beloved of the Elves (*LotR* I 479), but Elbereth has actually made him a star, "a sign of hope to the dwellers of Middle-earth" (*LotR* III 381). The sign of the star, omnipresent in the literary creation of Middle-earth, points also to Tolkien's Marian inspiration, manifest particularly in the figure of Varda/Elbereth.

Bibliography

BROWN, Carleton, ed. *English Lyrics of the XIIIth Century*. Oxford: Clarendon Press, 1932.

ed. *Religious Lyrics of the XVth Century*. Oxford: Clarendon Press, 1939.

ed. *Religious Lyrics of the XIVth Century*. Oxford: Clarendon Press, 1952.

CALDECOTT, Stratford. "Over the Chasm of Fire: Christian Heroism in *The Silmarillion* and *The Lord of the Rings*." *Tolkien. A Celebration*. Ed. Joseph Pearce. London: HarperCollins*Religious*, 1999. 17-33.

CHANCE, Jane, ed. *Tolkien the Medievalist*. London and New York: Routledge, 2003.

CHAUCER, Geoffrey. "The Prioresse's Tale." *The Riverside Chaucer*. Ed. Larry C. Benson. Oxford: Oxford UP, 209-212.

CLAUSEN, Christopher. "*The Lord of the Rings* and *The Ballad of the White Horse*." *South Atlantic Bulletin* 39/2, May 1974:10-16.

CLAYTON, Mary. *The Cult of the Virgin Mary in Anglo-Saxon England*. Cambridge Studies in Anglo-Saxon England. Cambridge: Cambridge UP, 1990.

Constantelos, Demetrios J. "Liturgy and Liturgical Daily Life in the Medieval Greek World – The Byzantine Empire." *The Liturgy of the Medieval Church.* Ed. Thomas J. Heffernan and E. Ann Matter. Kalamazoo, MI: Medieval Institute Publications, Western Michigan University, 2001. 109-143.

Coulombe, Charles A. "*The Lord of the Rings*: A Catholic View." *Tolkien: A Celebration*, ed. Joseph Pearce. London: HarperCollins*Religious*, 1999. 53-66.

Dante Alighieri. *The Divine Comedy of Dante Alighieri*, 3 vols. *Inferno, Purgatorio, Paradiso* [dual-language editions]. Trans. and comments by John D. Sinclair. New York, 1939.

Dobbie, Elliot Van Kirk, *The Anglo-Saxon Minor Poems.* The Anglo-Saxon Poetic Records, 6. New York: Columbia University Press, 1942.

Donovan, Leslie A. "The Valkyrie Reflex in J.R.R. Tolkien's *The Lord of the Rings.*" *Tolkien the Medievalist*, ed. Jane Chance. London and New York: Routledge, 2003. 106-132.

Duncan, Thomas G., ed. *Medieval English Lyrics 1200-1400.* London: Penguin Books, 1995.

Duriez, Colin. *The J.R.R. Tolkien Handbook: A Comprehensive Guide to His Life, Writings, and World of Middle-earth.* Grand Rapids, MI: Baker Book Mouse, 1992.

Fiałkowski, Tomasz. "Oxfordzcy mistrzowie wyobraźni. An interwiew with prof. Przemysław Mroczkowski." *Tygodnik Powszechny* 14, 1994.

Flieger, Verlyn. *Splintered Light: Logos and Language in Tolkien's World.* First edition 1983. Kent, OH: The Kent State UP, 2002.

Flint, Valerie. *The Rise of Magic in Early Medieval Europe.* Princeton: Princeton UP, 1991.

A Gest of Robyn Hode. Ed. Stephen Knight and Thomas H. Ohlgren. Kalamazoo, MI: Medieval Institute Publications, 1997.

Grosseteste, Robert. *On Light.* Trans. C. C. Riedl. Milwaukee, WI: Marquette UP, 1978.

Heffernan, Thomas J., and E. Ann Matter, ed. *The Liturgy of the Medieval Church.* Kalamazoo, MI: Medieval Institute Publications, Western Michigan University, 2001.

Helander, Sven. "The Liturgical Profile of the Parish Church in Medieval Sweden." *The Liturgy of the Medieval Church.* Ed. Thomas J. Heffernan and E. Ann Matter. Kalamazoo, Michigan: Medieval Institute Publications, Western Michigan University, 2001. 145-186.

The Holy Bible. The Authorised Version. Nashville and New York: Thomas Nelson, 1981.

HONEGGER, Thomas. "Tolkien Through the Eyes of a Mediaevalist." *Reconsidering Tolkien*. Ed. Thomas Honegger. Zurich and Berne: Walking Tree Publishers, 2005. 45-66.

The King of Tars. Ed. from the Auchinleck MS. Advocates 19.2.1 by Judith Perryman. Heidelberg: Carl Winter Universitätsverlag, 1980.

KÚTNIK, Rev. Jozef. *Litania loretańska*. Trans. from the Slovak by Juliusz Zychowicz. Kraków: Znak, 1983.

MAHER, Michael W., S. J. *"A land without stain*: Medieval Images of Mary and Their Use in the Characterization of Galadriel." *Tolkien the Medievalist*. Ed. Jane Chance. London and New York: Routledge, 2003. 225-236.

MALORY, Sir Thomas. *Works*. Ed. Eugène Vinaver. Oxford: Oxford UP, 1977.

NENNIUS. *The Historia Brittonum. Vol. 3: The 'Vatican' Recension*. Ed. David N. Dumville. Cambridge: Brewer, 1985.

Octavian. Ed. Harriet Hudson. *Four Middle English Romances*. Kalamazoo, Michigan: Western Michigan University for TEAMS, 1996.

PEARCE, Joseph, "Tolkien and the Catholic Literary Revival." *Tolkien: A Celebration*. Ed. Joseph Pearce, London: HarperCollins, 1999. 102-123.

ed, *Tolkien: A Celebration*. London: HarperCollins, 1999.

Pearl. Ed. E. V. Gordon. Oxford: Clarendon Press, 1980.

SAYER, George. "Recollections of J.R.R. Tolkien." *Tolkien: A Celebration*. Ed. Joseph Pearce. London: HarperCollins, 1999. 1-16.

Sir Gawain and the Green Knight. Ed. J. R. R. Tolkien and E. V. Gordon. Second edition rev. Norman Davis. Oxford: Clarendon Press, 1979.

TOLKIEN, John Ronald Reuel. *The Lord of the Rings*, Parts I, II, III. London: HarperCollins, 1999.

The Silmarillion. Ed. Christopher Tolkien. London: HarperCollins, 1999.

The Letters of J. R. R. Tolkien. Ed. Humphrey Carpenter with the assistance of Christopher Tolkien. London: HarperCollins, 1995.

VITZ, Evelyn B. "The Liturgy and Vernacular Literature." *The Liturgy of the Medieval Church*. Ed. Thomas J. Heffernan & E. Ann Matter. Kalamazoo, MI: Medieval Institute Publications, Western Michigan University, 2001. 551-618.

WIECK, Roger S. "The Book of Hours." *The Liturgy of the Medieval Church*. Ed. Thomas J. Heffernan & E. Ann Matter. Kalamazoo, MI: Medieval Institute Publications, Western Michigan University, 2001. 473-513.

WILSON, R. M. *The Lost Literature of Medieval England*, London: Methuen, 1952.

About the author

BARBARA KOWALIK is a professor in the Institute of English Studies at the University of Warsaw. She took her Ph. D. at the University of Łódź and for many years taught English language and literature at Maria Curie-Skłodowska University of Lublin. In 2003 she moved to Warsaw, where she has been teaching courses and seminars on English literature, particularly medieval literature and women writers. She has authored numerous articles and reviews, specialising in close readings of outstanding as well as underrated literary texts. Her articles include studies of *Pearl* and *St. Erkenwald* and selected works by Chaucer, Henryson, Shakespeare, Anne Finch, Charlotte Smith, Jane Austen, Edwin Muir, Ruth Pitter, C.S. Lewis, Charles Williams, and Neil Gaiman. Part of her doctoral dissertation was published in 1997 as *From Circle to Tangle. Space in the Poems of the Pearl Manuscript*. Her habilitation on Barbara Pym's fiction, *A Woman's Pastoral*, was published in 2002. Her most recent book, *Betwixt 'engelaunde' and 'englene londe': Dialogic Poetics in Early English Religious Lyric*, was published by Peter Lang in 2010. She currently works on Biernat of Lublin's fables seen against the medieval European beast fable tradition. Barbara Kowalik presides over the editorial board of *Acta Philologica*, a scholarly journal published by the Faculty of Neophilology at the University of Warsaw.

Katarzyna Blacharska

The Fallen: Milton's Satan and Tolkien's Melkor

Abstract

This paper presents an analysis of the depiction of Melkor in *The Silmarillion* (1977) by J.R.R. Tolkien and focuses on one aspect: the similarity between the fallen Ainur and the Devil of John Milton's *Paradise Lost* (1667). The aim is to demonstrate that while creating the figure of Melkor Tolkien not only followed the scriptural tradition but was also influenced by Milton's epic to a great extent.

The struggle between Light and Darkness, and between Good and Evil, has been one of the principal motifs present in imaginative literature throughout the ages. It seems that it is a trait of all societies to seek an explanation for the origin of evil in the world. At the same time, with the subject being so stimulating, it has been repeatedly used in fiction. *The Silmarillion*, which recounts the history of J.R.R. Tolkien's fictional universe, is to a great extent indebted to the Judeo-Christian tradition, not only as far as the whole structure of the universe and the very act of Creation are concerned but also in respect to the emergence of evil. In depicting the conflict between Good and Evil, Tolkien's work has much in common with one of the greatest poems in the English language, namely John Milton's *Paradise Lost*. Naturally there will be some who say that Milton "might seem the last English poet to resonate with Tolkien" (Holmes 428), possibly because of the Puritan poet's severe Protestantism (as compared to Tolkien's Catholicism) or due to his southern inspiration (Greek and Roman), and his simultaneous contempt for England's pagan Anglo-Saxon ancestors (Holmes 428; Shippey 257). Either way, there can be no doubt that throughout *The Silmarillion* we are able to find traces of Miltonian influence. The aim of this article is thus to demonstrate the close resemblance between *The Silmarillion*'s Melkor and the Satan of *Paradise Lost* and to show that the correspondences in their characteristics go beyond those ascribed to the Devil in biblical scripture. In the following, I will only focus on the most salient points since a comprehensive discussion of the topic would go beyond the scope of this paper.

In their description of evil Milton's *Paradise Lost* and Tolkien's *The Silmarillion* follow the theological tradition of the Hebraic account in Genesis, but they may possibly also reflect *Genesis B*, the middle section (lines 235-851) of the Old English poem *Genesis*,[1] which presents a "detailed account of the rebellion and fall of the angels that goes far beyond the biblical story" (Russell, *Prince of Darkness* 125). J. B. Russell describes how in the Old English poem an omniscient and omnipotent God creates the angels and bestows free will on them before creating the universe and its inhabitants. Motivated by pride and envy, one of the angels rebels and renounces his liege lord, sets up his own stronghold in the northwest of Heaven and summons other angels to join him. Eventually, Lucifer and his companions are cast by God into Hell, where they lose their angelic dignity. Aware that they are not able to defeat God in open battle, their leader decides to pervert the newly-created humans, turn them against God and enslave them. Subsequently, he sets out to tempt Adam and, having failed, he turns his attention to Eve, who succumbs to his influence (125-129).

Both *Paradise Lost* and *The Silmarillion* correspond with the *Genesis B* account insofar as the Fall of angels (Ainur) happens before the creation of the Earth (Arda) (see also Flieger 55-58).[2] However, the narratives do not give us occasion to see a good Satan or a good Melkor, and hence we are unable to witness them struggling with their previously reported good natures. The name traditionally accorded to the "good" Satan, the name he bears before his Fall, is *Lucifer* (Light-bearer).[3] However, throughout *Paradise Lost* the name is mentioned only three

---

[1] There has been some debate as to whether Milton knew the contents of the Junius Manuscript (including the Old English poems of *Genesis*, *Exodus*, *Daniel* and *Christ and Satan*), published in 1655, but nothing solid has been proven, other than the fact that Milton was a close acquaintance of Franciscus Junius, its publisher (see McGrath 142; Rumble 385-86).

[2] It is noteworthy that Angband, one of Melkor's domains, is in the northwest, which seems to parallel the *Genesis B* account. On the other hand, Melkor's first dwelling, Utumno, is in the north, just as Lucifer's palace in *Paradise Lost*. The notion of North as the representation of the realm of evil seems to be a common Christian tradition, probably stemming from Jeremiah 1.14. Interestingly, the concept is present also in other cultures (see e.g. Eliade 259-88; Wasilewski 148).

[3] "Light-bearer," Jerome's Latin translation of the Hebrew *Helel ben Shahar* (Forsyth 51), which roughly means "bright son of the morning" (Russell, *Devil* 195-96) or "Shining One, Son of the Dawn" (Forsyth 51).

times: in Books 5 (line 760: "The Palace of great *Lucifer*"), 7 (lines 131-34: "Know then, that after *Lucifer* from Heav'n / [...] Fell") and 10 (lines 424-425: "proud seate / Of *Lucifer*").⁴ In Milton's epic Satan is always fallen; even in Heaven he is already a fallen being. As Stanley Fish (xxv) writes, "[w]e never see him, but see only what he has become [...]. His former name is heard no more, not because it is anathema to pronounce it [...] but because *he* no longer exists." Consequently, the fallen angel is referred to as Satan, i.e. the "Adversary" (Turner 57), and along with his subsequent deterioration he is spoken of as the Devil and the Fiend, a deterioration which these names also serve to illustrate.

In the case of Melkor in *The Silmarillion* the situation is analogous: in Ilúvatar's Heaven he is already a fallen creature.⁵ Moreover, because of his evil deeds "He who arises in Might" (*S* 410)⁶ is cursed with the name Morgoth, "the Black Enemy" (*S* 412), and with his further degradation he is known only by the latter; interestingly, it is analogous to the meaning of the name *Satan*. By using the gifts bestowed upon him by Ilúvatar in a corrupt manner (for instance, under his control the gift of reason turns into cunning) Melkor evolves into a destructive and cruel figure, and his name reflects the darkening of his character.⁷

However, the change of names is not the only thing that Milton's Satan and Tolkien's Morgoth have in common as both authors favour the tradition that sees pride as the origin of sin. With Satan and Morgoth it starts as a belief in their own worth and independence (Augustine's "turning to oneself," instead of looking to the Creator, and valuing personal good above the good of others),⁸ and develops into a desire to triumph over their Creator. Satan,

---

4 This and all subsequent quotations from *Paradise Lost* follow Flannagan.
5 See Evans 194-224 for more information about the state of being fallen in Tolkien's work.
6 This and all subsequent quotations from *The Silmarillion* follow Christopher Tolkien's 1999 edition.
7 Regina M. Schwartz observes that having lost their positive identity, the fallen angels in *Paradise Lost* have also lost their names (Fish xxv). The notion of losing one's name seems to apply equally well to Melkor.
8 According to Augustine, Satan was to be cut off from God, the source of creation, as a result of the sin of pride, and consequently his nature was impaired as was the goodness of God, which he had possessed. For Augustine's contemporary, John Cassian, Satan started to believe in his own powers when he concentrated upon himself and chose his own benefits, and he was devoured by the untruth of it to the point where he was unable to free himself. Thus he did not achieve freedom but further degradation and instability of his nature (Revard, ch. 1-2). Also, in the aforementioned *Genesis B* Satan prefers to contemplate himself rather than his Creator (Russell, *Prince of Darkness* 125).

who "trusted to have equal'd the most High" (*PL* 1.40), led his followers to an "impious War" (1.43) as a consequence of which they were cast down into Hell. Melkor, in turn, wanted to enhance the power and glory that was assigned to his theme in Ilúvatar's music, and what is more, he wanted to incorporate into the music his own themes, independently of his Creator.[9]

Still, in accordance with the tradition, pride is not the only sin that Satan and Melkor might be accused of. Both Milton and Tolkien show pride to be interwoven with the sin of envy. It is pride that prompts Satan to rebel against the Omnipotent and urges him to reject the Son, of whom he is *envious* and whom he perceives to be unworthy of God's favour. Nevertheless, his envy is not restricted only to the Son as it also embraces the human pair, and it can be seen in the soliloquies of Books 4 and 9.

As we have seen, pride is also Melkor's flaw: in the Ainulindalë we witness the emergence of his belief in his own powers and his desire to create independently of the source of his being, but, similarly to Milton's fallen angel, the sin generates the feeling of envy as well. Already in Heaven, Ilúvatar shows his might over Melkor's continuous intrusions and silences the Music, and while other Ainur are terrified Melkor is filled with a shame that engenders a secret anger. He envies Ilúvatar's power of creation, and he wanders into the Void in search of the Imperishable Flame "for desire grew hot within him to bring into Being things of his own" (*S* 4). Nonetheless, his envy does not end with Ilúvatar. He is also envious of the Valar (especially Manwë)[10] and the Children of Ilúvatar, since they were to be endowed with so many favours.

Some manuscripts, most notably the Apocryphal Books of Enoch, allude to yet another sin of the fallen angels, lust. The fallen, named the Watchers or *Grigori*, were supposed to have become so not only as a result of pride but also as a consequence of having seen the beauty of women, mating with them and thus creating the race of *Nephilim* (Webster 70). The punishment

---

9 On the resemblance between the descriptions of Satan's and Melkor's fall see Watkins 3-4.
10 As Verlyn Flieger argues, although Manwë is "the chief of the Valar, lord of the earth, and Eru's deputy" (54), he is not God but a secondary figure (55): Manwë appears to be a Christ figure, but he cannot be found His equal, precisely because of this subordination. Interestingly, for Joseph Pearce Manwë is cast in the role of the archangel Michael (435).

they received for this crime was being chained in the depths of Hell for ten thousand years.[11]

The sin that the fallen angel of Milton and the fallen Ainur of Tolkien are capable of seems to be closely related to that of lust. In *Paradise Lost* passion and lust are already visible in the birth of Satan's daughter, Sin, and her subsequent violation by her father; later on the theme will be also covertly instilled in Book 9. We witness this in the scene where Satan espies Eve alone in the Garden, gets ready to corrupt her and subsequently succeeds in his temptation. The whole section abounds with mythological allusions, contanis puns and a certain ambiguity of language, which enhance the erotic atmosphere of the passage. Some critics propose particularly literal readings of the passage. For example, Kent R. Lehnhof shows how Milton follows the tradition which sexualized humanity's first sin, arguing, among other things, that, in a sense, Satan becomes Eve's first forbidden sexual partner when he "impregnates" her with his tongue (38).

Nonetheless, what is interesting is the fact that while contemplating the graceful form of Eve the fallen angel is momentarily stunned and becomes "Stupidly good, of enmitie disarm'd, / Of guile, of hate, of envie, of revenge" (*PL* 9.465-66). Her innocence and innate image of Heaven attract him and reverse, at least temporarily, the effects of evil (9.463-64). However, he is enslaved by his mental Hell, which will not let him stay in this state: "But the hot Hell that always in him burnes, / Though in mid Heav'n, soon ended his delight, / And tortures him now more, the more he sees / Of pleasure not for him ordain'd [...]" (9.467-70).

---

11 *The Book of Enoch* uses the term Watchers, while *The Second Book of Enoch* refers to them as *Grigori*. The term Watchers is used also in the *Book of Daniel* (4.13, 17, 23) and in the *Book of Jubilees* (4.15, 5:1), among others. 1 *Enoch* is supposedly based on the verse in *Genesis* 6 where "the sons of God came in unto the daughters of men, and they bare children to them, the same became mighty men which were of old, men of renown" (6.4) (see also Wright 20). On the numerous interpretations of the phrase "the sons of God" see Clines 33-46; Hendel 13-26; Kline 187-204; Wolf 115-19. According to Grant McColley, the *Book of Enoch* was attainable in Milton's times, but the manuscripts of the *Second Book of Enoch* were found only in the nineteenth century (Revard 30). Nevertheless, Revard (31) argues that Origen, who had a great impact on Milton, relied heavily on 2 *Enoch*. In fact some elements from the *Book of Enoch* and 2 *Enoch* might be tracked in Milton's description of Hell but also of Melkor's first dwelling, Utumno (*S* 134). Both include an icy region, with heat and frost under their masters' command.

Let us look at *The Silmarillion* in this context. Morgoth does not manifest any sexual lust[12] until the meeting with Lúthien, when he is overwhelmed by it at the sight of Lúthien's beauty: "Then Morgoth looking upon her beauty conceived in his thought an evil lust, and a design more dark than any that had yet come into his heart since he fled from Valinor" (*S* 212). However, in comparison to Milton's Satan there is no redeeming emotion in him – not even for a moment. Here we are able to witness how Melkor's perversity eventually brings about his ruin: while he takes delight in his despicable thoughts, his vigilance is dulled and Lúthien puts him to sleep. The existing situation is only a foreshadowing of his ultimate defeat.

At this point in both Milton's epic and in Tolkien's work the figures of the fallen are already seriously degenerated: they have lost most of their heavenly attributes and wasted the gifts bestowed upon them. Moreover, Satan in the shape of a snake is "mixt with bestial slime" (*PL* 9.165), while Melkor-Morgoth "became ever more bound to the earth" (*S* 113). Having been spiritual beings they are now debased enough as to feel lust, which has its roots in the animal instinct.

Despite the fact that each work presents us with a figure who is corrupted by the sins of pride and envy, and who subsequently engenders lust, both works are ambiguous as far as the origin of evil in the world is concerned[13] and in some way appear to suggest that it cannot be definitely explained.[14] Satan and Melkor are among the most powerful beings of their kind, perfect and rational. However much they are bestowed with the gifts of power, knowledge and reason etc., that which emerges from within their nature is something that is inexplicable: they refuse to submit to the Force by which they were created and, as a result of their refusal, are torn asunder from within.[15]

In general, *Paradise Lost* follows the Augustinian tradition asserting that since God is the eternal manifestation of goodness, there can be no iniquity found in

---

12 Before, however, he frequently manifests his lust for the Silmarils. It is not greed, as it does not have any material undertones, and for that reason it may be referred to as lust, an overwhelming desire to possess something. *Morgoth's Ring* in turn features another instance of Morgoth's corrupt sexual lust: the rape of the Sun maiden, Arie.
13 Also Jonathan Evans argues that *The Silmarillion* "doesn't give a satisfactory explanation" (207).
14 This in fact illustrates the attempts of theology to explain the origin of evil.
15 At the same time in both cases their rebellion is not a threat to God or Ilúvatar, but a tool for a greater good (see also Watkins 3).

Him. As such He cannot be the source of evil. However, Augustine's explanation of the existence of evil is rather obscure: it must come from His creatures and the free will they have been honoured with. Milton's epic parallels the tradition in this inconclusiveness: it is easy to say that Satan falls of his own free will. Nevertheless as John S. Tanner points out, "Satan's evil erupts in a vacuum, as it were, in a moment of radical self-determination" (45). It is not explained why the angel experiences it. Simultaneously, the evil begotten by Satan takes possession of him: it has all the characteristics of a compulsion and does not look solely like a consequence of a free choice. His sin then literally becomes an exterior entity which materialises in the form of a daughter, not accidentally named Sin.

Melkor's revolt embraces the elements of Augustinian theology[16] as well (Rosebury 113),[17] sharing also its ambiguity. As Jonathan Evans notices, all verbs referring to Melkor's transgression are passive or in the past-perfect form, which suggests that the Fall "happens" to him (209). Furthermore,

> Melkor himself might have objected (though he does not) that responsibility for the error that results from his exercise of the free will with which he was endowed must lie at least in part in his creation as a free being, and thus must have its ultimate source in the creator – Eru – himself. The very act of creation must contain within it at least the risk that something might go awry. (Evans 209)

Moreover, the critic suggests that Melkor behaves like Ilúvatar before the creation: "While in retrospect the attentive reader is able to reinterpret Melkor's actions as the self-alienating behavior of a being ultimately to be cut off from Eru, the ground of being itself, by being alone or thinking thoughts of his own, Melkor is behaving like Ilúvatar himself prior to the creation" (209), and similarly to Milton's Satan the fallen Ainur possesses some of his Creator's at-

---

16 For the discussion of different concepts of evil see Fornet-Ponse 2005.
17 For the differences between this story and Christian myths see Rosebury 113-115, and Flieger 124. Shippey, in turn, notices also Boethian and Manichean elements permeating *The Lord of the Rings* (170-176). Olszański's work "Evil and the Evil One in Tolkien's Theology" follows Shippey's view that in Tolkien's fiction we encounter a hint of a dualistic, Manichaean element (Rosebury 100), that is the Void: "The Void is not nothing, since Melkor (Morgoth) is able to go into it, and it is there that his estrangement from Eru and from the other immortals begins. While evil remains negation, and God does not create evil, it is not incomprehensible that good should become evil when God countenances the existence of a state outside himself" (113). Interestingly, also in Milton's epic there is the slightly puzzling figure of Chaos, whose sole aim is to wreak havoc, to spoil and to ruin (*PL* 2.1009).

tributes: "the first fall of a created being is shown as concomitant with an act of *making*" (Evans 209). Thus, Melkor's act of creation is not unsound in its nature; the problem is rather that his intentions and/or effects are the opposite of Ilúvatar's (Evans 209).[18]

Brian Rosebury reads Melkor's Fall in a similar vein. He argues that the Ainur's rebellion is not at first a declaration of war[19] but a creative revolt having its origin in the artistic nature which is bestowed upon Ilúvatar's beings and which urges them to rebel. This can be seen not only in the example of Melkor but also in the case of Fëanor, the Elves and the Dwarves in general, and Aulë. The two races are similarly affected by their creativity: their flaw is their unwillingness to part with what their creativity has produced,[20] and Fëanor and his Silmarils are an extreme case of this. While the issue may be found understandable with reference to inferior creatures, we also encounter another Ainu tempted by his own creativity, Aulë. His creation of the Seven Fathers of the Dwarves is condemned by Ilúvatar as they are not independent beings: "the creatures of thy hand and mind can live only by that being, moving when thou thinkest to move them, and if thy thought be elsewhere, standing idle" (*S* 37). Repentant, Aulë offers to destroy the Dwarves and explains he did not wish for lordship but for creatures to love and teach. Moreover, he says that the need to create was planted within him by Ilúvatar, and he, His child, wanted to imitate his Father without any mockery. It turns out that the Dwarves flinch at the sight of the hammer, which shows that Aulë's act of creation is accepted by Ilúvatar, who breathes life into them, and thus redeems them.

According to Rosebury, Melkor's case illustrates the "Power Bad, Creativity Good" polarity (115): because his behaviour is sullied by the sin of pride and desire for power from the beginning. While he starts as "an impatient creative

---

18 See also Huttar 11.
19 For Rosebury Melkor cannot declare war against Ilúvatar, simply because he does not know that such thing exists. Satan of *Paradise Lost* does know, for the Heaven of his God is of military structure; thus he uses vocabulary characteristic of this type of Heaven (115). Nevertheless, Watkins perceives Melkor's musical intrusions and disruptions as "close to actual battle than any other event in Ilúvatar's presence" (3).
20 Shippey, too, claims that in the case of the Elves it is not simply greed or pride in the strict sense, but an impatient desire to create things which are the reflection of their own image, the kind of pride not present, for instance, in *Paradise Lost*. The Fall occurs when the Elves become interested in the products of their hands, instead of God (Shippey 273-74).

spirit" (115), in the course of the story he becomes increasingly destructive: he wants to create beings, but instead of cherishing their existence for its own sake, he does it because of a desire of glorification and control over other creatures. Later, this attitude will lead to an even greater deterioration, and all he will be left with is a hatred of the independent will of others and of the results of their creativity. The difference between Aulë and Melkor is that the former loves creation and finds pleasure in it. He is not fascinated by his own craftsmanship. Seeing his fault, he is able to let go of the product of his hands even if it is paid for with excruciating pain. Melkor would not be capable of such sacrifice. He is intent only on self-satisfaction, at first through his own attempt at creation, and subsequently through his desire to destroy what others create. His descent onto Arda is followed by his continuous interferences and disruptions of the actions of other Valar, so that the outcome may suit his ends. Still, while Melkor aspires to be an independent source of creation, he is not able to produce anything original. Even in the beginning his music is already repetitious. Later, suffering from envy and hatred, he cannot create anything genuine: all he can bring forth are copies, mockery, and destruction. With his wickedness he contaminates whatever he comes across: nature, creatures, and still life. Not able to create life, he produces the race of Orcs by means of torture and corruption inflicted upon the Elves, which is one of the most perverse instances of his mimicry of his God.[21] What is more, Melkor even manages to sully Ilúvatar's gift of death, a gift of great mystery but one which initially was good in nature and inspired hope. It was a mysterious gift as no one knew what was to become of Men at the end of the world. Morgoth, not possessing this knowledge either, is successful in corrupting the gift, and changing hope into fear.

Unlike Melkor, Satan of *Paradise Lost* seems not to cherish any false hopes of independent creation. He does not hope to create new life nor does he envy

---

21 Tolkien's position on numerous issues changed throughout the process of the creation of his mythology. One of these is the question of the origin of Orcs. As Matthew Fensome (437) writes: "Tolkien, a devout Catholic, later found difficulty with the idea of irredeemably corrupt Elves, and an essay in 'Myths Transformed' argues that, since only Eru has the power and authority to create wholly new life, the Orcs must in fact have been 'beasts of humanized shape' made to speak by Morgoth (*MR* 410). Characteristically, Tolkien approaches the matter as if he were an outside observer, sifting the evidence and alternately formulating and dismissing theories – though he reaches no final conclusion." What is noteworthy, also the figure of Melkor-Morgoth himself is subject to many changes throughout *The History of Middle-Earth* (for example the enhancement of his powers in *Morgoth's Ring*); however, an in-depth analysis of the development of the character is beyond the scope of this paper.

this ability of God. What is more perverse, however, is his conviction and argument that God does not have such power: "who saw / When this creation was? rememberst thou / Thy making, while the Maker gave thee being? / We know no time when we were not as now; / Know none before us, self-begot, self-rais'd / By our own quick'ning power" (*PL* 5.853-61). Satan argues that angels were self-begotten and renounces God as their Creator. To crush his opponent in the discussion, Abdiel, an angel who remains loyal to God despite serving under Beelzebub, he resorts to an argument found by critics to be either "completely irrational reasoning" (Lewis 97-98), or a "masterstroke" (Wójcicka 62): the Foe answers that he does not remember anything before they had been created, and therefore they must have been begotten on their own.[22] After being cast into Hell, he goes as far as to assert that it is the space that creates new worlds, while the whole miracle is unduly attributed to God.

Although Satan is incapable of independent creation, we can see that he is very skillful as far as the corruption and influence of others is concerned, which is a feature shared with Melkor-Morgoth. As G.K. Hunter writes in his *Paradise Lost*, "the idea of something like an incurable virus with a virtually infinite capacity for mutation attaches to Satan in both his moral and narrative function" (60). This analogy serves as a perfect illustration of the infectuous nature of both Satan and Melkor. Milton shows the character of the fallen angel as being capable of adapting to various situations and of creating his own meanings and contexts (60). In the first two books Satan deliberately portrays himself as a mixture of the epic and the tragic hero, limited by his vices which are *imposed* on him by God. After all Satan is called the first liar and the master of disguise: he may be incapable of the creation of anything genuine, but he does copy God in many, always skewed ways: for instance when he creates Pandemonium in the image of Heaven, and when he fathers Death, which is generally seen as a parody of the begetting of the Son by the Father (Frye 19). As Christ is the Word of God, Death may be perceived as the Word of Satan. Thus Satan, his son Death, and his daughter Sin, who is simultaneously a mother to his son, form a perverted Trinity (Fowler 129n).

---

22 The interpretation of the scene is complicated due to Satan's ability to "dismiss unattractive facts from his consciousness" (Carey 137). We do not know if the fallen angel lies deliberately (which was seconded by Lewis) or believes the idea. Interestingly, the angels seem not to have any knowledge about their creation; similarly, the Ainur cannot penetrate some of the secrets of Ilúvatar.

The complication is that Satan does not do *everything* deliberately. Initially he *pretends* to be a hero who has taken arms against a merciless tyrant. The fallen angel covers himself in lies, but it turns out that at some point he must have started to absorb them himself. It seems that Stanley Fish is right when he claims that, having decided to separate from God, Satan alters his relationship both with the Omnipotent and with the universe (xxxii). He generates a new reality, where he encounters an authoritarian, unjust Father, who has a weakness for His younger (and unworthy) son. Because his sight is distorted by pride and envy (xxvi), Satan imitates the real world and its ideas (kingship, kingdom, loyalty, and the Trinity) in his own distorted image, and when he does this "he has no choice (he has already made it) but to live in it, to see what it allows him to see, to draw conclusions based on its assumed outlines, to read the present and project possible futures by its lights" (xxxiii). Hunter's comparison of the fallen angel to a virus is apt, as Satan manages to imprint his inner Hell on whatever he encounters, be this his companions, Eve, or even the animals in Paradise.[23]

The Devil succeeds in persuading his companions that they rebelled against a tyrant. Worse, he gradually transfers his own vision of the world onto them. His usual technique of temptation consists first of flattery, then the introduction of a sense of frustration with the state of things before and after the Fall, and in the final stage he directs the anger and frustration he has induced towards the alleged culprit, God. Satan manages to perfect the technique by using it on other rebel angels; however, he shows his mastery only when he directs the craft towards himself and succeeds (Wójcicka 61-66). The Foe will be able to seduce *himself* into believing that he actually *is* a tragic hero. Also with Eve he tries to achieve his goal by using this already triumphant strategy, but the situation will turn out to be more complicated and the Devil will have to use something more than pure flattery. In the end he will be successful in taking advantage of Eve's innocence and, perversely, intelligence. Nonetheless, it has to be emphasised that in *Paradise Lost* humans are no real enemies for Satan, and he never lowers himself to quarrel directly with them. His sole aim is to

---

23 He spreads his own sense of despair, which he can never be free from. Milton appears to foreshadow what Søren Kierkegaard will say in the nineteenth century: people in despair infect others with their sense of despair – not only do they confirm their state in others, the very act is simultaneously a temporary relief, but also a revenge on the world for this state (Zuziak 228).

take revenge on God: he wants to ruin the happiness of humans solely because he wants to cross God. He feels insulted at the sight of the human couple (he claims humans are inferior[24] material creatures, not so much advanced compared to angels, *probably* having been made of earth) but at the same time he is attracted to them due to their resemblance to the Creator.

Melkor, in turn, acts on his hatred towards the creation in general.[25] For him all beings created by Ilúvatar are only potential slaves, which reminds one of Satan's desire in *Genesis B* to enslave humanity. The fallen Ainur is only able to feel a mixture of hatred and fear towards humans. While Melkor's techniques of influence and corruption are seemingly more diverse than those of Milton's Satan they still possess the same basis: a mixture of truth and untruth[26] and the exploitation of the victim's weakness. At the same time he manifests extreme cruelty and violence through his actions, whereas Milton's Devil is generally a creature of great speeches but of little action – he talks a lot about his vicious plans, but for the most part he is passive. In comparison, Melkor is characterized by aggression and brutality; in addition he does not avoid inflicting tortures. In order to turn the Elves against Orome Melkor does not hesitate to send ghosts to spy and capture them, thus cunningly enhancing their fear and using it to his advantage (S 46). Attempting to obtain the Silmarils he seeks a way to ruin Fëanor. He does not act directly but rather chooses to spread lies in order to spread discord among the Noldor. Being able to inject his ideas into the hearts of others, he succeeds in winning many Elves. While they are certain these are their own thoughts, it is he who planted the idea that the Valar took the Elves to Aman out of jealousy, and that they deliberately hid from the Firstborn the future appearance of Men, who are to take their place.[27] All of the above il-

---

24 Flannagan claims that Satan perceives humans as a *little* inferior, which for him is a reflection of Psalm 8.5: "For thou has made him a little lower than the angels, and hast crowned him with glory and honour" (445). However, it may appear that although Satan sees the humans as a *little* inferior, what is most important for him is the fact that they *are* inferior. It is his understanding that the elevation of a creature inferior to him is done by God deliberately.
25 For comparison see Watkins 5.
26 Interestingly, similarly to Satan Melkor is called the master of lies and disguise.
27 Jonathan Evans is certainly right when he claims that the lie is quite believable, since there is a minuscule grain of truth in it: "Both the "Ainulindalë" and the "Valaquenta" describe a development that comes as a surprise to the Valar: the coming of the Elves and Men, children of Ilúvatar, the third theme in the cosmic music whose meaning and purpose the Ainur do not fully comprehend. Nor do the Elves, it seems" (199). The Elves are honoured with the gift of engendering more beauty than the rest of Ilúvatar's Children; however, Men are supposed to be blessed with another gift, the inextinguishable desire to "seek beyond the world" (S 35), which will be appeased only in death.

lustrate the fallen Ainur's ability to play upon the weaknesses of the creatures he wants to corrupt (for instance, the Noldors' pride, Fëanor's love for the Silmarils and his desire for freedom and power), a trait he shares with Milton's Satan.

Similarly, he tempts Ungoliant by making use of her insatiabile hunger. He says: "Do as I bid; and if thou hunger still when all is done, then I will give thee whatsoever thy lust may demand" (*S* 77), a blatant lie, and maybe a copy of the fallen angel's seduction directed towards his children, Sin and Death: "there ye shall be fed and fill'd / Immeasurably; all things shall be your prey" (*PL* 2.843-44).

It is worth noting at this point that Ungoliant herself is an intriguing figure: a being of unknown descent.[28] It is believed that in ages past "she descended from the darkness that lies about Arda, when Melkor first looked down in envy upon the Kingdom of Manwë, and that in the beginning she was one of those that he corrupted to his service" (*S* 76). She is begotten when Melkor feels envy towards Manwë for the first time, which is strangely analogous to the birth of Sin in *Paradise Lost*. This occurs during a conspiratorial debate in Heaven against God and His Son when Satan is surprised by a sudden pain and dizziness, which engenders a fair, goddess-like figure: Sin jumps out of the left side of her father's head.[29] Satan finds the new creature to be his "perfect image" (*PL* 2.764), becomes "enamour'd" (2.765) and violates her.[30]

Ungoliant, who at the beginning is *corrupted* by Melkor[31] and serves under his command, decides at one point to become the "mistress of her lust" (*S* 76), which is not only reminiscent of Sin's separation from her father but may also

---

28 This in a sense parallels the ambiguity of the origin of evil in the world.
29 Her birth is a parody of the creation of Athena (Flannagan 403), and of Eve (Grzegorzewska 22), but may also be a play on Gnostic myths about Sophia. Barbara Kiefer Lewalski argues, moreover, that Sin's meeting with her father is "a grotesquely comic reprise of those tender and pathetic scenes of familial love in the *Iliad* in which Andromache, Thetis, and Hecuba plead with their warrior husbands and sons to avoid battle" (60).
30 Flannagan suggests that the bond between Satan and Sin is not only incestuous but also narcissistic (403). As she is the fallen angel's perfect image, when he falls in love with her or lusts after her he reveals his passion and love of himself. Tanner, who proposes to read the myth as a representation of self-temptation (48), observes that by the story Milton demonstrates the ambiguity that pervades the notion of free will: the myth "acknowledges that, at the deepest level, complete self-determination begins to look more like compulsion than like free choice. [...] the evil to which Satan gives birth also possesses him; he does not appear so much to choose evil, rationally and deliberately, as to succumb to it in pain and lust" (49).
31 For a slightly different analysis of the character of Ungoliant see Sly 116-17.

be a play on Melkor's own act of estrangement from God. Meanwhile Sin gives birth to Death, which transforms her into "a formidable shape; / [...] Woman to the waste, and fair, / But ended foul in many a scaly fould / Voluminous and vast, a Serpent arm'd / With mortal sting [...]" (*PL* 2.649-653).

Ungoliant changes her shape, too: after the separation from Melkor she adopts the form of a spider "of monstrous form" (*S* 77). As far as her primary shape and emergence in the story remind us of Sin, her insatiability and successive metamorphosis is a trait of Sin's son, Death. Her gluttony and voracity is seen already in the beginning when she craves for light though hating it: she sucks up all the light she is able to find, up to starvation. When Melkor offers her unlimited sustenance, lust overcomes her fear. She weaves a cloak of darkness over Melkor and herself, *Unlight*,[32] and produces a ladder of woven ropes (*S* 77). This event corresponds with the scene in *Paradise Lost* where Sin and Death resolve to set off for the Earth and build a bridge over chaos (Book 10). Her subsequent transformation, resulting from ravenousness, "she swelled to a shape so vast and hideous" (*S* 80), evokes Melkor's terror. In the future, he will be almost defeated by her as a consequence of having endowed her with his own power.[33]

How is it possible that an Ainu is terrified at the sight of such a monstrosity and nearly overthrown by an inferior creature? Both Melkor-Morgoth and Satan provide a good illustration of Milton's words in *Samson Agonistes*: "All wickedness is weakness" (834). At first both are perfect, heavenly beings, but they decide to separate from their Creators, and while Satan is cast down to Hell, Melkor is allowed to venture into Arda with other Ainur. Yet every fall has its repercussions.

David Daiches and John S. Tanner argue that Sin's metamorphosis is an illustration of the fifteenth verse of the first chapter of the Epistle of James: "Then

---

32 Unlight provides yet another resemblance to the characters of Milton's epic. It is not known which substance Ungoliant is made of and what shape she has in the beginning. She takes on the form of a spider; however, she still possesses an unbelievable ability to expand, grow, transform (especially due to Melkor's powers). Thus she resembles Satan's child, Death: "The other shape, / If shape it might be call'd that shape had none / Distinguishable in member, joynt, or limb, / Or substance might be call'd that shadow seem'd, / For each seem'd either; black it stood as Night [...]" (*PL* 2.666-70). It is significant that Ungoliant possesses also the power to control the aforementioned Unlight ("in which things seemed to be no more, and which eyes could not pierce, for it was void," *S* 77).
33 It is interesting that she will take shelter in the place later called the Valley of Dreadful *Death* (*S* 86).

when lust hath conceived, it bringeth forth sin; and sin, when it is finished, bringeth forth death" (Daiches 176; Tanner 49). For Daiches the episode demonstrates "the true ugliness of all that Satan has done and produced" (176), and while initially the reader finds the Devil attractive, subsequently we are presented with "the true meaning of his actions. What is evil is unnatural and the unnatural is profoundly ugly" (176). The metamorphosis of Sin shows successive and inescapable changes which mark the nature of sin and, above all, the consequences of it.

A similar situation befalls the fallen angels (Lewalski 74), who are subject to gradual metamorphosis which is both moral and physical. Furthermore, the physical change seems to be a reflection of the moral transformation. In Book 1 the being that once was Lucifer is shocked when he notices in his lieutenant, Beelzebub, the change prompted by the Fall ("If thou beest he; But O how fall'n! how chang'd [...]," *PL* 1.84). Still, he rejects any possibility of a change inside himself, or he tries to suppress the thought, and he poses as strong and undefeated, as a magnificent "Arch Angel ruin'd" (1.594) who has not lost his "Original brightness" (1.593) or changed in his substance (1.256-57). He still possesses his remarkable ability to shape-shift (he pretends to be a Cherub, subsequently he transforms into a cormorant, abandoning the form in order to assume shapes of other animals, most notably a snake). Finally however, he will have to take note of his degradation: he does not remember his relationship with Sin until she enlightens him, and he is not recognized in Eden by the angelic guards, "Think not, revolted Spirit, thy shape the same, / Or undiminisht brightness, to be known / As when thou stoodst in Heav'n upright and pure; / That Glorie then, when thou no more wast good, / Departed from thee, and thou resembl'st now / Thy sin and place of doom obscure and foule" (4.835-40). At the same time, it is not only in stature and physical form that Satan is gradually eroded but also in his mind and character. Already during the War in Heaven he is able to experience the result of having been depraved of God's love and grace: he is felled by the supposedly weaker Abdiel, he feels pain, he is confused, and he tends to repeat phrases (God's or his own) like an echo, continuously changing meanings.³⁴ Soon, from the Promethean figure of Books 1 and 2, noble and indomitable on the surface, he degenerates into a frustrated creature of inner contradictions, torn between self-love and self-hate. In the last stage we witness him as a devious adversary of the human pair, manifesting atrocity, malevolence, and obsession with envy. The inner Hell that burns in him enfeebles him so much that he is afraid of Adam's strength and intellectual powers. He is in a state of permanent *katabasis* from the very moment he conceives pride and malice in his heart. Book 10 witnesses his transformation into a serpent, which enhances the sense of Satan's continuous Fall as even in the first lines of the poem Satan is already the Infernal Serpent (Daiches 154). He finishes where he starts and he has no possibility to repent.³⁵

Also Melkor is launched "on a downward moral trajectory, a 'ruinous path' leading twice to his imprisonment and ultimately to his banishment from Arda itself into the void of everlasting night" (Evans 208). However, whereas in Satan the mental change is gradual, in Melkor's case it is very radical: from the beginning he expresses only his hatred and malice towards the creation and is ready to commit whatever crime/sin it takes to achieve his goals. In *Paradise Lost* from the very start the reader expects to be able to condemn the Devil with ease, but it turns out that this is not the case, since Milton

---

34 It seems that Satan's situation is similar to that of humanity after the Fall. Falling, people lost contact with God, who withdrew from them, depriving them of His presence. With the long passage of time they forgot Him and forgot the truth, but they have been trying to reconstruct it with the use of myths.

35 Satan's redemption was a doctrinal issue. Carey claims that, according to Robins, Milton disagreed with Origen's theory of *apokatastasis*, while Patrides suggests that there had to be such a possibility in the poem (Carey 135). It would not be impossible for God, since the impossibility could be interpreted as an infringement on God's omnipotence. Thus Milton needed to show Satan as irredeemable but through his own fault. Indeed, it is the Devil himself who perceives his sin as absolute and irreversible. *The Silmarillion* seems not to provide any hope for Morgoth's redemption either – it is his nature that does not allow him to repent and be redeemed, no matter how many chances he has been given. At the same time, as Debbie Sly relates, "In his response to W. H. Auden's review of *RK*, Tolkien denies dealing 'in Absolute Evil' on the grounds that no 'rational being' can be 'wholly evil' (*L* 243); but he avoids any detailed examination of the nature of either Melkor or Sauron. They are never presented as suffering grief or remorse – when thwarted, they rage or sulk – and their original and fallen natures are represented symbolically in terms of the possession or forfeiture of fairness" (111). The issue of Melkor's end will return in Tolkien's other writings. In *The Lost Road* we may read: "In that day Tulkas shall strive with Morgoth, and on his right hand shall be Fionwë, and on his left Túrin Turambar, son of Húrin, coming from the halls of Mandos; and the black sword of Túrin shall deal unto Morgoth his death and final end; and so shall the children of Húrin and all Men be avenged" (333). Later on Tolkien will intend to enhance the power of Melkor: "Yet there is no power conceivable greater than Melkor save Eru only. Therefore Eru, if He will not relinquish His work to Melkor, who must else proceed to mastery, then Eru must come in to conquer him" (*MR* 322).

shows the fallen angel as a being torn by extremes, suffering from mental Hell, able to delude himself and simultaneously seduce the reader (Fish 19). Tolkien, by contrast, is quite explicit in his views on Melkor-Morgoth and never gives the fallen Ainur the chance to show himself in a different light. With the Fall all his attributes erode, and he does not exhibit any redeeming feelings. The only change that we can suspect him of is an ever growing desire for power, to the point of perverse infantilism (for instance when he announces himself the King of the World and forges an iron crown to be set with the Silmarils, which he "never took from his head, though its weight became a deadly weariness," *S* 86).

Nevertheless, a gradual deterioration is seen in Melkor's physical substance. At first, just like the other Valar, he is able to change his form, take on and abandon the visible frame, shape-shift (often in order to manipulate others), and to appear different than he really is (vide Satan as Leviathan, *PL* 1.203-08). Eventually, he will lose the ability when he joins forces with Ungoliant and thus stays in his visible form of a dark, terrible (a reflection of his malice and wrath) and colossal (manifestation of his aspirations) Lord.[36] Similarly to Satan, he wants to be seen as powerful and majestic, "as a mountain that wades in the sea and has its head above the clouds and is clad in ice and crowned with smoke and fire" (*S* 11),[37] but these are only appearances. Torn by his obsessions and cut off from the source of his creation, Ilúvatar, he is subject to fear and anger, which devour him from the inside. Gradually he will also suffer other changes: susceptibility to pain and wounds (for instance in his fight with Fingolfin, or the burns he receives from the Silmarils) and dispersion of power, "for as he grew in malice, and sent forth from himself the evil that he conceived in lies and creatures of wickedness, his might passed into them and was dispersed [...]"[38] (*S* 113). In the case of both the fallen angel and of the fallen Ainur the downfall is related to their negative development and may be described as exceptionally shameful. Satan arrives in Pandemonium with an air of triumph, but what he encounters is a concert of hisses. His rebel companions, and in a moment he himself, are transformed into serpents, and

---

36 See also Sly 111 and Watkins 4.
37 Compare the passage for instance with Milton's *PL* 1.195-98, 203-8, 286-89, or 292-94. In both cases the words resonate only with "Semblance of worth, not substance" (*PL* 1.529).
38 While his action is deliberate, it results in a weakening.

as such they are placed in a grove, among trees laden with numerous forbidden fruits. They suffer extreme hunger and thirst, and the only way to quench it is to eat the fruit; nonetheless, instead of Fruit they: "Chewd bitter Ashes, which th' offended taste / With spattering noise rejected: oft they assayd, / Hunger and thirst constraining, drugd as oft, / With hatefullest disrelish writh'd their jaws / With soot and cinders fill'd [...]" (*PL* 10.565-570). The punishment is thus absolutely grotesque since the Foe is confined to the shape he himself has chosen. Moreover, he is doomed to feed on the Fruit he has selected as the tool of temptation.

Morgoth's punishment is similarly appropriate. He had no qualms about inflicting suffering and torture, and he used physical force to achieve his aims: now he was going to be treated in the same way. Although he debases himself before the Valar as before and stoops to begging for pardon, this time no one heeds him. At first "his feet were hewn from under him, and he was hurled upon his face" (*S* 303), as if to punish his pride. Afterwards "he was bound with the chain Angainor which he had worn aforetime, and his iron crown," which he claimed was a symbol of his power over the Earth, "they beat into a collar for his neck" (*S* 303), a symbol of submission. Then "his head was bowed upon his knees" (*S* 303), as if in perpetual act of defeat. Finally he is cast through the Door of Night beyond the Walls of the World into the Timeless Void, the same Void he laboriously roamed in search of the Imperishable Flame.

John Milton's Satan and J.R.R. Tolkien's Melkor are two versions of the scriptural Devil. Even though the author of *Paradise Lost* was a Protestant and Tolkien a follower of Catholicism, they both make use of the same tradition in the construction of their figures. What is also interesting is the fact that Tolkien seems to be as much indebted to Milton as to Scripture. Not only is the rebellion in Ilúvatar's Heaven reminiscent of Milton's fallen angel's revolt but further correspondences between the characters have been found as well: the ability to shape-shift, followed by a physical and mental deterioration, which accompanies the change of names; ambitions of independence; the birth of Ungoliant (Sin/Death); the techniques of temptation and depravation; the corruption of Ilúvatar's Children;[39] irredeemability. The most significant differences include Milton's focus on Satan's psychological profile and hence the intended complexity of the character. Milton's fallen angel is able to convince the readers that he really believes his God is a tyrant. This figure of Satan, shown as someone who is occasionally capable of a "good" thought, might even, unlike Tolkien's Melkor, be capable of evoking the readers' sympathy. Other disparities between the two characters include Melkor's active, as opposed to Satan's passive, brutality, and his aspirations towards independent creation, which contrast with those of Satan, who does not cherish any such hopes and even refuses to acknowledge God's power of creation.

Bearing in mind the differences between Tolkien and Milton, it is telling that there is an underlying correspondence between the figure of the fallen angel and the fallen Ainu. What is more, both works manage to present certain ideas to be pondered upon, emphasizing the ambiguities that pervade the concepts elucidated by the tradition: the unclear origin of evil, the strength of temptation, or the weakness of humans. In both we may discern hope intermingled with despair: although the rebel creatures that bring ruin are finally punished, the sin they planted in humans will last.

---

[39] Both *Paradise Lost* and *The Silmarillion* show that the Fall of mankind was in some way initiated by an earlier Fall, that is of Satan and of Melkor. As has been noted by Jonathan Evans, Melkor manages to deprave "an originally sinless race – in Tolkien, *races*, including Men" (206). However, Tolkien does not incorporate the Fall of Men into the narrative, and the Men we encounter are already corrupted: "Like Milton, Tolkien assumes the Fall of Man to be predicated on a prior fall – Satan's/Melkor's. But unlike Milton, Tolkien chooses *not* to make this event the central conflict of his story but only one of its many effects" (206).

Similarities between Tolkien's Melkor in *The Silmarillion* and Milton's Satan in *Paradise Lost*

Ambiguity about the origin of evil	• Both works embrace the elements of Augustinian theology as far as the origin of evil is concerned, sharing also its ambiguity. • Satan and Melkor are among the most powerful beings of their kind, perfect and rational, but still they fall. In both works the Fall happens to them rather than being a consequence of a free choice.
Good nature before the Fall	• In both cases we find suggestive hints; there is, however, no possibility to verify them by means of a reliable account by a witness.
The Fall	• The Falls of Melkor and Satan happen before the creation of, respectively, Arda and the Earth. • The rebellions are not a threat to God / Ilúvatar, but a tool for a greater good. • In both works: "the first fall of a created being is shown as concomitant with an act of *making*" (Evans 209). • The Falls of Satan and Melkor indirectly initiate the Fall of mankind.
Change of names illustrating the darkening of character	• Melkor ("He who arises in Might") is cursed with the name Morgoth ("The Black Enemy"), which corresponds to Lucifer's ("Light-bearer") new appellation, Satan ("The Adversary").

Sins (Pride, Envy, Lust)	• Pride: In both cases we witness the emergence of the belief in one's own powers and a desire to become an independent entity. • Envy: Melkor's envy of Ilúvatar's power of creation; envy of the Valar (especially Manwë); envy of the Children of Ilúvatar. Satan's envy of Christ and of Adam and Eve. • Lust: in Melkor's case it is lust for the Silmarils; sexual lust at the sight of Lúthien. Satan's lust is visible in the birth of Sin and her subsequent violation by him; Satan is seen as Eve's first forbidden sexual partner, "impregnating" her with his tongue (Lehnhof 38).
Techniques of temptation and other abilities	• Both characters are called the masters of lies and disguise. Melkor's techniques of temptation possess the same basis as Satan's: untruth mixed with truth, the exploitation of a victim's weaknesses, injection of ideas, contamination. • Both characters possess a remarkable ability to shape-shift. • No ability to produce anything genuine: only (mocking) imitations and perversions of the original.
Hell	• Melkor's first dwelling, Utumno, and Satan's Hell comprise an icy region, with heat and frost under their masters' command.
North as evil	• Both works embrace the direction of North as evil: Lucifer's palace is in the north, just as Melkor's fortress, Utumno; another of Melkor's domains, Angband, is in the northwest.

| Degeneration | - In both cases the fallen angelic beings lose most of their heavenly attributes and waste the gifts bestowed upon them.
- Both are in the state of permanent katabasis: with the course of events they are subject to physical and mental degeneration. Satan: felled by (weaker?) Abdiel; feels pain; he is confused and tends to repeat phrases like an echo; he is afraid of Adam's strength and intellectual powers. Melkor: is subject to fear and anger, which devour him from the inside; gradual susceptibility to pain and wounds; dispersion of power and the ensuing weakening.
- In the final stage Morgoth "became ever more bound to the earth" (*S* 113), while Satan in the shape of a snake is "mixt with bestial slime" (*PL* IX, 165).
- Both experience a change of substance and the loss of ability to transform. |
|---|---|

The punishment – ironic and grotesque	• Satan and his companions are imprisoned in the shape of snakes, suffering extreme hunger and thirst. The only way to quench it is to feed on the fruit Satan has selected as the tool of temptation; nonetheless, it does not bring relief but intensifies the torment. • Morgoth's punishment is equally ironic: "his feet were hewn from under him, and he was hurled upon his face" (*S* 303), as if to punish his pride, afterwards "he was bound with the chain Angainor which he had worn aforetime, and his iron crown" (a symbol of his power over the Earth), "they beat into a collar for his neck" (*S* 303) (a symbol of submission), then "his head was bowed upon his knees" (*S* 303), as if in perpetual act of defeat. Finally he is cast through the Door of Night beyond the Walls of the World into the Timeless Void, the same Void he laboriously roamed in search of the Imperishable Flame. • Possible irredeemability.

The figure of Ungoliant, corresponding to that of Sin and Death	• The emergence of Ungoliant is analogous to the birth of Sin. Ungoliant "descended from the darkness that lies about Arda, when Melkor first looked down in envy upon the Kingdom of Manwë," while Sin springs from the left side of Satan's head during a conspiratorial debate in Heaven against God and His Son. • Separation of Ungoliant and Sin from their 'masters.' • Transformation of Ungoliant and Sin following the separation from their masters. Ability of expansion, growth, transformation – a trait Ungoliant shares with Death. • Insatiability – a trait shared by Ungoliant and Death. • The building of a passage: Ungoliant weaves a cloak of darkness over Melkor and herself and produces a ladder of woven ropes (*S* 77); Sin and Death resolve to set off for the Earth and build a bridge over chaos (Book 10). • Ungoliant poses a threat to Melkor, just as Death does to Satan. • After a confrontation with Melkor she takes shelter in the place later called the Valley of Dreadful *Death* (*S* 86).

Differences between Tolkien's Melkor in *The Silmarillion* and Milton's Satan in *Paradise Lost*

Psychology	• In-depth psychological view of Milton's Satan; in comparison, Melkor's inner life is not presented or commented upon in detail. • Redeeming moments in *Paradise Lost* vs. no redeeming feelings/traits in Melkor-Morgoth. • Satan's gradual mental change versus Melkor's 'more radical' one. • Attempts of Melkor at creation vs. Satan's disillusionment in this area and transferring the disillusionment onto his vision of God. • Satan's war is with God – he does not care about humans, they are only a means to thwart God's design; he is able to appreciate their beauty and the beauty of the Earth. Melkor's actions are based on his hatred against creation in general. He strives only for satisfaction of his selfish desires and is motivated by a lust for destruction. For him all beings created by Ilúvatar are nothing but potential slaves.
Actions	• Milton's Satan is a passive creature of great speech but little action; Melkor is driven by desire for destruction and manifests extreme cruelty and violence through his actions.

Bibliography

CAREY, John. "Milton's Satan." *Cambridge Companion to Milton.* Ed. Dennis Danielson. Cambridge: Cambridge UP, 1989. 131-145.

CLINES, David J. A. "The Significance of the 'Sons of God' (Gen. 6,1-4) in the Context of Primeval History (Gen. 1-11)." *Journal for the Study of the Old Testament* 13 (1979): 33-46.

DAICHES, David. *Milton.* London: Hutchinson University Library, 1968.

ELIADE, Mircea. "Shamanism and Cosmology." *Shamanism: Archaic Techniques of Ecstasy.* Princeton: Princeton UP, 1964. 259-288.

EVANS, Jonathan. "The Anthropology of Arda." *Tolkien the Medievalist.* Ed. Jane Chance. London: Routledge, 2002. 194-224.

FENSOME, Matthew. "Morgoth's Ring." *J.R.R. Tolkien Encyclopedia. Scholarhip and Critical Assessment.* Ed. Michael D.C. Drout. New York and London: Routledge, Taylor & Francis, 2007. 436-438.

FISH, Stanley. *Surprised by Sin: The Reader in "Paradise Lost."* Cambridge, MA: Harvard UP, 1998.

FLANNAGAN, Roy C., ed. *The Riverside Milton.* Boston, New York: Houghton Mifflin, 1998.

FLIEGER, Verlyn. *Splintered Light: Logos and Language in Tolkien's World.* Grand Rapids, MI: Eerdmans, 1983.

FORNET-PONSE, Thomas. "Different Concepts of Evil in *The Lord of the Rings.*" *The Ring Goes Ever On. Proceedings of the Tolkien 2005 Conference Vol. 2.* Ed. Sarah Wells. The Tolkien Society, 2008. 78-90.

FORSYTH, Neil. *The Old Enemy: Satan and the Combat Myth.* Princeton: Princeton UP, 1987.

FOWLER, Alastair, ed. *Paradise Lost.* London: Longman, 1971.

FRYE, Northrop. *The Return of Eden. Five Essays on Milton's Epics.* Toronto and Buffalo: University of Toronto Press, 1965.

GRZEGORZEWSKA, Małgorzata. "'What I will is Fate': O przeznaczeniu i wolnej woli w *Raju utraconym* Johna Miltona." *Odrodzenie i Reformacja w Polsce* 51 (2007): 21-36.

HENDEL, R.S. "Of Demigods and the Deluge. Toward an Interpretation of Genesis 6.1-4." *Journal of Biblical Literature* 106 (1987): 13-26.

HOLMES, John R. "Milton." *J.R.R. Tolkien Encyclopedia. Scholarhip and Critical Assessment*. Ed. Michael D.C. Drout. New York and London: Routledge, Taylor & Francis, 2007. 428-429.

HUNTER, G. K. *Paradise Lost*. London: George Allen & Unwin, 1980.

HUTTAR, Charles A. "Tolkien, Epic Traditions, and Golden Age Myths." *Bloom's Modern Critical Views: J.R.R. Tolkien*. Ed. Harold Bloom. Chelsea House Publications, 2008. 3-16.

KLINE, Meredith. "Divine Kingship and Genesis 6:1-4." *Westminster Theological Journal* 24 (1962): 187-204.

LEHNHOF, Kent R. "'Impregn'd with Reason': Eve's Aural Conception in *Paradise Lost*." *Milton Studies* 41 (2003): 38-75.

LEWALSKI, Barbara Kiefer. *"Paradise Lost" and the Rhetoric of Literary Forms*. Princeton, NJ: Princeton UP, 1985.

LEWIS, Clive Staples. *A Preface to Paradise Lost*. London: Oxford UP, 1944.

MCGRATH, Alister. *Christian Literature: An Anthology*. Oxford: Blackwell Publishers, 2001.

MILTON, John. *Paradise Lost*. In *The Riverside Milton*. Ed. Roy C. Flannagan. Boston, New York: Houghton Mifflin, 1998. 297-710.

Samson Agonistes. In *The Riverside Milton*. Ed. Roy C. Flannagan. Boston, New York: Houghton Mifflin Company, 1998. 783-844.

PEARCE, Joseph. "Morgoth and Melkor." *J.R.R. Tolkien Encyclopedia. Scholarhip and Critical Assessment*. Ed. Michael D.C. Drout. New York and London: Routledge, 2007. 435-436.

REVARD, Stella Purce. *The War in Heaven: "Paradise Lost" and the Tradition of Satan's Rebellion*. London: Cornell UP, 1980.

ROSEBURY, Brian. "Tolkien in the History of Ideas." *Bloom's Modern Critical Views: J.R.R. Tolkien*. Ed. Harold Bloom. Chelsea House Publications, 2008. 89-120.

RUMBLE, Alexander R. "Junius Manuscript." *Medieval England: An Encyclopedia*. Ed. Paul E. Szarmach, M. Teresa Tavormina, and Joel T. Rosenthal. New York: Garland, 1998. 385-386.

RUSSELL, Jeffrey Burton. *The Devil: Perceptions of Evil from Antiquity to Primitive Christianity*. Ithaca, NY: Cornell UP, 1977.

The Prince of Darkness: Radical Evil and the Power of Good in History. Ithaca and London: Cornell UP, 1988.

SHIPPEY, Tom A. *Droga do Śródziemia (Road to Middle-Earth)*. Trans. Joanna Kokot. Zysk i S-ka, 2002.

SLY, Debbie. "Weaving Nets of Gloom: 'Darkness Profound' in Tolkien and Milton." *J.R.R. Tolkien and His Literary Resonances: Views of Middle-earth*. Ed. George Clark and Daniel Timmons. London: Greenwood Press, 2000. 109-119.

TANNER, John S. "'Say First What Cause': Ricoeur and the Etiology of Evil in *Paradise Lost*." *PMLA* 103.1 (1988): 45-56.

TOLKIEN, John Ronald Reuel. *The Lost Road and Other Writings*. Ed. Christopher Tolkien. Boston: Houghton Mifflin, 1987.

Morgoth's Ring. Ed. Christopher Tolkien. London: HarperCollins; Boston: Houghton Mifflin, 1993.

The Silmarillion. Ed. Christopher Tolkien. London: HarperCollins, 1999.

TURNER, Alice K. *Historia Piekła (The History of Hell)*. Trans. Jerzy Jarniewicz. Gdansk: Wydawnictwo Marabut, 2004.

WASILEWSKI, J. S. *Podróże do piekieł: rzecz o szamańskich misteriach*. Ludowa Spółdzielnia Wydawnicza, 1979.

WATKINS, Zach. "Satan and *The Silmarillion*: John Milton's Angelic Decline in J.R.R. Tolkien's Melkor." *The Grey Book* 1 (2005): 1-6.

WEBSTER, Richard. *Encyclopedia of Angels*. Woodbury, MN: Llewellyn Publications, 2009.

WOLF, Herbert M. *An Introduction to the Old Testament Pentateuch*. Chicago: Moody Publishers, 1991.

WÓJCICKA, Maria. "The Strategies of Temptation in *Paradise Lost*." *Approaches to Literature Part 1*. Ed. Grażyna Bystydzienska. Warsaw: Department of English Literature University of Warsaw, 2001. 61-68.

WRIGHT, Archie T. *The Origin of Evil Spirits the Reception of Genesis 6.1-4 in Early Jewish Literature*. Tübingen: Mohr Siebeck, 2005.

ZUZIAK, Władysław. "Wiara rozpaczy i wiara nadziei." *Człowiek wobec rozpaczy w filozofii Sørena Kierkegaarda*. Ed. Marek Urban, Władysław Zuziak. Kraków: Wydawnictwo Naukowe PAT, 2004. 218-243.

About the author

KATARZYNA BLACHARSKA obtained her M.A. degree in British Literature at the University of Warsaw in 2009 for the thesis titled "The Image of a Sad Rebel – the Presentation of Satan in John Milton's *Paradise Lost*". At present she is a doctoral student in the Institute of English Studies, University of Warsaw. Her research focuses on the works of John Milton. She is also interested in the perception of evil throughout history, representations of evil and the figure of the Devil in literature, as well as magic, despair, and melancholy in history and literature. She has published two articles: "Two Sins of John Milton's Satan" (2010) and "Satan's Prayer: the First Soliloquy of John Milton's Fallen Angel from the Perspective of Paul Ricoeur's Notion of Lamentation as Prayer" (2011).

Renata Leśniakiewicz-Drzymała

Berserkir, Bödvar Bjarki and the Dragon Fáfnir. The Influence of Selected Medieval Icelandic Sagas on Tolkien's Works for Children

Abstract

The following paper deals with the impact of selected medieval Icelandic sagas on Tolkien's minor works which are usually considered to have been written for children, such as *The Hobbit, The Adventures of Tom Bombadil* and *Farmer Giles of Ham*. The paper starts with an analysis of the character of Beorn and compares his unpredictable mood and ability to change skin with the attributes of the Norse warriors known as the *berserkir*. Afterwards parallels are drawn between Smaug and Fáfnir of the *Völsunga saga*, proving that the character of Tolkien's dragon was deeply influenced by the description of the Norse beast. The subsequent subject of consideration concerns some references to the Völsung legend that are present in the collection of Tolkien's poems, *The Adventures of Tom Bombadil*. Finally the description of Giles' arrival at the dragon's lair is compared with the analogous scene from the *Völsunga saga*, leading to the general conclusion that Tolkien's wide knowledge of the Norse literature and language allowed him to refashion many forgotten motifs from the old sagas and use them in some of his own minor works, labeled as mere children's stories but in fact revealing a considerable degree of sophistication.

J.R.R. Tolkien's best known source of inspiration, next to Anglo-Saxon materials, is Norse mythology, literature, and language.[1] Apart from many valuable studies on Tolkien's influences,[2] there exist numerous of non-scholarly publications, such as Tolkien guides "for dummies" or popular publications about the origins of Middle-earth,[3] which discover the fact that the names of dwarves in *The Hobbit* are taken from *The Elder Edda*,[4] that the term *Middle-earth* is

---

1 See Risden 18.
2 Foremost among these works is Tom Shippey's *The Road to Middle-earth*.
3 See, for example, Colbert, Day (*Tolkien's Ring* and *World*), and Harvey.
4 *The Elder Edda*, also called *The Poetic Edda* or *Sæmundar Edda*, is one of the most important sources for Norse mythology. It is a collection of Old Norse poems preserved in the medieval Icelandic manuscript called *Codex Regius*, thought to have been written in the 1270s. One of the Eddaic poems, the *Völuspá* ("The Prophecy of the Seeress"), contains a section called *Dvergatal* ("Catalogue of Dwarves"), from which come the names of Tolkien's dwarves and the name of Gandalf.

a reflection of the Old Norse *Miðgarðr*,[5] that Gandalf is a type of Odin-like wanderer,[6] and that the difference between Tolkien's Light Elves and Dark Elves resembles Snorri Sturluson's distinction between *ljósálfar* and *dökkálfar*.[7] Tolkien's borrowing from Norse sources is a commonly known fact and one may well think that this matter is no longer a suitable field for further research. However, it seems a worthwhile project to examine Tolkien's Norse influences once more and determine how some medieval Icelandic sagas affected Tolkien's works that are usually thought to be intended for children, such as *The Hobbit*, *The Adventures of Tom Bombadil* and *Farmer Giles of Ham*.[8]

Tolkien's literary work that features most prominently Old Norse elements is *The Hobbit*, where we find the dwarves' names from *Dvergatal*.[9] However, in this paper we will not comment on the names of Thorin's companions. We shall rather start our considerations with the analysis of an enigmatic character, the skin-changer Beorn. Living alone in company of his animals Beorn is a strange creature, and full of contradictions.[10] His name comes from an Old English word for "bear", but it is also a poetic metaphor for "man" or rather "brave warrior" (as the Old Norse word *björn*). Despite his dangerous name, Beorn's lifestyle is quite idyllic – he keeps his bees, takes care of his sheep and ponies and looks after his

---

5 In Norse cosmology the universe consists of nine worlds: Miðgarðr, Ásgarðr, Vanaheimr, Jötunheimr, Álfheimr, Svartálfaheimr, Helheimr, Niflheimr and Muspellsheimr. They are all united by the cosmic ash tree, Yggdrasil. Miðgarðr, the realm of humans, is thought to be placed somewhere in the middle of the trunk of Yggdrasil and is surrounded by a great impassable ocean. Other worlds are inhabited by supernatural beings: gods, giants, elves, dwarves and dead men.

6 Odin was the most important god in Norse mythology during the Viking Age and the ruler of the Æsir, the major clan of the Norse gods. He was associated with dark magic, necromancy, poetry, war, battle rage and wisdom. He used to wander the world of men disguised as a lonely traveller – an old one-eyed man with a long beard and a staff, wearing a blue cloak and a wide-brimmed hat. However, during his visits in the underworld or in the world of giants, Odin mounted his eight-legged steed Sleipinir, the fastest of all horses. On Odin's influence on Gandalf, but also on Manwë, Makar and Meássë, see Burns, "Norse and Christian Gods" 169-170.

7 *The Prose Edda* of Snorri Sturluson (an Icelandic historian, poet, writer and politician) emphasizes the main differences between mythological light elves (*ljósálfar*) and dark elves (*dökkálfar*). This distinction, however, neither explains the existence of black elves (*svartálfar*) in Old Norse sources, nor does it give an answer to the question whether the dark/black elves are identical with the dwarves. On the differences between light and dark elves and on the ambiguity of Snorri's distinction see Motz 122 and Turville-Petre 231. On the influence of Snorri's problematic dichotomy on Tolkien's Elves see Shippey, "Light-elves" 1-15 and Wilkin 61-80. On Grimm's troubles with the terms 'elf' and 'dwarf' and on Tolkien's answer to this problem see Shippey, "Grimm" 90.

8 We will not include *Roverandom* in our discussion, although its plot also contains some Norse elements, such as Niord (Scandinavian sea god), Sea-serpent and the Viking master of mer-dog. However, the lack of references to Icelandic sagas excludes this novella from our sphere of interest.

9 On the names of Tolkien's dwarves and their connection with *The Elder Edda*, see Callahan 20; Brunsdale 49-50; Bryce 113-119 and Shippey, "Tolkien and Iceland" 195-196.

10 On the dichotomies in Beorn's personality see Burns, *Perilous Realms* 30-43.

beautiful garden. Nevertheless, Gandalf warns his companions that Beorn is a uniquely capricious host: "you must be careful not to annoy him, or heaven knows what will happen. He can be appalling when he is angry, though he is kind enough if humoured. Still I warn you he gets angry easily" (*H* 134-35). He also has an astonishing quality: "He is a skin-changer. He changes his skin: sometimes he is a huge black bear, sometimes he is a great strong black-haired man with huge arms and a great beard" (*H* 135). This ability evokes associations with a phenomenon encountered in Old Norse sources called *skipta hömum* ("to change the shape" / "to change the skin") and connects him with the warriors falling into battle fury, the *berserkir*.[11] According to Norse literature, they are elite warriors, who fight in the first ranks, cannot be hurt by any weapon and are immune to pain. The *berserkir* act like mad men, roar like animals, whose shape they are supposedly able to take, and kill everything on their way without distinguishing between friend and foe. The source of their battle rage is unclear, although there are several theories to explain their wild and uncontrolled behaviour, such as mental illness – schizophrenia or hysterical psychosis (Foote and Wilson 285) – hypnotic trance caused by ritual dancing (Davidson 87; Speidel 253-290) or state of intoxication induced by the consumption of alcohol and drugs, such as the highly hallucinogenic mushroom *Amanita muscaria* (Fabing 232). However, medieval Norse literature explains the madness of the *berserkir* in a different way. According to *YS*[12] their fury was caused by the influence and dark sorcery of Odin, since the *berserkir* were his chosen warriors, who "rushed forwards without armour, were as mad as dogs or wolves, bit their shields, and

---

11 The etymology of the term *berserkir* (sing. *berserkr*) is unclear and there are two highly probable hypotheses. The first assumes that the name of Scandinavian warriors comes from two words: *berr*, "naked", and *serkr*, "shirt" (Kuhn 218-27; Noreen 242-54), since the *berserkir* were thought to fight without shirts or armours, or even completely naked. The second hypothesis connects the name of these elite warriors with words *ber*, "bear", and *serkr*, "shirt" (See 129-36), since they usually wore bear skins. Another term associated in Norse sources with warriors falling into battle rage is *úlfheðnar* (sing. *úlfheðinn*), "men clothed in wolf skins".

12 *Ynglinga saga* was written by Snorri Sturluson around 1225 as the first part of his history of the ancient Norse kings, the *Heimskringla*. *YS* was based on the poem *Ynglingatal*, listing the kings of the Swedish royal House of Ynglings and written by the Norwegian 9th-century skald Thjódólfr of Hvinir. Snorri describes in his saga the arrival of the Norse gods from Asia to Scandinavia and tells how one of them, Yngvi-Freyr, founded the Yngling dynasty at Uppsala. Afterwards *YS* follows the line of the Ynglings from king Fjölnir, son of Yngvi-Freyr, to Rögnvaldr the Mountain-High. Some original stanzas from *Ynglingatal* were interwoven by Snorri into the content of his saga as a confirmation of the reliability of his record.

were strong as bears or wild bulls; they killed people, but neither fire nor iron could do them harm".[13]

The ability to change into a berserk was often inherited, and according to *ES*,[14] dealing with such a hot-headed member of a family was never an easy thing, even despite his other virtues.

> It was told of Úlf that he was a great householder. It was his custom to rise up early, and then go round among his workmen or his smiths, and to overlook his fields, and at times he would talk with such as needed his counsel. He could give good counsel in all things, for he was very wise. But everyday as evening drew on he became angry, so that few had courage to speak with him; he was sleepy, and it was commonly said that he was a great shape-shifter. He was called Kveldúlf [Evening-wolf].[15]

The same evening-anxiety characterizes Skalla-Grím Kveldúlfsson, who one day after dusk almost kills his son Egil in his fury (*ES* 117-118).

After the Christianization of Scandinavia the image of the elite warrior feeling neither pain no fear was replaced in sagas by the black legend of the berserk. Christian religion considered Odin with his tendency to cultivate dark magic as one of the servants of the devil and thus Odin's mad warriors were treated as allies of the demons. In Icelandic sagas the berserk is often depicted as the enemy of the true faith, who tries to destroy Christian morality by challenging one of the priests to an ordeal of fire.[16] Moreover, the berserkers seem to be possessed by evil forces, since they cannot control their attacks of blind fury

---

13 "Fóru brynjulausir ok váru galnir sem hundar eða vargar, bitu í skjǫldu sína, váru sterkir sem birnir eða griðungar; þeir drápu mannfólkit, en hvártki eldr né járn orti á þá" (*YS* 14). All quotations from Icelandic sagas, except for *The Volsunga saga*, have been translated from Old Norse by the author of this paper.

14 *Egils saga Skalla-Grímssonar* was written in the 12th century by an anonymous author and is considered to be one of the best of the Icelandic sagas. The plot of the saga is centered on the life of Egil Skalla-Grímsson, famous Icelandic skald and berserk, a very ambiguous character, who on the one hand is a great warrior and brilliant poet, but on the other a cruel, violent man, who commits his first murder at the age of seven. Egil's multi-faceted personality is reflected in the saga by ambivalent attributes of his family, consisting of men either handsome and noble or ugly, violent and able to go berserk.

15 "Svá er sagt, at Úlfr var búsýslumaðr mikill; var þat siðr hans, at rísa upp árdegis ok ganga þá um sýslur manna eða þar er smiðir váru ok sjá yfir fénað sinn ok akra, en stundum var hann á tali við menn þá, er ráða hans þurftu; kunni hann til alls góð ráð at leggja, því at hann var forvitri. En dag hvern er at kveldi leið, þá gerðist hann styggr, svá at fáir menn máttu orðum við hann koma; var hann kveldsvæfr; þat var mál manna, at hann væri mjǫk hamrammr; hann var kallaðr Kveldúlfr" (*ES* 2-3).

16 The idea of such an ordeal was to prove the weakness of the Christian God. However, when it comes to the trial, berserkers are always unable to cross the fire that was consecrated by a Christian priest, as it happens for example in *Brennu-Njáls saga* (*BNS* 242).

and thus do more harm than good in the ranks of their own allies. *HSH*[17] tells of twelve skin-changer brothers: "it was commonly said that they kill their own men and damage their own ship when they are taken by the fury of the berserkers."[18] Many sagas describe mad warriors not only as useless, but also as slow-witted or even hopelessly stupid, for their adversaries easily manage to deceive them, lure them into a cunning trap and kill them in a most foolish way, which is completely unsuitable for such great and strong fighters as the famous *berserkir* (*EBS*[19] 45-48; *GS*[20] 68-78, 151-53). Their almost supernatural powers are no longer desirable in the converted society, so the berserkers are no more involved in epic battles under the banners of famous kings. Instead they use their strength and invulnerability to challenge common people to duel under the veil of asking for the hand of their daughters, and seize their wealth after killing them in an unfair fight.[21] The picture of the berserk presented in Icelandic sagas shows vividly that the mad warrior became a relict of the pagan past, his unpredictable and dangerous attacks of rage were explained by the devil's influence, and he was considered as a dull-witted murderer with foam on his mouth, using his supernatural strength to kill weaker opponents and seize their property.

Such orc-like behaviour is obviously foreign to Beorn's nature, but still he is quite a sinister person. Although he is a good and caring householder like Kveldúlf, just as the latter he is also sometimes in a dangerous frame of mind and has to be treated with care, so that staying with him under one roof after

---

17 *Hervarar saga ok Heiðreks konungs* is a legendary saga from the 13th century. It deals with the cursed sword Tyrfing and the fate of its owners, but also describes the wars between Goths and Huns. *HSH* combines matter from several older sagas and contains valuable information about Gothic wars, and thus it is a very useful source for Swedish medieval history.

18 "Því at þeim hafði þat at váða orðit, at þeir höfðu drepit menn sína ok hroðit skip sín, þá er berserksgangr fór at þeim" (*HSH* 6).

19 *Eyrbyggja saga* was written by an anonymous author most likely at the turn of the 13th to the 14th century. Its plot is centered on a long-standing feud between two important chieftains of Iceland, Snorri goði and Arnkel goði, but the saga also includes numerous ghost-tales, such as the stories of undead men (*draugar*) coming into the house to warm themselves by the fire.

20 *Grettis saga Ásmundarsonar* was probably written at the beginning of the 14th century by an anonymous author, but it is believed that it may have been based on a previous account of Grettir's life written by Sturla Thórdarson, an Icelandic historian, writer and politician living in the 13th century. The saga deals with the life of Grettir Ásmundarson, an Icelandic outlaw, who was afraid of the dark due to the curse that gave him the unwanted ability of seeing ghosts after dusk. Grettir is often compared to the Anglo-Saxon hero Beowulf, since the basic situation for both heroes is similar, they have to fight similar enemies and suffer similar fates and the episode of Grettir's fight with a terrible she-troll bears considerable resemblance to the scene of Beowulf's fight with Grendel's mother.

21 On the motif of the unwanted berserk admirer see Blaney 279-94.

dusk can be perilous. Bilbo is fully conscious of this fact when he wakes up in the night and hears something strange. "There was a growling sound outside, and a noise as of some great animal scuffling at the door. Bilbo wondered what it was, and whether it could be Beorn in enchanted shape, and if he would come in as a bear and kill them" (*H* 150). The hobbit's fears are not completely unjustified because even if Beorn does not fall into a berserk's fury *sensu stricto*, he is still a fierce and merciless enemy. Those who were fighting in the Battle of Five Armies could find this out when he arrived among them, changing the course of combat.

> In that last hour Beorn himself had appeared – no one knew how or from where. He came alone, and in bear's shape; and he seemed to have grown almost to giant-size in his wrath. The roar of his voice was like drums and guns; and he tossed wolves and goblins from his path like straws and feathers. He fell upon their rear, and broke like a clap of thunder through the ring. The dwarves were making a stand still about their lords upon a low rounded hill. Then Beorn stooped and lifted Thorin, who had fallen pierced with spears, and bore him out of the fray. Swiftly he returned and his wrath was redoubled, so that nothing could withstand him, and no weapon seemed to bite upon him. He scattered the bodyguard, and pulled down Bolg himself and crushed him. Then dismay fell on the Goblins and they fled in all directions. (*H* 334-35)

The idea of a huge bear appearing on the battlefield and scattering the ranks of enemies may have been borrowed by Tolkien from *HSK*,[22] in which one of the devoted champions of the Danish king Hrólf is Böðvar Bjarki. His nick-name means "bear-cub" and he is a son of Björn ("bear") and Bera ("she-bear"). The father of our hero, in contrast to Beorn, is a bear during the day and a man at night, but Bjarki is capable of retaining his human form all the time. Since he came to Denmark from Gautland and defeated a terrible monster harassing Hrólf's court, he is sometimes considered to be an analogous hero to Beowulf (whose name also means "bear" – "bee-wolf"). However, the deed of Bjarki that is most important for our discussion took place during the last battle of king Hrólf against his treacherous brother-in-law Hjörvard. The combat was fierce and Hrólf's warriors were in great need.

---

22 *Hrólfs saga kraka ok kappa hans* is a late legendary saga describing the heroic deeds of the Danish king Hrólf Kraki and his champions. It is thought to have been written in the period between c. 1230 and c. 1450. Many of the characters from the saga are also known under corresponding Old English forms of their names from Anglo-Saxon poems. For example in *Beowulf* Hrólf Kraki appears as Hroðulf, his father Helgi as Halga, his grandfather Halfdan as Healfdene, his uncle Hróarr as Hroðgar, and the royal house of Hrólf, the Skjöldungs, as the Scyldings.

Then Hjörvard and his men saw a huge bear going before king Hrólf's men, always nearest to where the king was. He killed more men with his paw than any five of the king's other champions; strokes and projectiles glanced off him. He crashed under him both men and horses of king Hjörvard's army, and everything that came in his way he crushed in his teeth, so that panic seized king Hjörvard's army.[23]

Meanwhile another champion of Hrólf's, Hjatli, notices Bjarki's absence on the battlefield and finds him sitting motionless in the king's dwelling. Since Hjatli is mocking his courage, Bjarki stands up with a yawn and prepares himself to battle with words: "I tell you truly that now the help I can give the king is many times less than it was before you called me up from here".[24] The great bear disappears and the combat ends with the death of king Hrólf and his champions.

The bear is Bjarki's *fylgja*, a guarding being assuming the shape of a woman or an animal, a sort of spiritual emanation (*hamr, hugr*) of the hero. In sagas one may send one's *fylgja* to some distant place after falling into a kind of trance, the end of which is usually signalized by a languorous yawn. Thus it is obvious that by disturbing Bjarki, Hjatli deprives king Hrólf of his most powerful weapon and at the same time decides the fate of the battle.

Contrary to the bear of *HSK*, Tolkien's Beorn is no ghost, appearing as he does among warriors. He is a creature of flesh and blood, though his nature may be considered somewhat supernatural, and when he is furious weapons cannot harm him. One could argue that he is Tolkien's "answer" to the myth of the bloodthirsty berserk guided by his blind fury, a demon-worshipper and ruthless plunderer. Mumbling and impetuous, Beorn is simultaneously caring for his beloved animals, which he treats with great gentleness. He is some kind of Treebeard-like creature, very deeply tied to nature and friendly to those who are honest, but he can also be unpredictable and very perilous, particularly when someone poses a threat to his domain or wants to abuse his animals. Beorn

---

[23] "Þat sjá þeir Hjǫrvarðr ok menn hans, at bjǫrn einn mikill ferr fyrir Hrólfs konungs mǫnnum ok jafnan þar næst, sem konungrinn var; hann drepr fleiri menn með sínum hrammi en fimm aðrir kappar konungs; hrjóta af honum hǫgg ok skotvápn, en hann brýtr undir sik bæði menn ok hesta af liði Hjǫrvarðar konungs ok allt þat, sem í nánd er, mylr hann með sínum tǫnnum, svá at illr kurr kemr í lið Hjǫrvarðar konungs" (*HSK* 100).
[24] "Ek segi þér at sǫnnu, at nú má ek mǫrgum hlutum minna lið veita konunginum, en áðr þú kallaðir mik upp heðan" (*HSK* 102).

needs no tricks, like sending his spiritual emanation on the battlefield, because he can appear there by himself, assuming the shape of a terrifying huge bear. He needs no bear skins because he is a skin-changer, and he does not have to fall into fury that would give him the strength of a bear because he is the bear *par excellence*, the lord of bears. Such could have been a "reconstructed" berserk, a mighty, magnificent and perilous creature, before he shared the fate of the Norse gods, who were reduced to spiteful servants of the devil.

A real reconstruction that took place in Tolkien's mind concerned other powerful mythological creatures by which he has been fascinated since his childhood. "I desired dragons with a profound desire," he confessed in his essay "On Fairy-Stories". Unfortunately, early medieval literature of the North offered little for there were only two truly fearful dragons: the nameless beast in *Beowulf* and Fáfnir in the *Völsunga saga*.²⁵ According to Tom Shippey (*Road* 82), Tolkien's deep disappointment with Fáfnir's trivial personality was the very impulse that led to the creation of the mighty Smaug. But was Fáfnir really so disappointing? In a letter to Naomi Mitchison Tolkien wrote on the subject of his desire: "I find 'dragons' a fascinating product of imagination. But I don't think the *Beowulf* one is frightfully good. [...] Fafnir in the late Norse versions of the Sigurd-story is better; and Smaug and his conversation obviously is in debt there" (*L* 134). What was the "debt" mentioned in the letter? Was it only the inspiration for creating a creature more satisfying than its Norse prototype, or maybe Fáfnir had something more to offer? The answer is probably to be found in a section of *VS* which says a lot about the nature of dragons.

The saga describes how Fáfnir after receiving his death wound wants to find out the name and the family of his slayer, but Sigurd gives him an evasive answer: "Unknown to men is my kin. I am called a noble beast: neither father have I nor mother, and all alone have I fared hither" (*VS* 78). The dragon accuses Sigurd of telling lies and thus makes his slayer reveal his true identity. After that Fáfnir asks Sigurd another question: "Who egged thee on to this deed, and why wouldst

---

25 *Völsunga saga* is a legendary saga written c. 1200-1270 as a prose adaptation of Eddaic poems concerning the decline of the Völsungs. Its main character is the young hero Sigurd, probably the most famous dragon slayer in the European tradition. The plot of the saga centers on the fate of the families of the Völsungs and the Gjukungs, who are entangled in the terrible curse of the dragon's treasure. It echoes the destruction of the East Germanic tribe of the Burgundians during the Migration Period.

thou be driven to it? Hadst thou never heard how that all folk were afraid of me, and of the awe of my countenance? But an eager father thou hadst, O bright eyed swain!" (*VS* 79). Once again the beast gets an evasive answer that it was a "hardy heart", a "strong hand" and a "sharp sword" that urged the young hero to commit this deed. The angry dragon accuses Sigurd of being only a slave and doubts his courage, but quickly changes his mind and advises his slayer to leave the cursed gold in peace and to beware of Fáfnir's brother, Regin: "Such counsel I give thee, that thou take thy horse and ride away at thy speediest, for ofttimes it fails out so, [*sic*] that he who gets a death-wound avenges himself none the less" (*VS* 80-81). However, Sigurd does not listen to his words and takes the gold away, and at the same time the dragon dies.

At first sight the dragon's conversation with Sigurd seems to be far too long, boring and not quite comprehensible, and it has nothing to do with the brilliant dialogue between Bilbo and Smaug that takes place during their first meeting. Underneath this text, however, we may see the picture of a uniquely deceitful monster, showing at the moment of his death-agony all his might, malice and cleverness hidden from an inexperienced youngster. One can almost imagine how Fáfnir moderates his rage, lies motionless and observes his young slayer for the purpose of finding out who he is. The dragon behaves like a staid wise man and scolds Sigurd for his lie in order to confuse him and make him reveal his secrets. Using flattery he tries to learn about the initiator of the attack, and when he does not get a satisfying answer, he reveals his true nature by insulting Sigurd unfairly, calling him a bondsman and prisoner of war. Right after that he moderates himself once again and returning to his sweet tone he pretends to care for Sigurd's fate, and advises him to abandon the cursed treasure. However, by telling him about uncounted riches and by repeating simulated warnings, Fáfnir in fact skilfully feeds Sigurd's lust for gold and makes him fall under the spell of both his own speech and the glamorous dragon's treasure. In a moment the beast recklessly reveals itself when saying, "ofttimes it fails out so, that he who gets a death-wound avenges himself none the less". Fáfnir's revenge is the death of Regin, for he managed to make Sigurd distrust his fellow, as well as the pitiful doom of all holders of cursed treasure, which Sigurd rashly takes away. "That is the effect that dragon-talk has on the inexperienced" (*H* 261).

It is obvious how deeply the foregoing conversation has influenced the dialogue between Smaug and Bilbo. The hobbit also refuses to reveal his true name and uses fanciful riddles, while the cunning dragon presents a wide range of his abilities: sophisticated but shallow courtesy, malice and hypocritical empathy. He gives Bilbo good advice,[26] but at the same time, just as Fáfnir, he makes him distrust his friends by asking him seemingly caring questions.[27] Because of this speech Bilbo's trust in the dwarves' honesty is seriously impaired and he keeps the dragon's bitter words in his mind for a long time (*H* 267).

Smaug, however, despite his false politeness, reveals his true beastly nature when saying: "I know the smell (and taste) of dwarf – no one better" (*H* 259). These words, just as in the case of Fáfnir, expose Smaug as a uniquely perilous opponent, who is hiding his true intentions and ferocity beneath the mask of kindness and care, but still fails to play his role perfectly. A feature common to both dragons is also an inclination to boast about their strength and power. Even in his death-hour Fáfnir recalls his former might and refuses to believe in his defeat:

> A countenance of terror I bore up before all folk, after that I brooded over the heritage of my brother, and on every side did I spout out poison, so that none durst come anigh me, and of no weapon was I afraid, nor ever had I so many men before me, as that I deemed myself not stronger than all; for all men were sore afraid of me. (*VS* 80)

Smaug, confident in his invincibility, sounds very similar:

> 'The King under the Mountain is dead and where are his kin that dare seek revenge? Girion Lord of Dale is dead, and I have eaten his people like a wolf among sheep, and where are his sons' sons that dare approach me? I kill where I wish and none dare resist. I laid low the warriors of old and their like is not in the world today. Then I was but young and tender. Now I am old and strong, strong, strong. Thief in the Shadows!' he gloated. 'My armour is like tenfold shields, my teeth are swords, my claws spears, the shock of my tail a thunderbolt, my wings a hurricane, and my breath death!' (*H* 262)

These boasts will, however, become the very reason for Smaug's defeat and death, for he will accidentally uncover the secret of his diamond waistcoat to Bilbo.

---

26 "You'll come to a bad end, if you go with such friends" (*H* 259).
27 "I suppose you got a fair price for that cup last night?"; "But what about delivery? What about cartage?"; "And you will get a fair share? Don't you believe it!" (*H* 260).

It is obvious that both Fáfnir and Smaug have much in common – they are deceitful and malicious as well as perilously intelligent and capable of manipulating their opponents in a very cunning way. Moreover, they share another attribute – a kind of parsimoniousness, which manifests itself in useless ownership and in jealous guarding of gathered riches. In *VS*, Regin tells Sigurd of his own brother Fáfnir: "so evil he grew that he fell to lying abroad, and begrudged any share in the wealth to any man, and so became the worst of all worms, and ever now lies brooding upon that treasure" (*VS* 71). Smaug also sleeps on a bed of treasure, which no one must touch because "dragons steal gold and jewels [...] from men and elves and dwarves, wherever they can find them; and they guard their plunder as long as they live (which is practically for ever, unless they are killed), and never enjoy a brass ring of it" (*H* 28). When Smaug discovers the theft of a cup, "his rage passes description", and it is "the sort of rage that is only seen when rich folk that have more than they can enjoy suddenly lose something that they have long had but have never before used or wanted" (*H* 252). This envious desire of possessing and hiding the treasure, so that no one may use it, characterizes also the worm mentioned in the poem "The Hoard" from the collection *The Adventures of Tom Bombadil*, for "he knew the place of the least ring / beneath the shadow of his black wing" (*ATB* 54). The lust for gold, so typical of all of Tolkien dragons, fits well Smaug's evil nature inherited from his Norse prototype, Fáfnir.

Another element that influenced Tolkien's depiction of Smaug was the way Fáfnir died. According to *VS*, Sigurd used a trick to kill the gigantic beast – he dug several holes in the path of the dragon, so that he could strike at the worm's soft underbelly.

> Now crept the worm down to his place of watering, and the earth shook all about him, and he snorted forth venom on all the way before him as he went; but Sigurd neither trembled nor was afraid at the roaring of him. So whenas the worm crept over the pits, Sigurd thrust his sword under his left shoulder, so that it sank in up to the hilts; then up leapt Sigurd from the pit and drew the sword back again unto him, and therewith was his arm all bloody, up to the very shoulder. Now when that mighty worm was ware that he had his death-wound, then he lashed out head and tail, so that all things soever that were before him were broken to pieces. (*VS* 78)

It is probably worth mentioning that key elements of this description may be found in all versions of Tolkien's tale of Túrin the dragon slayer and his terrible opponent Glaurung: first, the monster's approach makes the earth shake; second, the hero thrusts his sword to the very hilt into the enemy's unprotected underbelly; and third the beast feeling its death-wound struggles and tosses in agony, burning and crushing everything within reach (*S* 222; *CH* 134-35; *LT* II 107). In *The Hobbit* these references to the Norse legend of the dragon can also be found, though they are somewhat modified. Tolkien, in early version, played with the idea of having Bilbo kill Smaug: "Bilbo [takes>] plunges in his little magic knife and it disappears. He cannot wield the swords or spears. Throes of dragon. Smashes walls and entrance to tunnel" (Rateliff 496; Carpenter 179). Tolkien eventually gave up this idea, but he kept the traditional motif of the dragon's soft underbelly as his main weakness. However, the black arrow of Bard vanishes to the feather in the hollow in Smaug's left breast, just as Sigurd's sword is thrust to the hilt into Fáfnir's left shoulder, and the defeated monster destroys the city of Esgaroth in his death-throes (*H* 289-90). Although the weapon used by Bard is quite different from famous swords mentioned in traditional legends of dragon slayers, the scene of Smaug's death still bears some resemblance to the *Völsunga saga*.

It is not difficult to notice how deeply the Fáfnir of Old Norse legends influenced Tolkien's creation of Smaug. Both dragons share such features as malice, deceitfulness, a greedy lust for useless possessions, and a dangerous intelligence. They also meet their death in a similar way. Smaug inherited all these attributes from Fáfnir, which makes him a perilous but truly fascinating creature and a formidable opponent for Bilbo and his companions.

Tolkien's fondness of the Icelandic saga of the Völsungs and the cursed treasure can also be seen in *The Adventures of Tom Bombadil*. In the poem "Bombadil Goes Boating" one may read: "I'll give your otter-fell to Barrow-wights. They'll taw you! / Then smother you in gold-rings! Your mother if she saw you, / she'd never know her son, unless 'twas by a whisker. / Nay, don't tease old Tom, until you be far brisker!" (*ATB* 19). These verses contain references to *VS*, and the whole poem is a bow of acknowledgment to Tolkien's scholarly erudition, as he wrote in a letter to his friend and publisher Rayner Unwin: "I am afraid it largely tickles my pedantic fancy, because of its echo of the Norse Nibelung matter (the otter's whisker); and because one of the lines comes straight, incredible though that may seem, from *The Ancrene Wisse*" (*L* 315). He addressed Pauline Baynes in similar tone: "The donnish detail is just a private pleasure which I do not expect anyone to notice (e.g. the hanging up of a kingfisher to see the way of the wind, which comes from Sir T. Browne; the otter's whisker sticking out of the gold, from the Norse Nibelung legends" (*L* 319). In both letters Tolkien alludes to the way in which the cursed treasure of dwarf Andvari became the property of mighty Hreidmar, whose sons were Fáfnir and Regin. His third son was called Otr, "otter", and he used to swim in this very shape in the pond of Andvari's waterfall. The Norse gods Odin, Hoenir and Loki accidentally killed Otr and showed his pelt to Hreidmar, who made them pay *weregild* for his murdered son. They were forced to fill and cover otter's pelt with gold. In order to do so, Loki took the golden treasure from the dwarf Andvari and soon the only thing sticking out of the pile of treasure was a single whisker, covered at once with the cursed ring Andvaranautr (*VS* 69-71). Hence, in Tolkien's poem Tom Bombadil speaks of tawing the otter-fell and smothering it in gold-rings.

Another "donnish detail" is to be found in *Farmer Giles of Ham*. It is even more interesting because the whole work is a kind of parody of heroic tradition (Wicher 67-76), and one of its main characters, the clumsy and amusing dragon Chrysophylax has little in common with the mighty and fearful beast of Norse legends.[28] His dwelling, however, makes a far better impression, which Giles and his old grey mare might have noticed when "at last on the west side of the mountain they came to the mouth of the cave. It was large and black and forbidding, and its brazen doors swung on great pillars of iron. [...] The doors of this deep house were set wide, and in their shadow they halted" (*FGH* 62). When Sigurd and his horse Grani ("grey") arrived at the gloomy dragon's lair, they also saw iron doors and an iron door-frame. Then Sigurd found so much gold and treasure inside

> that he thought verily that scarce might two horses, or three belike, bear it thence. So he took all the gold and laid it in two great chests, and set them on the horse Grani, and took the reins of him, but nowise will he stir, neither will he abide smiting. Then Sigurd knows the mind of the horse, and leaps on

---

28 On the comparison between Chrysophylax and Smaug, the epitome of a "good" dragon, see Honegger 27-59.

the back of him, and smites and spurs into him, and off the horse goes even as if he were unladen. (*VS* 84)

Tolkien seems to be joking about Grani's exaggerated behaviour by describing the anxiety of Giles' old mare when observing a tall pile of treasures rising in front of the dragon's dwelling.

> But by this time the grey mare was getting a bit anxious on her own account. 'Who's going to carry all this heavy stuff home, I wonder?' thought she; and she gave such a long sad look at all the bags and the boxes that the farmer guessed her mind.
>
> 'Never you worry, lass!' said he. 'We'll make the old worm do the carting'. (*FGH* 63)

The grey (which may be a reference to Grani's grey colour) mare is cut from a different cloth than the heroic and supernaturally strong steed of Sigurd's, but it has certainly more common sense. The passage describing the arrival at the monster's lair and the loading of the treasure is once again Tolkien's reference to Norse literary tradition. It is thus visible that even in his shorter popular works, as *The Adventures of Tom Bombadil* or *Farmer Giles*, Tolkien included "donnish details", which were probably incomprehensible for those of his readers who were unfamiliar with Icelandic literature, but which made seemingly trivial stories and poems far more interesting and tickled the author's "pedantic fancy", by giving him true "private pleasure".

Most readers know J.R.R. Tolkien as the author of the epic *The Lord of the Rings*, but he was also a respected scholar and brilliant linguist. As Christopher Tolkien says, his father's "erudition was by no means confined to 'Anglo-Saxon', but extended to an expert knowledge of the poems of the Elder Edda and the Old Norse language [...]. In fact, for many years after he became the professor of Anglo-Saxon at Oxford in 1925 he was the professor of Old Norse, though no such title existed; he gave lectures and classes on Norse language and literature in every year from 1926 until at least 1939" (*LSSG* 2). Yet Tolkien never treated Norse (or Anglo-Saxon) texts as mere materials for academic teaching, theorizing, disputing and arguing. He managed to include many plots of medieval Icelandic sagas in his own literary works, and to refashion in fascinating ways and give a new lease of life to creatures and characters that were almost forgotten. The examples discussed show vividly that even in those of his writings which are generally considered to be trivial and fit only (or primarily) for children, there are many references to the literary tradition of the North, such as the allusions to the Völsung legend in *Farmer Giles of Ham* and *The Adventures of Tom Bombadil*, or echoes of the berserk myth from Icelandic sagas in *The Hobbit*. Through them we may perceive that Tolkien was not only a fantasy writer, but also a brilliant scholar, whose academic knowledge of Norse literature, mythology and languages deeply influenced his popular writings.

Bibliography

BLANEY, Benjamin. "The Berserk Suitor: The Literary Application of a Stereotype Theme." *Scandinavian Studies* 54 (1982): 279-294.

BOER, Richard C., ed. *Grettis saga Ásmundarsonar*. Halle a.S.: Niemeyer, 1900.

BRUNSDALE, Mitzi M. "Norse Mythological Elements in *The Hobbit*." *Mythlore* 9 (1983): 49-50.

BRYCE, Lynne. "The Influence of Scandinavian Mythology on the Works of J.R.R. Tolkien." *Edda: Nordisk tidsskrift for litteraturforskning* 2 (1983): 113-119.

BURNS, Marjorie J. "Norse and Christian Gods: The Integrative Theology of J.R.R. Tolkien." *Tolkien and the Invention of Myth: A Reader*. Ed. Jane Chance. Lexington: University Press of Kentucky, 2004. 163-178.

Perilous Realms: Celtic and Norse in Tolkien's Middle-earth. Toronto: University of Toronto Press, 2005.

CALLAHAN, Patrick J. "Tolkien's Dwarfs and the Eddas." *Tolkien Journal* 15 (1972): 20.

CARPENTER, Humphrey. *Tolkien. A Biography*. Boston: Houghton Mifflin, 1977.

ed. *The Letters of J.R.R. Tolkien*. Boston: Houghton Mifflin, 1981.

COLBERT, David. *The Magical Worlds of the Lord of the Rings: The Amazing Myths, Legends and Facts Behind the Masterpiece*. New York: Berkley Books, 2002.

DAVIDSON, Hilda Ellis. *Myths and Symbols in Pagan Europe. Early Scandinavian and Celtic Religions*. Syracuse: Manchester UP, 1988.

DAY, David. *Tolkien's Ring*. London: HarperCollins, 1994.

The World of Tolkien: Mythological Sources of The Lord of the Rings. London: Mitchell Beazley, 2003.

FABING, Howard D. "On Going Berserk: A Neurochemical Inquiry." *Scientific Monthly* (Nov. 1956): 232-237.

FOOTE, Peter G., and David M. Wilson. *The Viking Achievement*. London: Sidgewick & Jackson, 1970.

HARVEY, Greg. *The Origins of Tolkien's Middle-earth for Dummies*. Indianapolis: Wiley Publishing, 2003.

HONEGGER, Thomas. "A Good Dragon is Hard to Find: From *draconitas* to *draco*." *Good Dragons are Rare. An Inquiry into Literary Dragons East and West*. Ed. Fanfan Chen and Thomas Honegger. Frankfurt am Main: Peter Lang, 2009. 27-59.

JÓNSSON, Finnur, ed. *Brennu-Njáls saga*. Halle a.S.: Niemeyer, 1908.

ed. *Egils saga Skallagrímssonar*. Halle a.S.: Niemeyer, 1894.

ed. *Hrólfs saga kraka og Bjarkarímur*. København: S.L. Møllers Bogtrykkeri, 1904.

KUHN, Hans. "Kämpen und berserker." *Frühmittelalterliche Studien* 2 (1968): 218-227.

MAGNUSSON, Eirikur, and William Morris, trans. *The Volsunga saga*. London: Norrœna Society, 1907.

MOTZ, Lotte. "Of Elves and Dwarfs." *Arv: Journal of Scandinavian Folklore* 29-30 (1974): 93-127.

NOREEN, Erik. "Ordet bärsärk." *Arkiv för nordisk filologi* 4 (1932): 242-254.

PETERSEN, Niels M., ed. *Hervarar saga ok Heiðreks konungs*. Kjøbenhavn: Brødrene Berlings bogtrykkeri, 1847.

RATELIFF, John D. *The History of The Hobbit. Part Two: Return to Bag-End*. London: HarperCollins, 2007.

RISDEN, E. L. "Source Criticism: Background and Applications." *Tolkien and the Study of His Sources: Critical Essays*. Ed. Jason Fisher. Jefferson NC: McFarland, 2011. 17-28.

SEE, Klaus von. "Berserker." *Zeitschrift für deutsche Wortforschung* 17 (1961): 129-136.

SHIPPEY, Tom. *The Road to Middle-earth*. London: Grafton, 1992.

"Light-elves, Dark-elves, and Others: Tolkien's Elvish Problem." *Tolkien Studies* 1 (2004): 1-15.

"Grimm, Grundtvig, Tolkien: Nationalism and the Invention of Mythologies." *Roots and Branches: Selected Papers on Tolkien by Tom Shippey*. Zurich and Berne: Walking Tree Publishers, 2007. 79-96.

"Tolkien and Iceland: The Philology of Envy." *Roots and Branches: Selected Papers on Tolkien by Tom Shippey*. Zurich and Berne: Walking Tree Publishers, 2007. 187-202.

SPEIDEL, Michael. "Berserk. A History of Indo-European Mad Warriors." *Journal of World History* 2 (2002): 253-290.

STURLUSON, Snorri. *Ynglinga saga*. Ed. Finnur Jónsson. København: G.E.C. Gadsforlag, 1912.

TOLKIEN, John Ronald Reuel. "The Adventures of Tom Bombadil." *The Tolkien Reader*. New York: Ballantine Books, 1969.

The Book of Lost Tales 2. London and Boston: George Allen & Unwin, 1984.

The Children of Húrin. London: HarperCollins, 2008.

"Farmer Giles of Ham." *The Tolkien Reader*. New York: Ballantine Books, 1969.

The Silmarillion. London: George Allen & Unwin, 1977.

The Hobbit. London: HarperCollins, 2006.

The Legend of Sigurd and Gudrún. London: HarperCollins, 2009.

TURVILLE-PETRE, E.O.G. *Myth and Religion of the North: The Religion of Ancient Scandinavia*. London: Weidenfeld and Nicolson, 1964.

VIGFÚSSON, Guðbrandur, ed. *Eyrbyggja saga*. Leipzig: F.C.W. Vogel, 1864.

WICHER, Andrzej. "J.R.R. Tolkien's *Farmer Giles of Ham* as an Anti-Beowulf – A Study in Tolkien's Comicality." *Shades of Humour*. Vol. 1/2. Ed. Alina Kwiatkowska and Sylwia Dżereń-Głowacka. Piotrków Trybunalski: Naukowe Wydawnictwo Piotrkowskie, 2008. 67-76.

WILKIN, Peter. "Norse Influences on Tolkien's Elves and Dwarves." *...Through a Glass Darkly: Reflections on the Sacred*. Ed. Frances Di Lauro. Sydney: Sydney UP, 2006. 61-80.

About the author

RENATA LEŚNIAKIEWICZ-DRZYMAŁA is a Cracow-based historian specializing in the history of medieval Europe. Her scholarship is focused on the history and broadly defined culture of Viking-age Scandinavia and Anglo-Saxon Britain, especially on the interplay between Norse mythology and Christianity. She is also interested in Tolkien studies, comparative mythology, and European folklore. She is the author of the Polish translations of Icelandic medieval sources: *Völsunga saga* and *Norna-Gests þáttr*. She served as a consulting historian for the Polish edition of *The Legend of Sigurd and Gudrún* by J.R.R. Tolkien.

Łukasz Neubauer

"He has gone to God glory seeking": J.R.R. Tolkien's Critique of the Northern Courage and Rejection of the Traditional Heroic Ethos in "The Homecoming of Beorhtnoth Beorhthelm's Son"

Abstract

The article examines one of the lesser known works of J.R.R. Tolkien, his 1953 post-combat sequel to *The Battle of Maldon* written in the form of an alliterative dialogue. While it is clearly overshadowed by his more famous epic works, "The Homecoming of Beorhtnoth" and its two accompanying essays cannot be ignored for their great philological depth and precision of critical analysis. In fact, the impact it has had on *The Battle of Maldon* scholarship since 1953 is frequently compared to that of Tolkien's other ground-breaking work, his earlier essay on *Beowulf*, which in so many ways opened the eyes of scholarly commentators to the genuine literary value of the poem. In "The Homecoming" Tolkien appears to put his own words of critique in the mouths of two solitary figures plodding through the corpse-strewn battlefield in search of their fallen lord's body. In this way, the writer implicitly succeeds in voicing his moral disapproval of what he aptly refers to as the 'northern heroic spirit', a highly distinctive trait (or, rather, 'defect') of character which is all too often almost uncritically accepted as an archetypal representation of the famed reckless heroism in early Germanic literature.

"From the world has passed / a prince peerless in peace and war" (HBBS 6).

With these words Torhthelm, a youthful poet and devoted retainer, bids farewell to the brave ealdorman Byrhtnoth,[1] the fallen hero of the battle of Maldon and principal figure of the late tenth- or early eleventh-century alliterative poem depicting the dramatic events of 991. "Alas, my friend, our lord was at fault [...]. Too proud, too princely!" (10), seems to reply (albeit not instantly) his more rational companion, an elderly farmer and retired warrior by the name of Tídwald. These two distinct – although not necessarily contradictory – voices of early medieval ethics, voices of both critique and praise, clearly resonate in the virtually noiseless gloom of post-combat reality "lit [only] by a faint beam [of] a dark-lantern" (4). First

---

1 Throughout "The Homecoming" Tolkien invariably spells the ealdorman's name 'Beorhtnoth'. Since his use of this diphthongised variation (not to be found in any Anglo-Saxon source) has never been successfully explained, I shall use the standardised form 'Byrhtnoth' when dealing with the character and only use 'Beorhtnoth' with reference to the title of Tolkien's work.

and foremost, however, they are the summing up of Tolkien's own attitude towards heroism, sacrifice and sense of duty towards one's men, an attitude he refers to in the second of two short essays accompanying "The Homecoming of Beorhtnoth Beorhthelm's Son" as the "northern heroic spirit" (13).

The historical battle of Maldon is believed to have taken place on 10 or 11 August 991,[2] somewhere near the present town of Maldon, by the low causeway linking Northey Island and the south bank of the river Pant (modern-day Blackwater). Standing on each side of the river were the *wicinga werod* (*Battle of Maldon*, 97) 'viking army'[3] and Byrhtnoth's *heorðwerod* (24) 'hearth-companions', probably hurriedly reinforced by some local troops of the greater *fyrd*. Once the negotiations had failed, there was no way of overcoming the looming conflict other than in open battle. Seeing that they would not be able to cross the narrow causeway without being decimated by the defenders' arrows, the heathen raiders *ongunnon lytegian* (86) 'began to use guile', asking Byrhtnoth to grant them safe passage across the water, and so permit them to have a fair fight. Unfortunately, all this seems to have only encouraged the proud ealdorman who, *for his ofermode* (89) 'from his overconfidence',[4] began to *alyfan landes to fela laþere ðeode* (90) 'allow too much land to the hateful people'. Leaving aside the evident ambiguity behind the poet's use of *ofermod*, it is obviously not possible to tell whether Byrhtnoth's decision was in any way motivated by strategic considerations or whether the aged ealdorman[5] simply wished to end his earthly life in the dramatic fashion of ancient heroes. Whatever the case may have been, the battle took an unfortunate turn for the defenders. Byrhtnoth himself was slain (164-84), most of

---

[2] This minor ambiguity with regard to the actual dating of the battle springs from the differences in three contemporary obits of Byrhtnoth produced in the monastic houses in Winchester, Ramsey (both of which have 11 August) and Ely (10 August).

[3] According to other accounts of the battle, the vikings may have been led by some Unlaf (*Anglo-Saxon Chronicle* MS A), often identified with the later king of Norway (995-1000) Olaf Tryggvason, or – perhaps even more puzzlingly – two otherwise unknown *duces* [...] *Justin et Guthmund filius Steitan* (John of Worcester's *Chronicon ex Chronicis*) 'dukes Justin and Guthmund the son of Steita'.

[4] Variously translated as "overconfidence" (Gordon 76), "arrogance" (Scragg, *Battle of Maldon* 100), "excessive courage" (O'Brien O'Keeffe 119) or "overmastering pride" (HBBS 13), the word *ofermod* has over the years become one of the most debated words in the entire corpus of Old English verse. In fact, as pointed out by Thomas Shippey, given its contextual connotations in secular poetry, "there is not enough evidence [...] to permit an absolutely reliable gloss" ("Boar and Badger: An Old English Heroic Antithesis?" 226) on line 89 of *The Battle of Maldon*.

[5] The *har hildenrinc* (169) 'gray-haired battle-hero' of *The Battle of Maldon* is generally held to have been in his mid-sixties in 991, a considerable age for any medieval warrior.

his men fled the battlefield (185-97), and the few loyal retainers who bravely chose to stay *be healfe [hira] hlaforde* (318) 'by the side of their lord' were all put to the ruthless edges of viking swords.

Despite the poem's regrettably fragmentary state,[6] *The Battle of Maldon* constitutes one of the most treasured works in the Anglo-Saxon canon, perhaps equally valued for its indisputable historical and cultural merits, as much as its literary ones. Other noteworthy aspects of *Maldon* are its relative linguistic simplicity and linearity of narration which make the poetic account of Byrhtnoth's last stand one of the most popular texts in Old English readers and grammars. In his earliest known encounter with the language of Cædmon, the sixteen-year-old Tolkien is said to have been assisted by George Brewerton, the English teacher and schoolmaster at King Edward's School in Birmingham, who lent him an Anglo-Saxon primer to boost his already impressive language skills (Carpenter 54). None of his, now numerous, biographers ever mentions the title, but it was most likely Henry Sweet's seminal *Anglo-Saxon Primer* (first published in 1882), perhaps accompanied by the same author's *Anglo-Saxon Reader in Verse and Prose* (first published in 1876). The latter contains selected works of Old English literature, including the complete *Battle of Maldon* (133-44) which young Tolkien may or may not have already come across in his independent studies.

The poem evidently made a life-long impression on the future Rawlinson and Bosworth Professor of Anglo-Saxon. Nearly three decades later, he would assist his friend E.V. Gordon (along with F.E. Harmer) in his work on the 1937 edition of *Maldon*[7] for Methuen's Old English Library, "read[ing] the proofs [...] and [making] many corrections and contributions" (Gordon vi) of a textual as well as a philological nature. It would also become a vital component of Tolkien's teaching repertoire, a stimulating starting point for many an academic discussion on the principles of courage, heroism and loyalty. Finally, the poem would constitute an important source of inspiration for some of his fictional works,

---

6 *Maldon*'s sole manuscript was already incomplete when it was destroyed in the disastrous fire at Ashburnham House on 23 October 1731. Fortunately, a few years earlier, a careful transcript had been made, possibly by David Casley, deputy keeper of the library.
7 Until 1981, when D.G. Scragg published his own edition in the Manchester University Series of Old and Middle English Texts, Gordon's work was in many ways the single most authoritative publication on *The Battle of Maldon*.

of which "The Homecoming of Beorhtnoth Beorhthelm's Son" is but the most evident, albeit not the only example.

First published in 1953 in the sixth volume of the scholarly journal *Essays and Studies by Members of the English Association*,[8] it is perhaps one of Tolkien's least characteristic literary creations in terms of form and style. Humphrey Carpenter refers to it as a "radio play"[9] and a "sequel" to *The Battle of Maldon* (286), Daniel Grotta sometimes calls it a "poem" (114), sometimes a "verse play" (158), while Tom Shippey applies the terms "poem-cum-essay", "coda" (*Road to Middle-Earth* 178) and "authorisation" ("Tolkien and The Homecoming of Beorhtnoth" 324). In fact, the exact nature of "The Homecoming" is very hard to pin down. It is a dramatic dialogue in alliterative verse which may be seen as an extended comment on the Old English poem with a particular emphasis on the meaning of *ofermod* and its possible cultural implications. It is accompanied by two rather condensed essays: "Beorhtnoth's Death" and "Ofermod", the former discussing the events of 991 (HBBS 1-3), the latter dealing with what Tolkien held to be the intended sense of the poem's most ambiguous word (13-18). The three components thus constitute a meaningful whole; a whole which can be best approached in its entirety and whose genuine philological value cannot be truly appreciated without at least a passing knowledge of the *Maldon* poem and its numerous textual allusions. It ought to be emphasised, though, that despite its being originally published in a scholarly journal, the central dialogue is not a piece of academic study, but rather – to use the words of Thomas Honegger – a "work of informed literary fiction" (189) set in the aftermath of the historical (as well as literary) battle of Maldon.

---

8 The complete "Homecoming" is said to have been in existence by 1945, although the dating of its first drafts points to the 1930s. Tolkien was always very careful about his choice of words and the whole work underwent several more or less significant revisions (including the names of its characters) before it was eventually printed in 1953.

9 It was, of course, never performed on stage, but a year after its publication, in 1954, "The Homecoming" was aired as a play on BBC Radio 3. Deeply dissatisfied with the quality of the production, Tolkien decided to make his own tape-recording at home, playing both parts and improvising additional sound effects.

"The Homecoming" recounts how two otherwise unknown men, Torhthelm and Tídwald,[10] servants of the late Byrhtnoth, are sent to the battlefield to recover the body of their fallen lord. In this respect Tolkien's narrative clearly contradicts the "late, and largely unhistorical account in the twelfth-century *Liber Eliensis*" (HBBS 2) where it is the Abbot of Ely himself who goes *cum quibusdam monachis ad locum pugne* (*Liber Eliensis* II. 62) 'with some monks to the place of battle' to find the ealdorman and have his headless body *ad hanc ecclesiam reporta*[*tur*] *et cum honore sepeli*[*tur*] (II. 62) 'brought to the church and buried with honour'. Tolkien's intention, however, as we shall see in the due course of this paper, was not to reconstruct the post-combat events of one night in the August of 991, but rather to give voice to his critical observation on the intricate nature of heroism in the Old English poem.

Even though there are few 'stage' directions throughout the entire "Homecoming", it is not difficult to conceive a dark, moonless night, occasionally lit by a "faint beam from a dark-lantern" (HBBS 4) or "candles in the dark" (12). The moments of grave silence are interrupted by ominous sounds such as the hooting of an owl (4), the fight with a corpse-stripper (8), the creaking of the wagon's wheels (11-12), the cracking of the whip (11), the clattering of the hooves (12) and the chanting of the monks (12-13). The two solitary figures make their way through the corpse-strewn battlefield, looking for the body of their dear lord. Every now and then, they recognise a face they once knew as a daring (and all too often) young lad or stumble upon some heathen warrior from across the sea. In the end, however, they come to see the horrible sight they have both been waiting for: the badly disfigured body of Byrhtnoth and his miraculously preserved sword. With heavy hearts and tear-filled eyes, they lift the heavy corpse and take it to the wagon they left standing by the fatal causeway, and then head for "Maldon and the monks, and then miles onward to Ely and the abbey" (11).

As has been indicated, the very reason why Tolkien decided to write "The Homecoming" was his wish to examine the ancient spirit of excessive, proud and, above all, self-centred heroism, the "northern heroic spirit" (13) and its very

---

10 The characters' full names are only listed on the margin as part of the stage headings. Throughout the entire "Homecoming" Torhthelm and Tídwald use hypocoristic forms of, respectively, 'Totta' and 'Tída'. In the earlier, pre-1953, versions Tolkien sometimes calls them 'Totta' and 'Tudda', sometimes 'Pudda' and 'Tibba'.

essence reflected in the ealdorman's *ofermod*. Before he formally does so in the third and final part of his work, however, Tolkien comments on Byrhtnoth's conduct in a somewhat less explicit way, by putting words of praise and criticism in the forthright mouths of young Torhthelm and old Tídwald.

Of the two men, Torhthelm (Old English for 'Bright Helmet') is the one whose youthful critical faculties allow him to find only little or no fault in the ways of his lord. His head is crammed with old tales concerning the heroes of the northern world and their invariably remarkable feats of courage. Accordingly, the young man idealises the battle and mouths elaborate (though at times fairly rash) words of praise in honour of Byrhtnoth, calling him "a prince peerless in peace and war" (6) and urging imaginary mourners to "build high the barrow his bones to keep" (7). In his naïve adoration of the fallen ealdorman, Torhthelm appears to be incapable of distinguishing between acts of reckless, self-centred heroism and a sensible but far less spectacular employment of down-to-earth tactics. Furthermore, in his dream he confuses the unavoidable post-combat pessimism of the defeated with a sweeping sense of devastation and moral decay which he imagines to be embodied in the tragic death of his lord:

"It's dark! It's dark, and doom coming!
Is no light left us? A light kindle,
and fan the flame! Lo! Fire now wakens,
hearth is burning, house is lighted,
men there gather. Out of the mists they come
through darkling doors whereat doom waiteth."
(HBBS 12)

Torhthelm's somnial anxieties are doubtlessly intensified by his vivid imagination as a gleeman and familiarity with the ancient lays of Beowulf and other great heroes in the same mould. His anticipation of a bleak future clearly echoes that of the suddenly leaderless Geats who, mourning the loss of their king, *hearde ondr[ædaþ] / wæl-fylla worn, werudes egesan, / hynðo ond hæft-nyd* (*Beowulf* 3153-55) 'are deeply frightened of massive slaughter, terror of troops, humiliation and captivity'. The elevated tone of his voice is indicative of Torhthelm's perception of the harsh reality – elegiac and contemplative, yet hardly ever rational.

Tídwald (Old English for 'Ruler of Time'), on the other hand, appears to be his exact opposite. An elderly peasant who has "seen much fighting in the English defence-levies" (HBBS 2), he turns out to be the actual voice of social critique in "The Homecoming" as well as Tolkien's own mouthpiece. Tom Shippey even argues that, unlike Torhthelm, Tídwald represents the more realistic side of Tolkien's inner dialogue. It is, in fact, a veiled attack on Old English poetry which in all likelihood provided the very motivation for Byrhtnoth's foolish decision to let the vikings cross the causeway ("Tolkien and The Homecoming" 329-33). In any case, Tídwald is far more rational in his judgement and does not let his feelings for the late ealdorman – "By the Cross Tída, / I loved him no less than any lord with him" (HBBS 5) – blind him to the fact that it was indeed Byrhtnoth's self-seeking desire to "give minstrels matter for mighty songs" (10) that ultimately led to the needless loss of so many lives. He deflates some of Torhthelm's heroic illusions and does not hesitate to make occasional sardonic remarks while carrying the lord's marred body: "Beorhtnoth we bear not Béowulf here: / no pyres for him, nor piling of mounds; / and the gold will be given to the good abbot" (7). This, of course, depends on whether the two men actually succeed in bringing it back, for, "by Edmund's head! though his own's missing, / [our] Lord's not light" (9).

The very clear distinction which Tídwald makes between Byrhtnoth and Beowulf is not only dictated by the evident cultural discrepancies that separate the two heroes – the Christian Saxon and the heathen Geat. Acting in the first part of the poem as *Higelaces / mæg ond magoðegn* (*Beowulf* 407-8) 'Hygelac's kinsman and young retainer', Beowulf is but a "subordinate with no responsibilities downwards" (HBBS 14), and does not put his own people directly in danger. Nor does he do so with regard to the helpless Danes who desperately seek his military assistance against the murderous *Caines cynne* (*Beowulf* 107) 'Cain's progeny' they call Grendel. In contrast, Byrhtnoth appears to do everything to boost his own heroic reputation, taking little heed of those who loyally stand by his side. "Let the poets babble" (HBBS 10), says Tídwald in reply to his younger companion's outburst of elegiac verse in praise of the ealdorman, "We'll praise his valour" (10), but not his tactics, almost utterly devoid of any "sense of what a responsible leader ought to do" (Bowman 95). Byrhtnoth's pride has overcome him when he let the vikings cross the fatal causeway, as "it should never have been" (HBBS 10). "Doom he dared," concludes Tídwald, "and he died for it" (10).

Tolkien's choice to place commoners at the very heart of his "Homecoming" and push the conventionally high-born hero to its margin is a prominent characteristic of his literary style. Both *The Hobbit* and *The Lord of the Rings* focus primarily on the adventures of the inhabitants of the Shire, rather than those of the apparently more heroic elves, dwarves and men (Rorabeck 42). In "The Homecoming", where the emphasis is primarily on the excess of heroic pride, the straightforward dialectic form featuring a youthful son of a minstrel and an old farmer not only facilitates the reader's insight into the average (if fictional) medieval mind, but also serves as a potent instrument of social criticism from those who are not normally part of the traditional heroic cast. It enables Tolkien to investigate the complex essence of northern heroism, a concept he further elaborates on in the third and final part of his work.

The "northern heroic spirit," maintains Tolkien in the second of the two short essays that supplement "The Homecoming", "is never quite pure; it is of gold and an alloy" (HBBS 14). In the case of Byrhtnoth, it is the "alloy of personal good name" (14), his excessive pride which has bred the insatiable "desire for honour and glory [both] in life and after death" (14). Being the ealdorman of Essex, his feudal responsibility – a fact he seems perfectly aware of in the early lines of the poem – is *gealgean eþel þysne, / Æþelredes eard, ealdres [his] / folc and foldan* (*Battle of Maldon* 52-4) 'to defend this homeland, Æthelred's country, his lord's folk and land'. In other words, Byrhtnoth ought to be directed in his deeds by a loyalty upwards (his king) and a responsibility downwards (his people). "In this situation," Tolkien says, "he was responsible for all the men under him, not to throw away their lives except with one object, the defence of the realm from an implacable foe" (HBBS 15).

Apart from his somewhat vague use of the word *ofermod*,[11] the anonymous English poet does not seem at any time to question Byrhtnoth's conduct at

---

11 Old English *ofermod* is of course etymologically analogous to Swedish *övermod* and German *Übermut*, but the actual reading of *Maldon* 89 will have to depend on a great deal of semantic subtleties intended by and only known to the anonymous poet. As a noun it appears three times (*Battle of Maldon* 89; *Genesis B* 272; *Instructions for Christians* 130) and once in a glossary where it is used to translate Latin *superbia*. The very same form, however, is also frequently used as an adjective, invariably meaning 'proud'.

Maldon.¹² Instead, he regards the ealdorman "with exaggerated favour" (Shippey, "Boar and Badger" 231), praising his indisputable valour in war and generosity in peace. Almost all the blame for the ultimate defeat is therefore placed on the horde of scheming vikings who did not hesitate to *lytegian* (*Battle of Maldon* 86) 'use guile' in order to get across the water unharmed and those of the defenders who, seeing their noble leader fall, *wendon fram þam wige and þone wudu sohton* (193) 'fled the battlefield and sought the woods'.

What was not too openly communicated by the *Maldon* poet (who may well have been an Ely monk writing his work in praise of the monastery's chief benefactor), could, of course, be safely explored nearly ten centuries later. Tolkien may perhaps have made a bit too much of merely one phrase, claiming that two lines could actually dominate the entire poem, but his reasoning is so convincing that it often seems difficult to question its validity. Byrhtnoth, he argues, treated the battle more like a "sporting match" (HBBS 15), failing thoroughly to remember his actual purpose and duty. The reasons seem perfectly obvious. Tolkien reduces them to the ealdorman's *ofermod*, the "defect of character [...] formed by nature [and] moulded [...] by 'aristocratic tradition' [...] enshrined in tales and verse of poets" (15). Byrhtnoth was therefore *lofgeornost* (*Beowulf* 3182) 'most eager for renown', far more chivalrous than actually heroic, seeking vain honour in placing both himself and his men at needless risk, a "truly heroic situation which they could redeem only by death" (HBBS 15) in combat.

For Tolkien the real heroes of *Maldon* are of course the "brave lads" (5) that Torhthelm and Tídwald find "silenced" (5) and "hewn out of ken" (4) while examining the battlefield. There is a good reason why he evokes the thoughtful words of Wiglaf who memorably reflects that *oft sceall eorl monig anes willan / wræc adreogan* (*Beowulf* 3077-78) 'oft must many an earl endure sorrow owing to the will of one man'. Wulfmær, Wulfstan, Ælfnoth, Offa, and other warriors, both named and unnamed, fell only because they chose (as was fitting) to remain faithful to the lord. "In their situation," Tolkien maintains, "heroism was superb" (HBBS 16). There is literally nothing they could be reproached

---

12 It may be, however, that if *The Battle of Maldon* had any "rounded ending and final appraisement" (HBBS 16) the brief mention of Byrhtnoth's *ofermod* contained in lines 89-90 could be resumed and further elaborated on. It may also be that the poet's intention was not to criticise the ealdorman, but rather praise his valour, in which case he would almost certainly suppress some of the awkward facts.

for on that fated day, as their heroism ensues solely from the noble causes of unwavering obedience to the rigorous code of honour and patient endurance of inevitable fatigue and pain. Their fortitude will not be rewarded with precious gifts of horses, swords or rings. For them the ultimate prize is to lie *be healfe [hira] hlaforde* (*Battle of Maldon* 318) 'by the side of their lord'.

It can hardly be argued now that in writing "The Homecoming" Tolkien made an ambitious and highly influential attempt to redefine the traditional heroic ethos of the north by distinguishing between the assumed social ills of Byrhtnoth's self-seeking wish to find glory in open combat and the poignant single-mindedness of his most faithful retainers who followed him in this daring but ultimately fatal effort. Despite its literariness, Tolkien's critical analysis of what prior to 1953 was almost universally held to be a celebration of "the spirit and essence of the Northern heroic literature in […] its invincible profession of heroic faith" (Ker 57) became yet another benchmark in Anglo-Saxon criticism. In several ways "The Homecoming" did to *The Battle of Maldon* what his 1936 lecture "*Beowulf*: The Monsters and the Critics" did to the epic tale of the Geatish hero – it opened the proverbial can of worms, provoking further arguments, analyses and discussions which definitely enriched our subsequent understanding of the *Maldon* poem with all of its countless cultural and historical implications.

Tolkien's critical opinion of Byrhtnoth evidently upset the hero's confirmed apologists who for the following two decades or so made numerous attempts to defend the ealdorman from the damning charges of "overmastering pride" (HBBS 13), needless nobility and foolishness. One of the most frequently used arguments in his favour was that of the dire strategic necessity to prevent the vikings from further plunder and pillage.[13] Other critics, however, adopted a tone similar to Tolkien's, often advocating alternative courses of action for the defenders which would have maximised the chances of their ultimate victory.[14] In any case, the growing interest in the battle

---

13 One of the most interesting analyses of Byrhtnoth's pre-combat motives may be found in Stephen Pollington's book *The Warrior's Way: England in the Viking Age*. There the English medievalist argues that the ealdorman may have actually taken the initiative and challenged the vikings in the hope that they would not be able to sack the nearby town of Maldon (64-66).
14 See, for instance, Edward B. Irving, Jr.'s paper "The Heroic Style in *The Battle of Maldon*", in which it is argued that "the English could have held the Vikings on the island until they starved them out" (462).

of Maldon brought forth a substantial body of academic literature on the subject, culminating around the millennial celebrations of Byrhtnoth's last stand in 1991, the year which saw the appearance of two very influential volumes of critical analysis – both literary and historical – *The Battle of Maldon AD 991* and *The Battle of Maldon: Fiction and Fact* edited, respectively, by Donald Scragg and Janet Cooper.[15] Stephen Pollington aptly sums up Tolkien's vast influence on *Maldon* scholarship in his now seminal book *The Warrior's Way*, observing that since the publication of "The Homecoming" the "views of the late Professor Tolkien have been widely regarded as the definite statement on the subject, and no treatment of the poem is complete without some reference to the professor and his paper" (66).

Distinct echoes of *The Battle of Maldon* may also be identified in most of Tolkien's fictional works, including *The Hobbit* and *The Lord of the Rings*. Byrhtnoth's tragic *ofermod* clearly evinces itself in, amongst others, Thorin's moral blindness (itself caused by the dwarven king's excessive pride and the stubbornness he displays in his later dealings with Bilbo and Gandalf), which only seems to increase with the dwarves' coming nearer to their abandoned Kingdom under the Lonely Mountain, and Boromir's vainglorious attempt to steal the Ring from Frodo and "use the power of the Enemy against him" (*LotR* 389) – an attempt which, to use Tolkien's words in "The Homecoming", was both "a noble error [and] the error of a noble" (HBBS 16).[16] Both heroes die, of course, for their "folly" and "overmastering pride" which the author evidently saw as corresponding to Byrhtnoth's utter "desire for honour and glory, in life and after death" (14). At fault they may be, then, yet neither of them is ever wholly condemned. Instead, they are inevitably provided

---

15 Despite the fact that Janet Cooper's volume was not published until two years later, it actually consists of the papers read between 5 and 9 August 1991 at the Battle of Maldon Millennial Conference organised in Colchester by the University of Essex.

16 Additionally, the High Warden of the White Tower also seems to combine a number of features from other literary/historical characters such as Roland (broken horn) or Seigneur de Bayard (death while seated against a tree, final confession). One other distinctive feature which equates Boromir with Byrhtnoth is their immense size. In his very first appearance in *The Lord of the Rings*, Boromir is described as "a tall man with a fair and noble face […], proud and stern of glance" (*LotR* 234). Once he is dead, three of his companions – Aragorn, Legolas and Gimli – carry his body to "the boat that was to bear him away" (406). Although they are no weaklings, their struggle to actually do so is highly reminiscent of that of Torhthelm and Tídwald, "for Boromir was a man both tall and strong" (406).

with one last chance of moral awakening, a chance they all take with a truly Christian humility.[17]

Tolkien's idea of heroism is much closer to that of pure and noble sacrifice, giving up one's life for the sake of others. Standing at one end of the crumbling bridge of Khazad-Dûm, Gandalf becomes a laudable alternative to Byrhtnoth's *ofermod*, fully replacing the ealdorman's decision to grant the vikings entry to the mainland with the wizard's unfaltering refusal to let the demonic Balrog come near the other members of the Fellowship. Byrhtnoth's *gað ricene to us* (*Battle of Maldon* 93) 'come quickly to us' thus exposes his pride, recklessness and vanity, while Gandalf's "you cannot pass" (*LotR* 322), responsibility, selflessness and a profound sense of higher purpose. Likewise, leading the combined forces of Gondor and Rohan in what appears to be a suicidal assault on the Black Gate of Mordor (*LotR* 868-74), Aragorn does not so much challenge the Dark Lord, as divert Sauron's attention from a far more important operation – Frodo's quest to destroy the Ruling Ring in the fires of Mount Doom. Unlike the proud ealdorman, the heir of Isildur does not seek chivalric glory in needless military bravado or any other form of unnecessary magnanimity, but *de facto* 'uses guile' to save the world from the destructive forces of ultimate Evil. Here, as in the dark mines of Moria, it is the end that justifies the means, not the other way round.

It cannot be denied that in "The Homecoming" Tolkien's response to Byrhtnoth's conduct at the battle of Maldon is mostly critical. The ealdorman's fatal decision, however, was not merely a moral and strategic failure which prompted a wave of unrestrained condemnation. Indeed, it was, perhaps more importantly, a starting point for Tolkien's reassessment of the "northern heroic spirit" (13), a reassessment further reflected in many of his highly admired works of fiction. Seen at face value, "The Homecoming" may obviously have the appearance of no more than a curious formal experiment undertaken by the popular author of *The Lord of the Rings*.[18] It is, however, a significant piece of literary criticism in which the voices of Torhthelm and Tídwald may be coming as much from the depths of a distant past as from the mouths of contemporary scholars (in-

---

17 Before he dies, Byrhtnoth also turns his eyes heavenwards, commending his soul to the mercy of God (*Battle of Maldon* 172-80).
18 Tolkien is said to have thoroughly disliked the dramatic genre and only used its conventions in the central part of his "Homecoming".

cluding, amongst others, Tolkien's friend and colleague E.V. Gordon), whose opinions Tolkien wished to comment on in the form of alliterative dialogue. His reading of the poem may have been fundamentally "coloured by his private views on personal morality" (Pollington 66), but, regardless of its actual value, it is a reading which appears to find resonances in almost every piece of literary criticism on *Maldon* published since 1953.

Bibliography

BLAKE, Ernest O., ed. *Liber Eliensis*. London: Royal Historical Society, 1962.

BOWMAN, Mary R. "Refining the Gold: Tolkien, *The Battle of Maldon*, and the Northern Theory of Courage." *Tolkien Studies* 7 (2010): 91-115.

CARPENTER, Humphrey. *J.R.R. Tolkien: A Biography*. London: HarperCollins, 2002.

CAVILL, Paul. "Interpretation of *The Battle of Maldon*, Lines 84-90: A Review and Reassessment." *Studia Neophilologica* 67.2 (1995): 149-164.

CHANCE, Jane. *Tolkien's Art: A Mythology for England*. Lexington: University of Kentucky Press, 2007.

DROUT, Michael D. C. "J.R.R. Tolkien's Medieval Scholarship and its Significance." *Tolkien Studies* 4 (2007): 113-176.

FOREST-HILL, Lynn. "Boromir, Byrhtnoth and Bayard: Finding a Language for Grief in J. R. R. Tolkien's *The Lord of the Rings*." *Tolkien Studies* 5 (2008): 73-97.

FRANK, Roberta. "*The Battle of Maldon* and Heroic Literature." *The Battle of Maldon AD 991*. Ed. Donald Scragg. Oxford: Basil Blackwell, 1991. 196-207.

"*The Battle of Maldon*: Its Reception, 1726-1906." *The Battle of Maldon: Fact and Fiction*. Ed. Janet Cooper. London: The Hambledon Press, 1993. 237-247.

GORDON, Eric V., ed. *The Battle of Maldon*. London: Methuen, 1954.

GROTTA, Daniel. *J.R.R. Tolkien: Architect of Middle Earth*. Philadelphia: Running Press, 1992.

HONEGGER, Thomas. "The Homecoming of Beorhtnoth: Philology and the Literary Muse." *Tolkien Studies* 4 (2007): 189-199.

IRVING Jr., Edward B. "The Heroic Style in *The Battle of Maldon*." *Studies in Philology* 58 (1961): 457-467.

KER, William P. *Epic and Romance: Essays on Medieval Literature*. London: Macmillan, 1897.

O'BRIEN O'Keeffe, Katherine. "Heroic Values and Christian Ethics." *The Cambridge Companion to Old English Literature*. Ed. Malcolm Godden and Michael Lapidge. Cambridge: Cambridge UP, 2002. 107-125.

ROBINSON, Fred C. "God, Death, and Loyalty in *The Battle of Maldon*." *Old English Literature*. Ed. Roy M. Liuzza. New Haven: Yale UP, 2002. 425-444.

POLLINGTON, Stephen. *The Warrior's Way: England in the Viking Age*. London: Blandford Press, 1989.

RORABECK, Robert. *Tolkien's Heroic Quest*. Maidstone: Crescent Moon Publishing, 2008.

SCRAGG, Donald G., ed. *The Battle of Maldon*. Manchester: Manchester University Press, 1984.

The Return of the Vikings: The Battle of Maldon 991. Stroud: Tempus Publishing, 2006.

SHIPPEY, Tom. "Boar and Badger: An Old English Heroic Antithesis?" *Leeds Studies in English* 16 (1985): 220-239.

The Road to Middle-Earth. London: HarperCollins, 2005.

"Tolkien and The Homecoming of Beorhtnoth". *Roots and Branches*. Zurich and Jena: Walking Tree Publishers, 2007. 323-339.

SWANTON, Michael, ed. *Beowulf*. Manchester: Manchester University Press, 1997.

TALIAFERRO, Charles and Craig Lindahl-Urben. "The Glory of Bilbo Baggins." *The Hobbit and Philosophy*. Ed. Gregory Bassham and Eric Bronson. Hoboken: John Wiley & Sons, 2012. 61-73.

TOLKIEN, John Ronald Reuel. "The Homecoming of Beorhtnoth Beorhthelm's Son". *Essays and Studies N.S.* 6 (1953): 1-18.

The Hobbit. London: HarperCollins, 1993.

The Lord of the Rings. London: HarperCollins, 1995.

About the author

ŁUKASZ NEUBAUER is a senior lecturer in the Institute of Neophilology and Social Communications at the Technical University of Koszalin, Poland. He specialises in early medieval history and Old Germanic literatures, in particular English poetry and Norse sagas. His publications include academic papers on the metrical structure of Anglo-Saxon verse and animal imagery in Old English battle poems. He is also interested in the Icelandic language and onomastics, and so has written a number of articles on place as well as proper names in Iceland.

Andrzej Wicher

What Exactly Does Tolkien Argue for in "*Beowulf*: The Monsters and the Critics"? An Attempt at a Metacriticism

Abstract

The present paper tries, first of all, to define the scope of J. R. R. Tolkien's achievement in his famous essay "*Beowulf*: The Monsters and the Critics", and also to consider the possibility of regarding this essay as an incomplete success in defending the value of the poem in question. According to the author of the paper, Tolkien's strategy is basically to admit the existence of specific limitations and deficiencies in the Old English poem, and then argue that those very deficiencies, in the context of the poem, should be regarded as strengths rather than as weaknesses. This appears to open a new perspective on existentialist, or quasi-existentialist, ramifications of Tolkien's thought, and may also call for a new way of looking at Tolkien's own works, and particularly at *The Lord of the Rings*. The paper includes also a brief analysis of Tolkien's theoretical essay "On Fairy-Stories", which shows that the approach to *Beowulf* shown in "*Beowulf*: The Monsters and the Critics" is only a symptom of Tolkien's general attitude to literature, and to life, an attitude that is typified by attention to detail and respect for the feelings and intentions of other people, provided they are not ruthless manipulators. From this we may also derive Tolkien's conception of magic in his books, where magic is not an independent force but rather an aspect of a character's personality.

One

The essay entitled "*Beowulf*: The Monsters and the Critics" is often praised as a work that reveals the beauty and the complexities of the Old English poem it is discussing. Although I don't want to question fundamentally this opinion, it seems that many aspects of this essay are not given the attention they call for. The essay, in its very title, appears to equate the monsters with the critics, elevating the author of the essay almost to the role of another Beowulf, who bravely confronts the incompetent critics of the poem, in a manner suggestive of Beowulf's own bravery when confronting the three monsters that posed a serious threat not only to the well-being but even to the survival of human society. Tolkien's principal charge against the critics of *Beowulf* is not so much that they criticize the poem incompetently, but rather that they fail to criticize it at all:

> But I have read enough, I think, to venture the opinion that *Beowulfiana* is, while rich in many departments, specially poor in one. It is poor in criticism, criticism that is directed to the understanding of a poem as a poem. (Tolkien, *MC* 5)

The critics are then accused of failing to give proper attention to the most central aspects of the poem. This accusation sounds familiar to anybody interested in the Anglo-American school of criticism known as the New Criticism. In the well-known essay, "Criticism, Inc." by one of that school's chief exponents, John Crowe Ransom, we find a scathing attack on university professors specializing in the history of literature:

> Professors of literature are learned but not critical men. The professional morale of this part of the university staff is evidently low. It is as if, with conscious or unconscious cunning, they had appropriated every avenue of escape from their responsibility which was decent and official; so that it is easy for one of them without public reproach to spend a lifetime in compiling the data of literature and yet rarely or never commit himself to a literary judgment. (Ransom 1109)

It is interesting that Ransom's seminal work was written only about two years (in 1938) after Tolkien's "Monsters and the Critics", which seems to show that the author of *The Lord of the Rings* was not so out of touch with various tendencies in the critical thought of his contemporaries as he is sometimes taken to be.

Tolkien's main quarrel with the Anglo-Saxonists of his day is expressed in the following statement:

> It has been said of *Beowulf* that its weakness lies in placing the unimportant things in the centre and the important on the outer edges. I think it profoundly untrue of the poem, but strikingly true of the literature about it. *Beowulf* has been used as a quarry of fact and fancy far more assiduously than it has been studied as a work of art. (Tolkien, *MC* 5)

The monstrous critics of *Beowulf*, then, confuse the centre with the margins when dealing with *Beowulf* and, perversely enough, accuse the poem itself of the same kind of transgression.

Further on, Tolkien gives us a delightful allegorical vision that is meant to illustrate the fate of the poem in the hands of the modern critics. The story he here makes use of is naturally the beginning of the popular fairy tale *Sleeping Beauty*, as told by Charles Perrault:

> As it set out upon its adventures among the modern scholars, *Beowulf* was christened by Wanley[1] Poesis – *Poeseos Anglo-Saxonicae egregium exemplum*. But the fairy godmother later invited to superintend its fortunes was Historia. And she brought with her Philologia, Mythologia, Archaeologia, and Laographia.[2] Excellent ladies. But where was the child's name-sake? Poesis was usually forgotten; occasionally admitted by a side-door; sometimes dismissed upon the door-step. 'The *Beowulf*', they said, 'is hardly an affair of yours, and not in any case a protégé that you could be proud of. It is an historical document. Only as such does it interest the superior culture of today.' And it is as an historical document that it has mainly been examined and dissected. (Tolkien, *MC* 6)

Tolkien's list of *Beowulf*'s rather irrelevant god-mothers may, again, remind us of the list of the so called "exclusions" provided by Ransom in "Criticism, Inc.", that is, of subjects and considerations that should not distract the attention of a professional critic. These exclusions include: "Personal registrations [...] Synopsis and paraphrase [...] Historical studies [...] Linguistic studies [...] Moral studies [...] Any other special studies which deal with some abstract or prose content taken out of the work" (Ransom 1115-1116). It can easily be seen that Ransom's and Tolkien's lists overlap in a high degree. Both critics, in keeping with the spirit of the New Criticism, advocate concentration on 'the work itself', or rather on what seems to be the work's most intimate and unique property, that is, its poetical or aesthetic value, to the exclusion of the apparently extraneous matters, even though Tolkien is, in fact, significantly less dogmatic in this than Ransom. The latter probably would not have used the adjective "excellent" with respect to his "exclusions".

At the same time, it is not my intention to claim that Tolkien was a kind of New Critic. I fundamentally agree with the following statement by Michael Drout:

> He [Tolkien] paid more attention to the monsters than had been done previously, but he did not neglect the historical elements in *Beowulf* in his analysis (anyone

---

[1] Tolkien refers here to Humfrey Wanley (1672-1726), an Oxford librarian who was responsible for the first catalogue of Anglo-Saxon manuscripts.
[2] By this, rather abstruse, term, not listed in the *Oxford English Dictionary*, and taken, apparently, from Modern Greek, Tolkien means, as far as I can see, folklore studies.

who thinks that Tolkien was a New Critic who only cared about the literary object in isolation needs to read *Finn and Hengest*). (Drout, "Brilliant Essay")

Tolkien's approach was, in my opinion, eclectic, he was interested in the main issues raised by the poem, but, being an Anglo-Saxonist worth his salt, he was naturally attracted to any aspects of the text that could throw some light on the history and culture of that distant epoch. The impression, however, that Tolkien could occasionally sound like a New Critic is confirmed, in my view, by Tom Shippey's following words:

> It has been said that Tolkien was himself a New Critic, just like F. R. Leavis and W. K. Wimsatt, and though I think Tolkien would have viewed such a label with absolute horror – he really did not like literary critics, or professors of literature – he certainly opened the door for a whole rush of Beowulfian New Critics. (Shippey, "Tolkien's Two Views")

To this I could only add that, as is clear from the above-provided quotation from "Criticism, Inc.", J. C. Ransom – no doubt a central figure in the American New Criticism – also did not like, or at least was highly critical of, professors of literature. Naturally, both J. C. Ransom and J. R. R. Tolkien were themselves, in a sense, professors of literature,[3] but one can argue that Ransom was, first of all, a poet, and Tolkien was, first of all, a linguist and an artistic writer.

Two

Tolkien insists that the poetical value of *Beowulf* is far greater than the poem's other qualities, and that it is indeed just that which can hardly fail to impress the reader:

> So far from being a poem so poor that only its accidental historical interest can still recommend it, *Beowulf* is in fact so interesting as poetry, in places poetry so powerful, that this quite overshadows the historical content, and is largely independent even of the most important facts (such as the date and identity of Hygelac) that research has discovered. (Tolkien, *MC* 7)

---

[3] This is of course more true of J. C. Ransom than of J. R. R. Tolkien, whose basic subject has always been historical linguistics, but it is hard to deny that Tolkien did lecture on literary subjects: his essay on *Beowulf*, discussed in the present article, was originally a lecture "delivered to the British Academy on 25 November 1936" (cf. Carpenter 143).

And yet it is difficult for Tolkien to deny that the scholars' undignified escape, as Ransom would have called it, into research concerning marginal aspects of *Beowulf* is, at least partly, caused by their being disappointed with exactly the poetical effect of the poem. The reason for this disappointment boils down to the statement that Tolkien quotes from the still popular enough book by W. P. Ker entitled *The Dark Ages* (1904):

> The fault of *Beowulf* is that there is nothing much in the story. The hero is occupied in killing monsters, like Hercules and Theseus. But there are other things in the lives of Hercules and Theseus besides the killing of the Hydra or of Procrustes. Beowulf has nothing else to do, when he has killed Grendel and Grendel's mother in Denmark: he goes home to his own Gautland, until at last the rolling years bring the Fire-drake and his last adventure. It is too simple. (Tolkien, *MC* 7)

In the recent re-makes and film adaptations of *Beowulf* (such as John Gardner's novel *Grendel* [1971], or the novel *Beowulf* [2007] by Caitlín R. Kiernan based on the screenplay by Neil Gaiman and Roger Avary), we can see very clearly the results, not always felicitous, of the modern writers' ambition to slake this intense thirst for more that the modern reader seems to suffer from when confronted with the Old English epic. Gardner, Gaiman, Kiernan and others are doing their best to make the story of Beowulf and the monsters more satisfying to the reader, or viewer, by providing them with all kinds of material, such as psychological analysis, erotic interest, or a conflict of loyalties, which the original *Beowulf* does not contain, or which is only faintly suggested there. Ker was probably the first critic who tried to describe *Beowulf* in terms of this thirst, or the unsatisfied feeling that the poem awakens. The readers are no doubt spoiled by such epic works as Homer's *Iliad* and *Odyssey*, or Virgil's *Aeneid*, which, even though much older than *Beowulf*, do contain most of the things that *Beowulf* seems to be so woefully deficient of, and the modern reader would so much like to find there.

Tolkien clearly tries to show that it is wrong to look at *Beowulf* mainly with regard to what it does not, rather than to what it does, contain. Yet he cannot ignore such a perspective completely, or rather, he is too good and honest a critic to be able to gloss it over. He grapples with it in a number of ways. One of them is to demonstrate the matter by means of another allegorical parable, this time filled with a haunting beauty, and reminiscent of the New Testament parables, of a man who built a tower overlooking the sea:

> A man inherited a field in which was an accumulation of old stone, part of an older hall. Of the old stone some had already been used in building the house in which he actually lived, not far from the old house of his fathers. Of the rest he took some and built a tower. But his friends coming perceived at once (without troubling to climb the steps) that these stones had formerly belonged to a more ancient building. So they pushed the tower over, with no little labour, in order to look for hidden carvings and inscriptions, or to discover whence the man's distant forefathers had obtained their building material. [...] And even the man's own descendants, who might have been expected to consider what he had been about, were heard to murmur: 'He is such an odd fellow! Imagine his using these old stones just to build a nonsensical tower! Why did not he restore the old house? He had no sense of proportion.' But from the top of that tower the man had been able to look out upon the sea. (Tolkien, *MC* 8)

The author does not fully explain the images used in the above parable, but we may try to do so. "An older hall" must be the ancient Germanic, pagan culture untouched yet, or almost untouched, by the influence of Christianity and Mediterranean civilization. "The house in which he lived" seems to be early medieval England; "the old house of his fathers" may be the original, continental home of the Anglo-Saxons, for example, the Southern Scandinavia, where the action of *Beowulf* takes place; "the man" and his "tower" are of course the anonymous author of the poem (or the culture to which he belonged), and the poem itself. The man's friends are surely the readers of *Beowulf*, while the man's descendants are, presumably, the English critics of *Beowulf*, who might be expected, at least from Tolkien's point of view, to be slightly more patriotic and refrain from attacking too viciously the oldest monument of epic poetry in the English language. What is not clear is the allegorical meaning of the sea in this parable. By saying that the tower, however imperfect in itself, enabled the man to watch the sea, Tolkien suggests that he is half-ready to admit that "the tower is nonsensical", that is, that the poem may appear nonsensical, or at least highly defective, in the eyes of many readers, and yet, with the help of it, one can gain some unique insight, or acquire some rather special, though unspecified, value.

The New Testament parable that this little story seems the most similar to is probably the parable of the mustard seed, which goes as follows:

> The kingdom of heaven is like to a grain of mustard seed, which a man took, and sowed it in his field: Which indeed is the least of all seeds: but when it is grown, it is the greatest among herbs, and becometh a tree, so that the birds of the air come and lodge in the branches thereof. (Matt. 13.31-32)

This is one of many New Testament parables that are meant to familiarize Christ's audience with the rather new, or even revolutionary, especially in the Jewish context, concept of the kingdom of heaven. What matters here, from our point of view, is, first of all, the contrast between the unprepossessing outer appearance of the mustard seed and its potential. Tolkien's "nonsensical tower" can also be easily destroyed, but it enables its builder to have access to a radically other dimension of the world. This dimension is, in "The Monsters and the Critics", symbolized by the sea, and in the Gospel according to St. Matthew, by "the birds of the air", where the air may be regarded as similarly vast and uncontrollable an element as Tolkien's sea.

Three

The novelty of Tolkien's approach to *Beowulf* seems to stem, in a high degree, from the assumption that this poem is a product of a mature culture and a mature mind that nobody needs to look upon condescendingly:

> Beowulf is not, then, the hero of an heroic lay, precisely. He has no enmeshed loyalties, nor hapless love. *He is a man, and that for him is sufficient tragedy.* It is not an irritating accident that the tone of the poem is so high and its theme so low. It is the theme in its deadly seriousness that begets the dignity of tone: *lif is læne: eal scæceð leoht and lif somod* [Life is fleeting, all departs, light and life together].[4] So deadly and ineluctable is the underlying thought, that those who in the circle of light, within the besieged hall, are absorbed in work or talk and do not look to the battlements, either do not regard it or recoil. Death comes to the feast, and they say He gibbers: He has no sense of proportion. (Tolkien, *MC* 18-19)

Thus, *Beowulf* appears as an existential, one might even say, existentialist tragedy. We may compare Tolkien's above statement with the following comment on Kierkegaard's philosophy:

---

4 I owe the translation of this Old English sentence, left untranslated by Tolkien, to: M.Drout, "Spliced Quotation" 149.

> The very word 'existence', for him, has exciting and adventurous connotations. 'To exist' is to face the uncertainties of the world and to commit oneself passionately to a way of life. (Mautner 187)

The monsters of the poem would then be allegories of "the uncertainties of the world", or simply of Time and Death, and the fact that they exactly are supernatural monsters, and not some human enemies, may be seen as emphasizing the irreducible and inexplicable strangeness of the human condition, some kind of quasi-Heideggerian abandonment in a world that cannot be made familiar, or rather in a world that we would be foolish to try to make appear familiar because its essential strangeness is bound, sooner or later, to manifest itself, to appear and re-appear. In *Beowulf*, the monsters appear three times, which may be understood as meaning that they are associated with the beginning, the middle, and the end, that is, with the whole of life's experience. This experience is then at each point exposed to a most destructive and uncanny irruption from outside the *oecumene* which the people in the pre-Conquest England called the Middle-earth.

Tolkien insists that it is the monsters that lend the poem its already mentioned "deadly seriousness" and "dignity of tone":

> I would suggest, then, that the monsters are not an inexplicable blunder of taste; they are essential, fundamentally allied to the underlying ideas of the poem, which give it its lofty tone and high seriousness. (Tolkien, *MC* 19)

The use of the term "high seriousness" may naturally remind us of Matthew Arnold and his theory of high seriousness and grand style, which are the notions that the Victorian critic used with reference to Homer, Virgil, and Dante, and was rather reluctant to find in English literature, with the exception of Milton, even though, in keeping with his habit to disparage his native culture, Arnold finds even Milton's grandeur to be far inferior to that of Homer or Dante. It is dubious that Arnold would be much impressed by the Beowulfian monsters because for him the problem of high seriousness was, first of all, a problem of style, rather than that of subject matter. Describing Homer's "grand style", Arnold, for example, says:

> For Homer is not only rapid in movement, simple in style, plain in language, natural in thought; he is also, and above all, noble. (Arnold 273)

From his point of view, the monsters, surely, cannot give any poem its "high seriousness" any more than the motif of the Cyclops guarantees this quality to Homer's *Odyssey*.

And yet, it is possible that Tolkien endows the term "high seriousness" with a slightly different shade of meaning. Let us look at the way time, according to Tolkien, is treated in *Beowulf*:

> As the poet looks back into the past, surveying the history of kings and warriors in the old traditions, he sees that all glory (or as we might say 'culture' or 'civilization') ends in night. The solution of that tragedy is not treated – it does not arise out of the material. We get in fact a poem from a pregnant moment of poise, looking back into the pit, by a man learned in old tales who was struggling, as it were, to get a general view of them all, perceiving their common tragedy of inevitable ruin, and yet feeling this more *poetically* because he was himself removed from the direct pressure of its despair. He could view from without, but still feel immediately and from within, the old dogma: despair of the event, combined with faith in the value of doomed resistance. He was still dealing with the great temporal tragedy, and not yet writing an allegorical homily in verse. (Tolkien, *MC* 23)

The meaning, or rather one of the meanings, of this, rather convoluted, passage seems to be that the poetical effect of *Beowulf*, its very special dignity and seriousness, is the result of a delicate equilibrium between what might be called, following Tolkien, "feeling from within" and "feeling from without", or rather "from outside". The *Beowulf* poet is sufficiently an outsider, in relation to the represented world of his poem, to see the general meaning of his subject matter, but, at the same time, he is enough of an insider to feel strongly about the characters and events he is describing, including of course the monsters. In other words, the poem seems to offer a possibility of an allegorical interpretation, but does not impose it on the reader.

But the phrases "the pregnant moment of poise" and "looking back into the pit" seem to refer also to the ability to see things *sub specie aeternitatis* (under the aspect of eternity), and under their temporal and transient aspect. A similar description of a paradoxical experience of time may be found in *The Lord of the Rings* and it is put in the mouth of the elf Legolas:

> Legolas stirred in his boat. 'Nay, time does not tarry ever,' he said; 'but change and growth is not in all things and places alike. For the Elves the world moves, and it moves both very swift and very slow. Swift, because they them-

selves change little, and all else fleets by: it is a grief to them. Slow, because they do not count the running years, not for themselves. The passing seasons are but ripples ever repeated in the long long stream. Yet beneath the Sun all things must wear to an end at last.' (Tolkien, *LotR* I 368; ch. 9)

In other words, the elvish idea of the passage of time combines again a, generally painful, awareness of inexorable going by, that is, usually, of fading and waning, with an unconcerned 'nothing new under the sun' attitude. This is typical of creatures that do not have to measure time, as they are immortal, or almost immortal, because Tolkien's elves, apparently, can be killed, but they cannot die from natural causes. At this point, we might try to re-introduce the monsters who, just like the elves, seem to be longeval creatures who may have an end, but whose beginning is buried in a very dim and distant past. The monsters contribute to the "high seriousness" in that they substantiate the long temporal perspective, and, as we remember, the monster Grendel is in *Beowulf* derived from the accursed Cain, the proto-murderer. A similar role is played in *The Lord of the Rings* by such longeval and primeval characters like the Elves, the Ents, or Tom Bombadil, but also by the Balrog and Shelob whose monstrosity makes the idea of long duration into something like a nightmarish "looking back into the pit". The monsters show a possibility for Time itself to be treated as an all-devouring monster, which you can resist, but only for a time, as it appears in the last sentence of Tolkien's essay:

> Yet it [*Beowulf*] is in fact written in a language that after many centuries has still essential kinship with our own, it was made in this land, and moves in our northern world beneath our northern sky, and for those who are native to that tongue and land, it must ever call with a profound appeal – until the dragon comes. (Tolkien, *MC* 23)

Thus, the poem itself becomes a time-conquering, and a monster-conquering, device and a product of "northern skies" that can reconcile us, or rather the critic's compatriots, with those skies, rather than with the Christian Heaven, "until the dragon comes".

A critic, Barry Langford, talks about a "Tolkienesque perspective", which he defines as follows:

> [...] a vast reach of time to which the present is not only inheritor or successor, but to which it is bound in active and conscious relation. (Langford 37)

It seems, then, possible to argue that this "Tolkienesque perspective", present in *The Lord of the Rings*, and in Tolkien's other works of fiction, could have been inspired by *Beowulf*, and particularly by Tolkien's understanding of it.

It is naturally also remarkable that Frodo, the protagonist of *The Lord of the Rings*, is, like Beowulf, a man (or rather a hobbit) with "no enmeshed loyalties, nor hapless love", even though the theme of the conflict of loyalties appears in this book (it is enough to think of Boromir the son of Denethor, the Steward of Gondor, who is torn between the loyalty to his boundlessly ambitious father, and to the Fellowship of the Ring), just as the theme of thwarted love (such as the love between Arwen Evenstar, an elven-daughter, and Aragorn, which can be fulfilled only at the price of Arwen's giving up her immortality; a story that is, in fact, only an echo of a much more dramatic and difficult love affair between Beren and Lúthien, told in *The Silmarillion*). Like Beowulf, Frodo ventures out of his native land on a mission to help members of other nations, or races. The difference is of course that Beowulf helps only the tribe of the Danes, closely related to his own tribe of the Geats, while Frodo manages to contribute decisively to the liberation and victory of all the Free Peoples, including his own race of the hobbits.[5] The psychological portrait of Frodo is, admittedly, much more complex than that of Beowulf, but it seems possible that Tolkien wanted to show in *The Lord of the Rings*, among other things, that man's predicament may be shown as dramatic enough without taking recourse to the devices and themes that the great Anglo-Saxon poem so signally lacks, while emphasising the ones that it does possess, such as fighting with supernatural enemies, or, in other words, that he wanted to repeat, in a sense, the achievement of *Beowulf*. It is not perhaps an accident that *The Lord of the Rings* ends with a vision of the main characters "passing over Sea" to reach some, rather melancholy, Kingdom of Heaven, more similar to the ancient Elysian Fields, and called the Blessed Realm, or the Undying Lands. Thus the trilogy becomes itself "the top of that tower [from which] the man had been able to look out upon the sea".

---

5 Frodo may be said to be involved then, to use an old Polish insurrectionist slogan, in a fight "for your freedom and ours".

Four

A similar way of thinking can be observed in the most important theoretical work on literature that Tolkien has produced, that is, in his essay "On Fairy-Stories" (1947). There the author refuses to provide a definition of the fairy-story, saying:

> The definition of a fairy-story – what it is, or what it should be – does not, then, depend on any definition or historical account of elf or fairy, but upon the nature of *Faërie*: the Perilous Realm itself, and the air that blows in that country. I will not attempt to define that, nor to describe it directly. It cannot be done. *Faërie* cannot be caught in a net of words; for it is one of its qualities to be indescribable, though not imperceptible. (Tolkien, *MC* 33-34)

Like the metaphorical tower in "The Monsters and the Critics", the fairy-story is there to provide, for those who care about such things, an insight into the enchanted land of *Faërie*. We underestimate perhaps the originality and, should I say, peculiarity of Tolkien's approach to the problem of the tale of magic (a more precise term than *fairy tale* or *fairy-story*). The two most famous synthetic theories concerning the tale of magic are probably Vladimir Propp's *Morphology of the Folk-Tale* (1928), and Max Lüthi's *The European Folktale. Form and Nature* (1947). Propp's approach is structural and concerned mainly with the typical plot of the tale of magic, while Lüthi's approach is stylistic, and, to some extent, phenomenological. Tolkien's approach is clearly neither: it is much more concerned with what might be called the social function of the tale of magic. This is first of all because, unlike Propp and Lüthi, Tolkien does not attempt to define the tale of magic. Moreover, he declares that this "cannot be done", and that "*Faërie* cannot be caught in a net of words". We do not know what he would have said about Propp's or Lüthi's, or other scholars', descriptions of this genre. Tolkien when writing "On Fairy-Stories" certainly had no knowledge of either Propp's or Lüthi's books, for the former became known in the West only in the 1950s, while the latter was published in the same year as "On Fairy-Stories".

Tolkien's negative declaration should, I think, be understood as meaning that one cannot capture, by discursive means, the essence of the magic of the tale of magic. He admits that the notion of *Faërie* should be understood as a kind of magic:

> *Faërie* itself may perhaps most nearly be translated as Magic – but it is magic of a peculiar mood and power, at the furthest pole from the vulgar devices of the laborious, scientific, magician. There is one proviso: if there is any satire present in the tale, one thing must not be made fun of, the magic itself. That must in that story be taken seriously, neither laughed at nor explained away. (Tolkien, *MC* 114)

It seems possible to describe Tolkien's approach to the tale of magic as didactic and religious. His obvious disgust with what he calls the vulgar conception of magic is, I think, an expression of his rejection of what commonly goes by the name of magic. Sir James Frazer, in his seminal book, *The Golden Bough*, established a standard way of distinguishing between magic and religion, according to which the former stands for a rather arrogant and manipulative attitude towards the forces of nature, roughly analogous to that of a scientist, while the latter is based on humility and reverence. As he puts it:

> This radical conflict of principle between magic and religion sufficiently explain the relentless hostility with which in history the priest has often pursued the magician. The haughty self-sufficiency of the magician, his arrogant demeanour towards the higher powers, and his unabashed claim to exercise a sway like theirs could not but revolt the priest, to whom, with his awful sense of the divine majesty, and his humble prostration in face of it, such claims and such a demeanour must have appeared an impious and blasphemous usurpation of prerogatives that belong to God alone. (Frazer 52)

It seems that what Tolkien calls "magic of a peculiar mood and power" is in fact magic tinged with elements of religion, specifically of Christianity, providing a special kind of redemption which Tolkien calls "eucatastrophe", and as distant as possible from the cold, manipulative magic based on the knowledge of the right kind of spells and magical formulas. The closest approximation of that Tolkienian "peculiar magic" is perhaps the kind of magic practised by the chief positive characters of *The Lord of the Rings*, Gandalf and Galadriel. They are not, strictly speaking, religious worshippers, indeed they both, particularly Galadriel, are more often themselves revered and looked up to, as figures of great authority, though not quite as gods. And yet if they manage to produce magical effects of any kind, they have nothing to do with "an arrogant exercise of a sway over the higher powers", but rather their magical powers seem to originate from a great concentration of psychic energy motivated by a strong desire to serve and be of some help to their friends. An example of this may be Gandalf's use of his magical staff in the hall of King Theoden, when he is enraged by the devious rhetoric of Wormtongue, a secret agent of the evil magician Saruman. The latter is, incidentally, a good example of a magician who embodies Frazer's famous equation between magic and science, his magic being only a means to increase his material power.

While it is assumed that a true magician remains in some fundamental collusion with the forces that rule over the world, the forces that, in *The Lord of the Rings*, are usually called the Valar, it is also clear that a Tolkienian magician is far from adopting the attitude of "humble prostration". Instead of trying to propitiate the supernatural forces with prayers, rituals, or offerings, he behaves as someone who has to solve a riddle, which requires neither abject humility, nor high-handedness, but rather a philologist's ability to enter the mind and the intention of the author, or even the great Author, an ability that is based on a mixture of empathy, self-forgetfulness, and perspicacity, offering something that seems to be half-way between the Frazerian extremes of magic and religion. This attitude is defined in "On Fairy-Stories" as a variety of childlikeness that is peculiar to fairy tales:

> But humility and innocence – these things 'the heart of a child' must mean in such a context – do not necessarily imply an uncritical wonder, nor indeed an uncritical tenderness. (Tolkien, *MC* 136)

A case in point is the scene in the first volume of *The Lord of the Rings*, when Gandalf manages, with considerable difficulty, to open the Door of Moria. The inscription on the door reads: "The Doors of Durin, Lord of Moria. Speak, friend, and enter" (*LotR* I 290; ch. 4). Gandalf, on deciphering this inscription, declares that it contains nothing of importance, but he is wrong. Only after a period of fruitless efforts, during which he and his companions hear the howling of magical wolves drawing near, efforts that include saying all kinds of magical spells, which, as usual in Tolkien, are of no use, does he finally manage to find the right solution. To do this, he has to realize that in translating the inscription from the Elvish tongue, he made a mistake, and that the correct translation should have been: "Say 'Friend' and enter" (*LotR* I 293; ch. 4). In other words, the mystery of the magical door was that there was no mystery, just a plain piece of information. Gandalf, powerful wizard that he is, has to admit that it was Merry, one of the little hobbits, who was on the right track when he asked the question: "What does it mean by *speak, friend, and enter?*". This is the logic Gandalf at first does not want to accept, as he prefers to interpret the words on the door egocentrically, that is according to what they seem to mean to him,[6] whereas Merry's question emphasizes the empathetic idea of inquiring about the author's intention, or rather about the intention of the text, or behind the text. Gandalf's final comment is:

> I had only to speak the Elvish word for *friend* and the door opened. Quite simple. Too simple for a learned loremaster in these suspicious days. Those were happier times. Now let us go! (Tolkien, *LotR* I 293; ch. 4)

Again Gandalf emphasizes the necessity to penetrate empathetically into the mentality of people living in different times in order to understand the texts produced by them, even though one might accuse him of following the much denigrated nostalgic stereotype of the Golden Age or the good old times. It is also probably significant that the correct password is the word *friend*, the meaning of which includes the principle of mutual understanding.

Beowulf, a poem that is as much about friendship as it is about enmity, contains a memorable line showing Beowulf as someone who feels a need to enter the mind even of those whom he intends to kill – this time in order to facilitate the killing. Thus he decides not to use a sword in his fight with Grendel, knowing that Grendel would never use a sword himself:

Ac wit on niht sculon Secge ofersittan, gif he gesecean dear Wig ofer wæpen: (*Beowulf*, verses 683-685, 1995: 46)	No, we'll at night play Without any weapons – if unweaponed he dare to face me in fight (*Beowulf*, verses 683-685, 2001: 26)

This is a rather peculiar logic, for an ordinary warrior would rejoice at the prospect of using a weapon that his enemy does not possess and cannot use. But Beowulf feels, even though he cannot, apparently, verbalize it precisely, that his enemy has to be fought in the way he himself fights, and that it was a mistake inherent in the former attempts to kill Grendel that they were based on an arrogant assumption that a civilized man should not stoop to the methods

---

6 In this way Gandalf seems to commit the mistake that Tolkien, in "On Fairy-Stories", calls "appropriation" (*OFS* 146).

adopted by a mere beast. T. A. Shippey calls Beowulf's declaration a boast,[7] and no doubt it is a boast, but a well reasoned one, and perhaps even based on a touch of humility.[8]

Ultimately, Beowulf's logic cannot be completely 'explained away', because it is much more intuitive than rational, but it is Tolkien's search for such a liberating logic, or rather magic, that seems to lie behind the mysterious formula of "the top of that tower [from which] the man had been able to look out upon the sea". It has to be concluded that the overall impression that Tolkien's approach to criticism makes is clearly different, in spite of certain similarities mentioned at the beginning of the present chapter, from the critical methods of New Criticism or Structuralism. Unlike those schools of criticism, Tolkien is looking in literature for a moral inspiration and guidance, and he probably would not have had much time for the notion of pure form, or literature as a purely linguistic phenomenon.

---

7 Cf. Shippey, *Beowulf* 15: "After Beowulf has made his boast that he will fight weaponless against Grendel, he disarms and lies down to sleep in Heorot".
8 Shippey in another place speaks interestingly about the absence, in *Beowulf*, of the modern taboo against boasting, and a much greater tolerance for what might be called heroic self-confidence. Cf. Shippey, *Beowulf* 8-9.

Bibliography

ARNOLD, Matthew. *Essays*. London, Edinburgh: Oxford UP, 1914.

Beowulf. Ed. Michael Alexander. London: Penguin Books, 1995.

Beowulf. A Verse Translation. Ed. Michael Alexander. London: Penguin Books, 2001.

The Bible. The Authorized King James Version. Ed. Robert Carroll and Stephen Prickett. Oxford: Oxford UP, 1998.

CARPENTER, Humphrey. *J.R.R. Tolkien. A Biography*. London, Boston, Sydney: Unwin Paperbacks, 1978.

DROUT, Michael D.C. "A Spliced Old English Quotation in *"Beowulf*: The Monsters and the Critics." *Tolkien Studies* 3 (2006): 149-156.

FARACI, Mary E. "'I Wish to Speak': Tolkien's Voice in His Beowulf Essay." *Tolkien the Medievalist*. Ed. Jane Chance. London: Routledge, 2003. 50-62.

FRAZER, James. *The Golden Bough. A Study in Magic and Religion*. Ware, Herfordshire: Wordsworth Reference, 1993.

GARDNER, John. *Grendel*. New York: Vintage Books, 1989.

KER, William Paton. *Epic and Romance. Essays on Medieval Literature*. London: Macmillan, 1931.

KIERNAN, Caitlín R. *Beowulf*. Trans. Małgorzata Dobrowolska. Warszawa: Prószyński i S-ka, 2007.

LANGFORD, Barry. "Time." *Reading 'The Lord of the Rings'*. Ed. Robert Eaglestone. London and New York: Continuum, 2005. 29-46.

LÜTHI, Max. *The European Folktale. Form and Nature*. Trans. John D. Niles. Bloomington, Ind.: Indiana UP, 2009.

MAUTNER, Thomas. *The Penguin Dictionary of Philosophy*. London: Penguin Books, 1997.

PROPP, Vladimir. *Morphology of the Folktale*. (Second edition). Trans. Laurence Scott. Ed. Louis A. Wagner. Austin: University of Texas Press, 2009.

RANSOM, John Crowe. "Criticism, Inc." *The Norton Anthology of Theory and Criticism*. Ed. Vincent B. Leitch. New York and London: W. W. Norton & Company, 2001. 1108-1118.

SHIPPEY, T. A. *Beowulf*. London: Edward Arnold, 1978.

TOLKIEN, John Ronald Reuel. *The Monsters and the Critics and Other Essays*. London: HarperCollins, 1997.

The Lord of the Rings, Part I. London: Unwin Books, 1976.

The Silmarillion. Ed. Christopher Tolkien. Boston and Sydney: George Allen & Unwin, 1977.

Electronic Sources

DROUT, Michael D.C., "*Beowulf*: The Monsters and the Critics: The Brilliant Essay that Broke *Beowulf* Studies." 01.Dec.2012. <http://www.lotrplaza.com/showthread.php?17739-Beowulf-The-Monsters-amp-the-Critics-Michael-Drout>

SHIPPEY, Tom. "Tolkien's Two Views of *Beowulf*: One hailed, one ignored. But did we get this right?" 01.Dec.2012. <http://www.lotrplaza.com/showthread.php?18483-Tolkien's-Two-Views-of-Beowulf-Tom-Shippey>

About the author

ANDRZEJ WICHER is professor in the Institute of English Studies at Łódź University, where he lectures on the history of English literature and theory of literature. He published a book entitled *Archaeology of the Sublime. Studies in Late-Medieval English Writings* (Katowice 1995) and another one under the title *Shakespeare's Parting Wondertales – a Study of the Elements of the Tale of Magic in William Shakespeare's Late Plays* (Łódź 2003). He also published a volume of Polish translations of Middle English literary works, including *Sir Gawain and the Green Knight and Pearl*. His new book entitled *Selected Medieval and Religious Themes in the Works of C.S. Lewis and J.R.R. Tolkien* is forthcoming. Prof. Andrzej Wicher took part in many international conferences; he is a member of the International Shakespeare Association, PASE (Polish Association for the Study of English), and the Scholarly Society in Łódź. He has so far published three books, and 65 scholarly articles and essays, seven of which appeared outside Poland. Besides, he took part in various academic exchange schemes and was a visiting lecturer at a number of British universities. Prof. Andrzej Wicher's professional interests include medieval and Renaissance studies, cultural studies, and modern fantasy literature, with special emphasis on the presence of folktale motifs in works of literature.

Walking Tree Publishers

Walking Tree Publishers was founded in 1997 as a forum for publication of material (books, videos, CDs, etc.) related to Tolkien and Middle-earth studies. Manuscripts and project proposals can be submitted to the board of editors (please include an SAE):

Walking Tree Publishers
CH-3052 Zollikofen
Switzerland
e-mail: info@walking-tree.org
http://www.walking-tree.org

Cormarë Series

The *Cormarë Series* collects papers and studies dedicated exclusively to the exploration of Tolkien's work. It comprises monographs, thematic collections of essays, conference volumes, and reprints of important yet no longer (easily) accessible papers by leading scholars in the field. Manuscripts and project proposals are evaluated by members of an independent board of advisors who support the series editors in their endeavour to provide the readers with qualitatively superior yet accessible studies on Tolkien and his work.

News from the Shire and Beyond. Studies on Tolkien
Peter Buchs and Thomas Honegger (eds.), Zurich and Berne 2004, Reprint, First edition 1997 (Cormarë Series 1), ISBN 978-3-9521424-5-5

Root and Branch. Approaches Towards Understanding Tolkien
Thomas Honegger (ed.), Zurich and Berne 2005, Reprint, First edition 1999 (Cormarë Series 2), ISBN 978-3-905703-01-6

Richard Sturch, *Four Christian Fantasists. A Study of the Fantastic Writings of George MacDonald, Charles Williams, C.S. Lewis and J.R.R. Tolkien*
Zurich and Berne 2007, Reprint, First edition 2001 (Cormarë Series 3), ISBN 978-3-905703-04-7

Tolkien in Translation
Thomas Honegger (ed.), Zurich and Jena 2011, Reprint, First edition 2003 (Cormarë Series 4), ISBN 978-3-905703-15-3

Mark T. Hooker, *Tolkien Through Russian Eyes*
Zurich and Berne 2003 (Cormarë Series 5), ISBN 978-3-9521424-7-9

Translating Tolkien: Text and Film
Thomas Honegger (ed.), Zurich and Jena 2011, Reprint, First edition 2004 (Cormarë Series 6), ISBN 978-3-905703-16-0

Christopher Garbowski, *Recovery and Transcendence for the Contemporary Mythmaker. The Spiritual Dimension in the Works of J.R.R. Tolkien*
Zurich and Berne 2004, Reprint, First Edition by Marie Curie Sklodowska, University Press, Lublin 2000, (Cormarë Series 7), ISBN 978-3-9521424-8-6

Reconsidering Tolkien
Thomas Honegger (ed.), Zurich and Berne 2005 (Cormarë Series 8),
ISBN 978-3-905703-00-9

Tolkien and Modernity 1
Frank Weinreich and Thomas Honegger (eds.), Zurich and Berne 2006 (Cormarë Series 9), ISBN 978-3-905703-02-3

Tolkien and Modernity 2
Thomas Honegger and Frank Weinreich (eds.), Zurich and Berne 2006 (Cormarë Series 10), ISBN 978-3-905703-03-0

Tom Shippey, *Roots and Branches. Selected Papers on Tolkien by Tom Shippey*
Zurich and Berne 2007 (Cormarë Series 11), ISBN 978-3-905703-05-4

Ross Smith, *Inside Language. Linguistic and Aesthetic Theory in Tolkien*
Zurich and Jena 2011, Reprint, First edition 2007 (Cormarë Series 12), ISBN 978-3-905703-20-7

How We Became Middle-earth. A Collection of Essays on The Lord of the Rings
Adam Lam and Nataliya Oryshchuk (eds.), Zurich and Berne 2007 (Cormarë Series 13), ISBN 978-3-905703-07-8

Myth and Magic. Art According to the Inklings
Eduardo Segura and Thomas Honegger (eds.), Zurich and Berne 2007 (Cormarë Series 14), ISBN 978-3-905703-08-5

The Silmarillion - Thirty Years On
Allan Turner (ed.), Zurich and Berne 2007 (Cormarë Series 15), ISBN 978-3-905703-10-8

Martin Simonson, *The Lord of the Rings and the Western Narrative Tradition*
Zurich and Jena 2008 (Cormarë Series 16), ISBN 978-3-905703-09-2

Tolkien's Shorter Works. Proceedings of the 4th Seminar of the Deutsche Tolkien Gesellschaft & Walking Tree Publishers Decennial Conference
Margaret Hiley and Frank Weinreich (eds.), Zurich and Jena 2008 (Cormarë Series 17), ISBN 978-3-905703-11-5

Tolkien's The Lord of the Rings: Sources of Inspiration
Stratford Caldecott and Thomas Honegger (eds.), Zurich and Jena 2008 (Cormarë Series 18), ISBN 978-3-905703-12-2

J.S. Ryan, *Tolkien's View: Windows into his World*
Zurich and Jena 2009 (Cormarë Series 19), ISBN 978-3-905703-13-9

Music in Middle-earth
Heidi Steimel and Friedhelm Schneidewind (eds.), Zurich and Jena 2010 (Cormarë Series 20), ISBN 978-3-905703-14-6

Liam Campbell, *The Ecological Augury in the Works of JRR Tolkien*
Zurich and Jena 2011 (Cormarë Series 21), ISBN 978-3-905703-18-4

Margaret Hiley, *The Loss and the Silence. Aspects of Modernism in the Works of C.S. Lewis, J.R.R. Tolkien and Charles Williams*
Zurich and Jena 2011 (Cormarë Series 22), ISBN 978-3-905703-19-1

Rainer Nagel, *Hobbit Place-names. A Linguistic Excursion through the Shire*
Zurich and Jena 2012 (Cormarë Series 23), ISBN 978-3-905703-22-1

Christopher MacLachlan, *Tolkien and Wagner: The Ring and Der Ring*
Zurich and Jena 2012 (Cormarë Series 24), ISBN 978-3-905703-21-4

Renée Vink, *Wagner and Tolkien: Mythmakers*
Zurich and Jena 2012 (Cormarë Series 25), ISBN 978-3-905703-25-2

The Broken Scythe. Death and Immortality in the Works of J.R.R. Tolkien
Roberto Arduini and Claudio Antonio Testi (eds.), Zurich and Jena 2012
(Cormarë Series 26), ISBN 978-3-905703-26-9

Sub-creating Middle-earth: Constructions of Authorship and the Works of J.R.R. Tolkien
Judith Klinger (ed.), Zurich and Jena 2012 (Cormarë Series 27),
ISBN 978-3-905703-27-6

Tolkien's Poetry
Julian Eilmann and Allan Turner (eds.), Zurich and Jena 2013
(Cormarë Series 28), ISBN 978-3-905703-28-3

O, What a Tangled Web? Tolkien and Medieval Literature. A View from Poland
Barbara Kowalik (ed.), Zurich and Jena 2013, (Cormarë Series 29),
ISBN 978-3-905703-29-0

J.S. Ryan, *In the Nameless Wood* (working title)
Zurich and Jena, forthcoming

Paul H. Kocher, *The Three Ages of Middle-earth*
Zurich and Jena, forthcoming

Beowulf and the Dragon

The original Old English text of the 'Dragon Episode' of *Beowulf* is set in an authentic font and printed and bound in hardback creating a high quality art book. The text is

illustrated by Anke Eissmann and accompanied by John Porter's translation. The introduction is by Tom Shippey. Limited first edition of 500 copies. 84 pages.

This high-quality book will please both Tolkien fans and those interested in mythology and Old English. It is also well suited as a gift.

Selected pages can be previewed on: www.walking-tree.org/beowulf

Beowulf and the Dragon
Zurich and Jena 2009,
ISBN 978-3-905703-17-7

Tales of Yore Series

The *Tales of Yore Series* grew out of the desire to share Kay Woollard's whimsical stories and drawings with a wider audience. The series aims at providing a platform for qualitatively superior fiction that will appeal to readers familiar with Tolkien's world.

Kay Woollard, *The Terror of Tatty Walk. A Frightener*
CD and Booklet, Zurich and Berne 2000, ISBN 978-3-9521424-2-4

Kay Woollard, *Wilmot's Very Strange Stone or What came of building "snobbits"*
CD and booklet, Zurich and Berne 2001, ISBN 978-3-9521424-4-8